Other Titles by TW Brown

The DEAD Series:

DEAD: The Ugly Beginning
DEAD: Revelations
DEAD: Fortunes & Failures

DEAD Special Edition

DEAD: Steve's Story
DEAD: Vignettes
DEAD: The Geeks

Zomblog

Zomblog
Zomblog II
Zomblog: The Final Entry
Zomblog: Snoe (coming October 2012)

Miscellaneous

Gruesomely Grimm Zombie Tales Vol. I
That Ghoul Ava
Dakota (as Todd Brown)

Zomblog:
The Final Entry

Written by: TW Brown

Zomblog: The Final Entry

©2011 May December Publications
2nd Edition

The Split-tree logo is a registered trademark of May December Publications LLC.

Printed in the U.S.A.

ISBN—978-1-936730-08-7

Dedication

To all my friends who have never stopped believing in me and supporting me...even when I didn't really deserve it.

ZOMBLOG:
The Final Entry

Friday, January 1

Happy New Year.

Two years ago, Samuel Todd started a blog. He had no idea the world was about to die. Within a month, the dead were walking the earth. Seven months later, he was dead and I was pregnant.

In the past two years, the world has changed dramatically. Humanity holds out…mostly in small pockets of survivors who cling to each other in desperation and try valiantly to create something resembling something we all knew. Others have taken advantage of the lack of authority figures, wreaking death and chaos wherever they go. These people prey on those deemed weaker. In many cases, that means women and children.

Make no mistake, nobody is innocent anymore. In this world, you kill to survive and you do it without hesitation…or you die. A few months into this whole drama, somebody told me that the estimated ratio between the living and the living dead had exceeded 13000:1. I'm sure that number is much bigger now.

The walking dead show no signs of just falling down. There was hope that, when food became scarce, they would just wither away. They haven't. What has gone away is almost any source of fuel, transportation, power—electric, battery or otherwise—and ammunition. Like the Romans, Vikings, and Knights of the Round Table, we battle hand-to-hand. In that sense, we have devolved.

The walking dead travel in singles and small groups, but they've also coagulated into larger groups that sometimes number in the thousands called herds or mobs. If they get on the trail of something (usually one of us) they pursue with a mindless determination. That is a blessing and a curse. You can ditch them if you're clever, but if they trap you somewhere…suicide is the quickest and easiest way out. They don't tend to leave once they have you trapped. Zombies do not feel frustration.

A few more things about the undead; they must suffer massive brain trauma to be put down. Their bite is the normal way for them to pass on the infection. Although, like any other blood-borne illness, open wounds and contaminated blood are bad deals. The good news is that this contamination is not one hundred percent. There have been cases where individuals have survived an attack and not turned. Nobody knows how or why, and medical science has gone the way of central air conditioning. Even after all this time, their stench gives them away. They're slower moving than the rising tide and have been known to make an unsettling sound that is likened to a baby cry. They don't freeze or become immobile in the winter, at least not in any of the winters I've experienced. I couldn't tell you about places like Alaska or Siberian.

A few months ago I set down my journal. The journal I took over when Sam died. Honestly, I didn't expect to pick it back up. However, I've found a therapeutic outlet in my life to be blatantly missing once I stopped writing. I've found I needed the catharsis of putting pen to paper.

I will not bore you with the mundane events of the past months. Actually, I've spent most of it recovering from a wicked ass-kicking after going heads-up with a cult of lunatics that happened to include a young girl who, at one time, traveled with me. I've been living in a mansion-turned-fortress for the past few months. Had I been writing in my journal it would have read mostly something like this: Woke up, stupid dog peed on the floor again, watched a group leave on a supply run again, couldn't help…again.

Get the picture?

However, I've been getting better. I've rehabbed until I'm as close to a hundred percent as I can be. As I've gotten healthier, my desire to get out in the mix again has grown. I don't do well being confined. It's one of those things you never learn about yourself until an extreme event occurs. Like, would you return the bag of money that fell out of an armored truck? Would you rush into that burning building to save a helpless stranger? Or could you stay monogamous and happily married?

I've decided to strike out for Las Vegas as soon as I feel the weather will allow me. Until it was deemed a waste, and the radio here was shut off—when wind and solar become your only source of power, you are forced to prioritize—we used to pick up an occasional message from somebody who claimed to be in

Las Vegas. What's more, they claim to have electric power. I need to see for myself.

I'm not sure if I'll travel alone or not. I haven't mentioned it to anyone in a while. Maybe they think I've learned my lesson. Maybe they think I will learn to be happy with this new life. I think I understand how Lewis and Clark, Christopher Columbus and Neil Armstrong felt. Sitting here...not knowing isn't an option.

My name is Meredith Gainey, and my New Year's resolution is to see Las Vegas for myself.

Saturday, January 2

This morning I took my dog for a walk...well...he isn't quite a dog yet, but he's too freakin' big to be called a puppy anymore. His gigantic feet keep getting in the way of his legs, and I have never in my life seen a dog trip as often as this one.

However, Sam's a good dog. He already knows to growl any time one of those walking meat bags gets close. Eric Grayfeather takes him out on patrol sometimes. I think he does it to piss me off. He knows how bad *I* want to be out there, so he takes Sam. Then, when everybody gets back, I get to hear all the neat things *my* dog did while I sit here on my ass.

That reminds me...the road (Highway 26) is now drivable from here to The Warehouse Complex. I am able to make trips to there or The Sunset Fortress. (Hey, they picked the names; not me.) It allows me to go see Baby Snoe whenever a patrol or convoy heads in that direction. I don't go very often because I wouldn't want the baby to become too attached to me. Also, I think it makes Janie and Lindsay, her adoptive mommies, very nervous.

The road clearing detail turned out to only be phase one. The two big communities—as well as the few dozen folks who live in the walls of the Mitchell mansion—are serious. They are using the plethora of abandoned vehicles to reinforce the barriers they create and continually expand. Both sides of the highway are walled off with them. It does keep the zombie traffic to a minimum while giving The Corridor (another of their catchy names), which is what they now call Highway 26 along this stretch, a very art deco sort of look. I bet some freaky artist back in the Before did a painting like this and idiots stood around some art studio reading all sorts of meaning into it.

And my contribution to all this hoopla? I was "allowed" to sit in an armored bank truck and be ready to drive if the work detail needed to make a hasty retreat. Woo-freaking-hoo!

In other news…Jenifer is recovering, but the scarring is severe. She was really upset when she discovered that she could only grow hair back on one side of her head (and that is patchy at best). Eventually she decided to adopt the clean-shaven look. Also, she is completely blind in her left eye. It—the eyeball—is all shriveled like a raisin in the socket and looks hideous. She wears an eye patch most of the time, but sometimes she either forgets…or enjoys freaking people out when they see her. I think it is more the latter. She moved to The Sunset Fortress a few weeks ago.

I talked my plans for leaving this place over with Jeff and Rodney earlier today. I made certain that they understood that I have not dismissed that idea. They both have women now! When did that happen? To their credit, neither tried to talk me out of it. I have set my date for departure at February 1st.

Oh…I got my medical clearance form Dr. Gene and Dr. Dennis last night. Of course, I immediately signed up for the next team leaving on a run. I will venture out on the 9th! It will serve two purposes: I will get to see how my dog operates 'in the field' during this excursion, and—more importantly—I will be finding out a few things about myself. I never realized what a toll it took on me just simply being out there. Even when you are in down time…there is no actual break. You must always be alert for trouble.

Every time I think about my upcoming Vegas run, I get butterflies in my stomach. I am about a dozen different types of nervous now. I chalk most of it up to being just a teensy bit stir crazy. This is the longest I've stayed put since all this began a couple years back. God! Has it been that long? I started to believe that the injuries I suffered in the fight with The Genesis Brotherhood might force me to become sedentary. However, I am a resilient girl. So there, World! Take that.

Sunday, January 3

Spent the day in the wooded hills behind the mansion. It's taken me all damned evening to defrost. It was windy, and freezing rain fell most of the time I was out. Sam and I were soaked by the time we came in. I loved it! The only thing that would've made it better is if we'd killed a zombie or ten.

Monday, January 4

Jeff and Rodney came to see me this morning. They came with a rather interesting proposal. I guess Jeff has been doing some research. He found an old phone book and tracked down Erin…Sam's ex-wife. They showed me on a map approximately where it would be.

Since I am leaving on a run anyways, and there are no restrictions as to where we can and can't go, the decision has been made to hit Samuel Todd's ex-wife's old residence and the surrounding neighborhood. It would be quite a luxury if we could find any of his old things like photos and such. I could make a nice package for Baby Snoe.

Here is a weird note; they have had nine births at The Sunset Fortress (that survived). Three were boys, of those three, two were named Sam. Of the six girls, three—that's half!—were named Meredith. Word came to me in a letter from Jenifer. (She also wished me luck with my trip, though I'm not sure if she meant my upcoming run or the impending Vegas journey. She didn't specify.) I guess news travels fast. Nothing like it was just before the Gates of Hell opened, but lots quicker than the Pony Express.

Did I mention that there are nightly runs made between the two main complexes and the mansion? What a difference two years makes.

Wednesday, January 6

Doctor Dennis gave me a check-up today. I got the feeling that he doesn't approve of my plans to leave. In fact, I got the distinct impression that he believed I would be sticking around …having babies! *Well, isn't that a bit Genesis Brotherhoody.*

It made me wonder. I know that there were people who listened to the broadcasts that those crazy people put out there on the airwaves. Did some of that madness stick to several of the listeners? Are there people at either of the complexes or here at the mansion that bought into that crap?

I do have to give this to all the survivors…they are trying very hard to bring back the Old Ways. Does the phrase "Those who do not learn from history are condemned to repeat it," mean anything to these folks?

Thursday, January 7

The team is set.

Jeff, Rodney, Eric Grayfeather, Tina Capps—at twenty-five years old, her meth days have her looking fifty…and not a healthy Susan Sarandon fifty—and I will leave with the midnight transport. We will be dropped off at the 170th Street exit on The Corridor. As much as I am sick to death of rest, I will try my best to get as much as possible in the next twenty-four hours. I seem to remember that you don't get much out there in the wilderness of a dead world.

Saturday, January 9

First night out.

I am sitting on the very same couch that Sam sat on when he held his daughter Beth after she had been bitten by her own mother, Sam's ex-wife Erin. Tina is acting like we're in a damn church. Hmmm…I know I probably shouldn't say 'damn' and 'church' in the same sentence, but sheesh!

It is normal to speak in hushed tones or whispers out in the wilderness because of the fact that noise brings trouble. Zombies are very Pavlovian insomuch that they are very responsive to sound. Yet, this gal Tina is walking around the house and won't speak above a barely audible whisper. I don't know why, but it is annoying the crap out of me. She's read a copy of his journal (which became mine and still is by the way). I lived with the man, sorta. She is acting like we are in the Vatican…and I am sprawled on the Holy Couch flipping through a photo album.

It was really bad when we went upstairs to the bedroom. To Sam's credit, he put them both—Erin and Beth—to rest just like he said…er…wrote. They both had pillowcases over their heads. I imagine that might've made it easier, but I can't imagine what he must've felt using a baseball bat on his loved ones so early on in the zombie rising. Sure, as time has passed, those tasks have gotten easier. If it is a total stranger, it is practically perfunctory. Only, when it is somebody you know or care about…even now it can be rough in the best of circumstances.

This house has very little in the way of salvageable or scavengeable goods. This photo album and a couple others are about it. It seems odd looking at Sam's face again. I'd all but forgotten what he looked like to be honest. What really hit me were the pictures of his daughter Elizabeth. She and Baby Snoe could be twins.

Tomorrow we move through this neighborhood in an indirect way back towards The Corridor. Tonight, however, we sleep in this place. I'm trying to understand how people can see it as some sort of shrine, but honestly, it is just another empty house that used to belong to somebody who eventually turned into one of the walking dead. It is just a house containing long-since-dead corpses that have dried up and barely stink at all anymore.

I will say that I am amazed at how little zombie traffic we encountered on the way here. Also, Eric has done a wonderful job training my goofy dog. Sam—the dog to be clear—is exceptional at sniffing out creepers. Creepers are what we call the ones missing lower extremities. They like to hide in tall grass and under cars. That makes me wonder if they possess some sort of rudimentary reasoning skill. Anyways, Sam made sure we were never surprised.

Tomorrow afternoon we will venture out and do the modern day version of shopping. One final note…I went out to the backyard and put down that female zombie that was *still* hanging from the fence. That was one of the ones that initially convinced Sam that really bad things were happening.

Sunday, January 10

It just can't be this easy. Each of us has a backpack and one of those nifty all-terrain carts that can be hitched to your backpack—each fitted with a quick-release just in case a fight kicks off—that we use to maximize what we can return to base with.

We haven't seen anything larger than a group of seven. They were wandering down a street with no real apparent purpose. We didn't even have to take them out. They were heading the other direction down a cross street.

At this rate, we'll be at The Corridor by tomorrow. Once we reach our spot, we hang a banner that will let any passing vehicle cruising The Corridor know that there is a team ready for pick up. I was more than a little surprised when I discovered that they were using *my* symbol; the one I devised with Jenifer and Dominique.

I'm not trying to come off as too weird, but I have this dread that, now that we've found Erin's residence, there will be a push to locate Sam's. Worse still, I fear that they will turn it into something like a holy relic and attempt to deify the man. Already, his (our) book is given to every survivor on The Corridor. It isn't required reading…yet. I can just see a hundred or so years down the road when he has been turned into a statue, every school that starts up in this area is named for him, and my little pattern is turned into some sort of holy symbol with all these deep meanings. Honestly, all I tried to do was create a design that was easy to recreate, but distinct enough to recognize.

Geez! Somebody is thinking highly of herself tonight. Right? I don't know…maybe. Or maybe I am just being weird.

Monday, January 11

Finally! Some real action. Sam is such a good doggy. Eric, Sam, and I were poking around a small twenty-unit apartment complex. We were coming up pretty big with canned food and even some cleaning supplies. The Warehouse has been great about sharing the wealth, but all manufactured resources are now very finite. You can never have enough toothpaste.

I found a one bedroom place that obviously belonged to one of those role-playing geek-types. It seems he had a real passion for collecting a variety of actual medieval weaponry. That is why I now have a pair of curved blades sheathed on my hips. (Eric called them scimitars.) I also have a spiked-headed mace dangling from a strap on my shoulder.

I was sitting on a rumpled bed prying open the black case that ended up revealing the scimitars. The lock wasn't very impressive, but it still took some jimmying. I guess that is why I didn't see the zombie walk through the front door that we'd left wide open. Eric was in the bathroom pulling stuff out of a cabinet under the sink, so he didn't see or hear it pass him as it trudged down the hallway.

Then Sam growled.

I've gotten sloppy during all these days behind the relative safety of the walls of the Mitchell mansion or inside the confines of an armored truck. I know Sam must've reacted sooner, but I was in serious tunnel-vision mode as I pried open that black case.

I looked up as the middle-aged man stumbled through the door. Sam was already at its feet, tugging on the hem of heavily frayed dress slacks. He growled louder and let loose with a single, sharp bark. I had the mace sitting on the bed beside me, so I grabbed it and brought it down hard with an overhead swing that also scraped away a bunch of that popcorn stuff that most apartments have coating the ceiling.

Every zombie can tell a little story if you look close enough. This guy knew he was turning and tried to kill himself. His mouth is a misshapen mess. Most of his teeth are shattered, and the tongue—what is left of it—is black and crispy looking. There is a nasty hole in the back of the throat that you can see through. This poor guy tried to eat a bullet and didn't put enough angle on the barrel of the pistol he used. He shoved that thing straight back and pulled the trigger. *"How do I know it was a pistol?"* you might ask. It is still dangling from his twisted and broken hand. Two years of God-knows-what has rendered the weapon useless just like most other firearms and ammo these days.

Back to what happened…

I brought that mace down hard on the top of the thing's head and it shattered like an overripe melon at a Gallagher show…and stunk worse than rotten eggs. This was my first field kill since taking on The Genesis Brotherhood. It felt invigorating.

Say what you want, and judge if you like, but THIS is where I belong. Out in the world...killing zombies. After it was over, Sam looked up at me as if to say, "Hey, lady, you better pay better attention if you want to live." Is it natural for a dog to have what appears to be a look of disgust? I scratched those soft ears and gave him a treat from the pouch that Eric told me to carry for just such occasions.

Searching the rest of the apartments, Sam's hackles rose at the doors of five of them. We went in ready for a fight. I got to try out all of my new toys. Whoever that geek was, he kept his weapons in excellent condition. Those scimitar blades were sharp enough to shave with.

We hung the banner an hour ago. Now we wait. When a vehicle passes and sees it, whoever is driving will wait five minutes. If we don't make it to the road in that time, we have to do it over again.

Tuesday, January 12

Back at the Mitchell's place.

I packaged up the stuff I found for Baby Snoe. Yes, I did consider making the trip to The Warehouse myself one last time, but decided against it in the end. I suck at goodbyes. It may be the cowardly thing, but I asked Jeff to deliver it for me.

I thought about just sending it with a supply run, but the way people seem to totally weird out over anything to do with the journal, I thought those photo albums might send them into a fervor. I looked things over one last time, added a copy of my journal and her dad's, and called it good. This one is coming with me to Vegas. Personally, I doubt she will ever see any of this stuff. I don't give humanity, no matter how organized they try to be, a chance in hell of surviving this ordeal.

Oh! How could I forget? Eric gave me a lovely sketch done in pencil. It was of me. I have no idea how or when he had time to do it, but it was creepy good. I put that in the box, too. Now, if she makes it that long, Baby Snoe will have an idea what her mommy looked like. And having both of our journals, hopefully she will feel just a little bit better about how things worked out.

Now it is time to give Sam a bath. I am pretty sure he rolled in dead people guts at some point. There is no way he will be allowed into the house smelling the way he does.

I got my first mission out of the way! It might've been a bit of a cake walk, and I think it was planned that way on purpose because I was coming along. At least I did it. I'd like to make one more before I head out. I think I will go check the sign-up sheets after I bathe Smelly Dog.

Wednesday, January 13

A light snow is falling. Even wearing four layers of clothing, I'm still cold. Being out in this is gonna take some getting used to. I am reminded of this one time when my best friend Katy and I decided that, during the third season of *Survivor*, we would live off of rice and rough it with the cast. It was only thirty-nine days...we knew we could do it. By day four we were sitting shame-faced in Mickey Dees.

I went outside today and cleared an area, made a small fire, and tried to get in sync with Mother Nature. I am now sitting inside in a rocking chair with a thick comforter over my legs and Sam curled at me feet. I've turned into an absolute sissy-girl.

Friday, January 15

I just had the strangest talk.

Eric Grayfeather came into my room after breakfast. He stared at me with those big, dark eyes of his for a few moments (which began to feel like an eternity). Finally, he asked if it was true that I was leaving for Las Vegas soon. I told him it was.

We spent an hour talking. He said that if I equip properly, Highway 26 through Mount Hood and all the way to Madras would be an ideal first leg. I told him I wasn't interested in becoming a Meredith Popsicle, nor did I want to try and recreate some sort of Donner Party adventure considering Sam was currently my only guaranteed company.

He explained that I could use the snow and weather to my advantage. Also, it would be less likely that I would encounter other living people that way. Since dealing with zombies has never been a problem for me and most of my problems have stemmed from encounters with the living…he had a point.

I listened and found myself starting to agree. Cities are still war zones: Living versus Dead; Living versus Living…*et cetera.* Eric helped me make a pretty impressive list of essentials. The good thing is that almost everything that I need is available here or at one of the other compounds.

As he was walking out my door, he stopped. Again I got that long, silent stare. Finally, he said, "I will go with you to Las Vegas." Then, just like that, he left!

That guy is so weird. Don't get me wrong; it'll be nice to make this journey with somebody alongside, but he is probably the last person I would've picked for company.

Saturday, January 16

The Warehouse sent a bus today. One of the scavenger teams came back early this morning to the mansion on foot. They had a small group of survivors along with them. Of the eighteen, two are *ZIPs: Zombie Immune Persons.* (I have no idea when we started attaching catchy acronyms to things again, nor do I care.) One of the ZIPs is a little boy no older than six. I tried to imagine what it must be like for a third of your life to be a citizen of this hellish apocalypse. He's seen things in real life that parents of the Old World would've called a shrink about if he'd been caught watching on television.

I was chosen to help examine all the females. (There are five.) It was not the most exciting day, but I did hear something interesting. There have been a flood of survivors heading east. Word is that the government has secured Rhode Island; actually, Aquidneck, wherever that is. I have no idea if that is true. I quickly realized that I didn't care. So this Aquidneck is cleared of zombies…has power…medical facilities. Big deal. Of course nobody who ever left for this place has come back to confirm the validity of the rumor. Anyways, who wants to live in Newport?

True or not, I imagine that whatever supposed government is in place, it's not for me. Also, it might as well be on the moon. Crossing the city of Portland is a daunting enough task. An entire continent? Not likely.

Sunday, January 17

Doctor Gene came to see me today and asked why I was so intent on leaving. He wanted to know what I hoped to find out there. The first part was easy to answer: stir-crazy. The second part was a little more difficult. There is something inside me that wants to get out there and just *see* things. It isn't just Vegas...it is everything.

The Grand Canyon.

Yellowstone National Park.

The World's Biggest Ball of String.

Still, I've always wanted to see Vegas. I used to watch shows about it. I loved the online poker. It intrigued me to no end. I can't explain it in any way that sounds rational. After the zombie outbreak, it was easy to forget about that city. That was until the radio message. Who knows? If that message would've never come that night, I'd be on my way someplace else with no better explanation. However, for over a year that place has been in my head like a Siren's song. I've been accused of being stubborn and bull-headed. Not once have I tried to deny it.

Tuesday, January 19

A small herd found our little retreat today. It happened early this morning several hours before sunrise. (Not that there was much of one with all the heavy, gray clouds that have been dumping snow on us all damn day.)

Sam's growls are what woke me even before Randy stuck his head inside my room and told me to suit up. In fact, by the time he did, I was pulling on my boots and inspecting my gloves for any rips.

I climbed up on the platform built along the inside of the wall. It allows you to see over the wall and lets you hold a steady position while you jab an approaching zombie in the head. Easypeazy-one-two-threezy! Only…to do that for over three hours really makes you think your arms might fall off. I don't understand how the zombies aren't simply frozen!

Right now, with the threat dealt with, my shoulders feel like they have a billion knots in them. My arms feel like overcooked noodles, and I have cramps because my period started at some point during the battle. Yay!

Wednesday, January 20

It actually feels like the weather is trying to conspire against me. Not a day has been above the low teens for three days now. There is also an additional two feet of snow on the ground. For those of you who didn't grow up in the Portland area…that is unheard of.

Eric came in from the drag-and-burn detail a little while ago to express his doubts as to our projected date of departure. Am I the only person who, once she sets her sights on something, can't let it go? I am feeling that supercharged mix of adrenaline and anticipation as I wait for my target date.

Sure, February was kinda arbitrary; and these days, what is the difference between the first and the twenty-first? I'll tell you what the difference is: I set a date and that is when I told myself that I was leaving. That may be one of the problems with writing this stuff down…I always have my own words staring back at me.

Friday, January 22

Spent the day outside the fence with Sam.

Everybody is kinda pissed at me right now. Okay! So I kinda forgot to tell anybody I was leaving. Last time I checked, I was an adult.

***

Now that I have cooled off mentally and warmed up physically, I made my apologies. I get it. We tell people we are leaving so that they don't worry. It isn't about being beholden to others…it is simply courtesy.

That said…it was so much FUN! Sam and I slipped out to the neighborhood next to the school we got trapped in back when I was pregnant. I shuddered just a little when I walked past that gymnasium where I almost died.

I should back up a bit. Last night, Eric came in with a cross-bow for me. It is rigged with a spool of nylon line that is a *Wham* video Day-Glo green. It is similar to fishing line. All I have to do is attach it to the bolt I am about to fire. Once I shoot, I can actually pull the bolt back. That is handy in so many ways. If I am low on ammo and there are zombies…I can reuse my ammo. It is like a video game power.

"MEREDITH HAS UNLIMITED AMMO." You use your own video game voice there. I always hear the voice from *Mortal Kombat.*

So, once I got down to that neighborhood, I actually had to search for a target. The first test went well. Sam growled and I just went in the direction he was pointing. Initially, I didn't see anything, and then this ponytailed, middle-aged yuppie guy came struggling through the bushes. I tagged it on the third shot (my aim is a little rusty). I kept reeling in my shot, reloading, and firing. Once I scored the hit, I had to actually use my hands to tug the bolt free.

Here's what I don't get. Pulling the bolt back, the head seemed to come apart like wet *papier-mâché.* It wasn't like the bolt had to line up and come back through the hole it made going in. I had to give a few hefty yanks, but eventually I had my bolt back. I kept thinking that the line would snap from my pulling so hard. After a dozen or so firm yanks, the skull sorta split, and my bolt came free. So…why don't these things just rot and fall over? I'm no Bill Nye, hell, the only reason I passed my high school science class is because the teacher made a pass at me. I was failing at the time. We made a deal. I got a "C" and he got to stay out of prison and off the six o' clock news. (He got busted two years later in the back of his car with a member of the girl's JV basketball team, so all I did is postpone the inevitable.)

Huh…got off track there for a second. My question was: How come those things aren't all just puddles of rot by now?

It's not like they have a plentiful food source any longer. It just doesn't make sense. But I guess neither does the whole 'dead getting up and eating the living' thing. Am I right?

After my first field test of the weapon and retrieval line, I started wading out deeper into the surrounding areas. Eventually, I found what I was looking for. Nine of those things were shuffling through a small park. I got their attention with a little whistle. The moan they cut loose with might be the same as it always has been, but the muffled quality of a snow-covered world made it extra creepy.

I climbed on top of one of those big wooden play structures. Once I found a spot, I made Sam sit and stay inside this reeking plastic bubble with lens-shaped oval windows. Then I stood on the platform attached to the rusted monkey bars. I was almost concerned that I was too close. Their fingertips—or what was left of them in most cases—brushed the bottom lip of the platform. I fired down into their heads from above. The ground actually helped here. There was a bit of a slope, and these things fell away. That kept the others from using the downed bodies to get a better swipe at me.

Getting the bolt free was work, but doable. The nasty part was cleaning them off between each use. It is time consuming, but in a world where consumables have stopped being mass-produced, you need to adapt. Next time out I will try it from the roof of a building.

Saturday, January 23

Started gathering things for the trip. Eric has ski attachments for the harness carts. It will make moving through the snow a lot easier. We have some awesome sub-zero outdoor equipment. As a test, tonight we're making a snow shelter and sleeping outside. I'm actually giddy. Eric seemed less enthused, but he never shows any emotion, and certainly not excitement. He always looks so solemn. At least I won't have to worry about him talking my ear off when we are out in the wilderness.

Monday, January 25

The sleeping bags work great! I also learned how to make a really ghetto version of an igloo. Sam seemed to enjoy climbing down into the foot of my sleeping bag. I was actually worried about that; the whole part of how to keep my dog safe and warm that is. Between the awesome sleeping bag and my dog, I was quite toasty.

Thursday, January 28

Just returned from The Sunset Fortress. They threw some sort of crazy party. There was quite a bit of homemade hooch being sampled and traded.

Yes. I was a naughty girl. No. I don't remember his name. Yes. I used protection. Jeez! I'm giving myself the third degree. All I will say is that he was quite *enthusiastic*. Only had to redirect him once. What is it about when things get a teensy bit nasty…men always go for the ass?

Friday, January 29

The weather conspiracy seems to be fading. It has rained all day. Not enough to wash away all the snow, but enough to diminish it so that we don't have to trudge through knee-deep drifts. That will wear you out quick.

In case you are wondering, Eric and I don't ski. And I don't have the patience to learn. It would probably come in handy, but we voted and it was unanimous. Besides, I would feel like my mobility was seriously hampered if I was on skis. When zombies pop up, you need to be flexible. A novice skier would be the equivalent of a free zombie buffet.

Sure, I've seen those movies where the action hero has a shootout with the bad guys while he is on skis, careening down a pine-freckled mountain. I've seen lots of things in movies. However, I've watched enough episodes of *MythBusters* to know that a lot of it is a bunch of hooey.

I loaded my harness cart today. I have an assortment of weapons, plenty of food (not looking forward to eating MREs again), filtration canteens, and an impressive amount of gear to help me stave of freezing to death.

Everybody here at the Mitchell place has made a point to stop in and say goodbye, give well-wishes, all that stuff. I would've liked to have seen Jenifer one last time before leaving. She is at The Warehouse for some reason. I did look for her at Sunset before the drinking kicked into high gear and had been a shade disappointed. Maybe she's no good at saying goodbye either. I will miss her.

I'm not trying to sound fatalistic, but I do not believe that I will never see this place again. Sure…that's where the ominous music plays…the foreshadowing of my eventual fate. Blah, blah, blah. Actually, it is that I don't plan on coming back. This is the start of the next phase of my adventure. There is a whole big world out there that I haven't seen. Getting Vegas out of the way sorta kicks off my checklist.

Sunday, January 31

This will be my last night in a bed for a while. I hope I can sleep, I'm so excited! This is really going to happen. Tomorrow morning I will put on my gear, check everything out, and Eric will join me and Sam at the gate.

I don't have any idea what I will find *out there*. I only know that I will be *out there*. I understand the idea of safety…but with an entire world *out there*, how can anybody simply hide behind the walls and live in one tiny space?

Monday, February 1

Made it all the way to the outskirts of Portland on the first day! Of course, most of the day was spent crossing the West Hills. We can see Mount Hood against a perfect frame of blue sky. It is crystal clear…and FREEZING!

We stopped midday in the neighborhood that I hid in with Lynn when I first passed through this way and our group got separated. Lynn's is just one of the many faces that haunt my nightmares. I can't really recall the face of any zombie I've killed—and there have been hundreds, if not thousands—but I can clearly see Lynn's. To put that in clearer perspective, I've once again all but forgotten what Sam's—Baby Snoe's dad, not my dog's—face looks like. But when I close my eyes, Lynn is there. Killing her haunts me worse than anything else I've seen or done.

***

Got a little morose for a moment there. That's one of the problems with solitude and aloneness (I don't know if that's really a word, but I like it). Left to your thoughts, it is easy for some of the worst to demand center stage in your mental theater.

Travelling with Eric Grayfeather is exactly how I imagined: quiet. Sometimes I actually forget that I am with another person. He rarely walks within twenty yards of me. Then, out of the blue, he will grab my arm and point something out to me. Half of the time I don't know what I am supposed to be looking at because he doesn't say anything. Like, one time, he did that grab-the-arm-and-point thing. So I am trying my hardest to see something. Then, this deer bounded out of some bushes. I don't know how in the hell he saw it *before* it came out of those bushes…but it was the biggest deer I've seen in my life. A few zombies popped up along the way, but nothing that even registered as interesting. Killing them has a tendency to be about as normal as swatting mosquitoes. You learn to ignore the ones that are far off and only administer death to those who may be buzzing in for a drink. Then, if they bite you, it is all you can think about. See? Zombies are just like mosquitoes.

Moving back through the city and out of the relatively well-patrolled area I've called home for the past several months, I heard something I haven't heard in a long time. In fact it was conspicuous in its absence...gunfire. Yep, folks are still out here in pockets of who-knows-how-many. Some still have good ammo to use in their fight to live just one more day.

Funny. If humanity as a whole were a dog or horse or something, we'd say put it out of its misery. There is something to be said about either our ability to survive (like the cockroach), or our refusal to accept death as an alternative.

Tuesday, February 2

THAT was more like it!

We crossed the bridge today. I came close to actually considering my chances with the ice cold water of the Willamette River (which has chunks of ice the size of cars floating in it).

We got up early because Eric said he wanted to cross the bridge *before* sunrise. So, after I was done cursing at him, we packed up and got moving. Sam didn't seem to mind and was bounding along like we were going to the park. He sniffed and peed on everything.

As we moved up the on-ramp, my happy puppy suddenly switched into Growly Dog. All the hair on his back was standing up, and he stepped back to be right at my side. I already knew from my previous crossing of the bridge that some of those things were trapped inside their vehicles. I thought that was what Sam had started growling at. (Apparently someplace where it is okay to end a sentence with a preposition.)

Silly Meredith.

We were actually on the bridge just as the eastern horizon was turning a lovely shade of pink. The appearance of a few bobbing shadows had me drawing my scimitars. (Did I mention that I'd taken time practicing using them in both hands simultaneously? I'm still a bit awkward, but steadily improving.) Eric drew this really sweet looking saber he found at a museum. Just like that, we were ready.

He moved to the left side of the bridge and I took the right. Fighting close has its uses at times, but outside like this, it is often better to have some space between yourself and your companions. Sam stayed glued to my side—good doggy!—and I readied myself for the fight. I counted an even dozen coming just for little old me. Eric looked like he would be facing double that.

The first one closed to within range, a black kid in what looked to have been his early teens. He was wearing a Portland basketball jersey with the number twenty-two. My blade caught him in the temple. Ah yes…the stinging buzz…how I've missed it so. I snapped my wrist back to keep the blade from catching in the skull as the zombie dropped at my feet.

Ducking beneath the outstretched arms of the next one, I popped up and simultaneously brought my blade under the chin of one zombie and straight up into the brain while kicking back at the one I'd ducked, sending it over the rail and to the river below.

It took me a few seconds to realize that Sam was facing back the way we'd come. He was hunched over and snarling something fierce. I glanced, and had to do a double-take. They were rail-to-rail, and coming for us. So much for them being scattered to the Four Winds after two years. I gave a warning whistle to Eric and he responded with an acknowledging hoot; Eric can't whistle.

I transformed into a dervish. That was a mistake. I have not been out in a while and forgot that, in situations like the one we were facing, you need to remain methodical and even. Not only did I have to spend energy on hitting a zombie for a second or even third time because I wasn't aiming, but I wore down from the constancy of the fight.

The ground became so slick that I started having difficulty with my footing. Then there was the creeper that I totally missed. It grabbed my left wrist—the little girl couldn't have been more than six years old when she'd been pulled apart—and yanked me off balance as I was trying to recover from one of the times when I'd slipped. I drove one of my blades into the top of her skull and rolled away as two more zombies sorta belly flopped right where I'd just been sprawled.

Getting to my knees, I felt something grab my left hand. My scimitar clattered to the pavement and I screamed as I felt teeth grinding down on my bones. Thank God for the mesh lining in the gloves. I made eye contact with Eric, and even from this far across the bridge, I could see the concern clearly etched in his face. I shook my head and went back to fighting. I started by punching the zombie gnashing on my hand square in the nose. Next, I shoved my other blade into his face. It fell...taking my glove with it. I absolutely did not have the time to retrieve it.

I was now surrounded.

That was when I considered the rail. By now, Sam was going berserk. He was growling, nipping, and tugging at the hems of these things that had me surrounded. I quickly realized that if I jumped, my chance of survival was zero. It wasn't just how high up we were, but that combined with the ice chunks made for a bad situation. I sought the thinnest point in their little line, and burst through the shrinking circle of undead. I still get the heebie-jeebies thinking about all those dead hands brushing my skin.

Ewww!

When I popped out the other side, I discovered Sam bounding around in a tizzy. He was giving this lady bus driver a real problem. I planted my blade in the back of her skull on the way past. Eric had fared much better. A pile of corpses were strewn about him.

We jogged the rest of the way across the bridge and decided to zig through a ruined neighborhood where we found an empty two-story house that looked exactly like every other house we passed. I have no explanation or logic behind our choice, it was simply luck. We totally scored!

We didn't have to touch any of our supplies and I am stuffed. It will almost suck to leave this place tomorrow. I just polished off two cans of mandarin oranges, a jar of sundried tomatoes in olive oil, and a tin of smoked oysters. Right now I am snacking on some magnificently stale Grandma's oatmeal cookies. (Don't knock wax packaging.)

It only gets better. I found a Sony Discman portable CD player. Right now I am curled up in a wicker Papasan chair with overstuffed cushions. Sam is in my lap under the blankies, and I am listening to Mozart. The disc says this is *Requiem*, which I realize is somewhat ironic giving the state of things. Eric said it was creepy, but I think it is beautiful. I found a package of a dozen batteries that work, but I will use this sparingly. It is an absolute treasure. There was a cd wallet with a few dozen discs in it. I plan on finding a way to bring this with me.

We really did take a lot of things for granted in the Old World. So much was readily available that it didn't require thought…just want. And now, music like this might be gone forever. *This* is what I meant about living. The simple act of finding this and hearing the music brought real tears to my eyes.

Eric is in the next room snoring. Every time I change the discs or there is a break between tracks on the cd, I hear him. Is there a more abrasive sound than snoring in this world? I think not. I'll even take wailing zombies over that sound.

It is almost dark outside. From my seat, I can look out the window to the street below. The dead stroll by like there is a twenty-four hour block party happening. Sometimes, one comes up to this house in particular. It paws at the door or scratches at the boards covering the windows, and then it wanders off. I think I'll stop writing for a bit and just enjoy this little luxury.

Friday, February 5

Someplace close there is a freakin' war goin' on! We've taken refuge in—of all things—a trailer park beside the highway. From here we can see an apartment complex across the way. Five of the three-story units are ablaze. Occasionally I can see shadowy forms dashing one way or the other. Also, we keep seeing bright flashes arc through the sky. (I think it is Molotov cocktails.)

Obviously this place has been picked clean. The trailer we are hiding in is nothing more than a shell. Even the wiring is gone. Sam doesn't like it at all.

The best thing about what is going on out there right now is that the zombies are drawn to all the activity on the other side of the highway. I haven't heard any sounds to indicate that either side has firearms. It is actually sort of creepy. Sometimes there is screaming. I can remember a time when I might've felt the need to go over there and get involved…pick a side. Not anymore.

Saturday, February 6

Highway 26 is also called Mount Hood Highway. We are out of the more densely populated areas and now camped in a farmhouse. The sign we passed, and eventually decided to turn down, said this is 'SE Stone Rd.' It intersected the highway and seemed as good of a place as any to turn off and look for our nightly lodgings.

There has been a herd through here recently. You can tell it is recent because the swathe of destruction isn't all mucky and full of puddles from this morning's rain shower. (Actually, that was Eric's observation, but once I looked and gave it some thought, it was kind of obvious.) The rain came early, but it has been sunny all day. Well, at least until about five minutes ago. Now all the trenches made by an undead army on the move are filling with water.

The field out back has about a twenty-yard-wide 'path' trampled through it. I wonder what started them this way. The reason I am curious is that, whatever used to grow in that field, it's now a head-high jungle. I've seen a few herds, and they always take the path of least resistance. The main body usually sticks to the road and the overspill will flow into the adjacent yards or fields. This group turned off the road and went into the field…like it was in pursuit of something or somebody.

Of course we checked it out up close. Not even a straggler in sight. There were the usual bits and pieces. Sam wouldn't step a foot in the area. Eric had a moment of unusual mirthfulness. We were poking around and he came up to me with an arm! After I gave an embarrassing shriek—and he stopped laughing—he held out the arm to me and insisted that I look. I did, but was obviously missing something.

"The watch," he said, holding the arm up for closer inspection. I looked and shrugged. "It's a Montblanc," Eric snickered as he pointed to the grime-smeared timepiece.

I still didn't get what the dickens he was trying to say.

"This watch was worth more than I made in a year…and I had a decent job." He chuckled, and then tossed the arm into the tall growth.

I watched it sail, proud that I refused to make a comment about how time flies. As we resumed our search for a place to sleep, I began to wonder. What was wrong with our society that a man—it was definitely a man's arm—could wear a watch that cost more than what a "normal" person made in a year? I mean, I get the whole "haves" and "have nots" thing. It is a fact of life…even today. I have seen groups come in with people on the verge of starvation, teeth falling out, skin laced with lesions. Meanwhile, those living along the corridor are eating three meals a day and holding parties complete with alcoholic beverages.

Perhaps we are unredeemable.

Sunday, February 7

Haven't gone far today. The night brought in some more nasty weather. Everything is coated with about a quarter inch of ice. It looks beautiful, but it is all but impossible to move around in. And as for fighting zombies in it? That's just asking for trouble.

I spent this afternoon cleaning and sharpening weapons. There wasn't much to glean from this place, but it was kinda interesting flipping through photo albums. I played a little game, giving each picture a story and some dialog. Eric was a curiously attentive audience. Sam, on the other hand, could've cared less. All that mattered to him was the occasional scratch behind the ears.

Monday, February 8

Outside, the sounds of Mother Nature kicking ass can be heard. Branches and all sorts of hanging and dangly things are popping, snapping, and breaking. We've been lucky, this old house is holding up fine. There weren't any trees in the yard that could prove a hazard. That had nothing to do with our choice when we picked it, but it gives us something to actually be aware of next time.

We are keeping a fire blazing around the clock. It is FUH-REE-ZIN outside!

Tuesday, February 9

Somebody died late last night. Sam woke me with his growls. Eric and I were up and armed in a flash before either of us realized what was going on. Peeking out of the tarp-covered window (we do that to hide the light from our fire) we couldn't see anything in the absolute darkness of a dead world. Then we heard it: The Scream.

I won't ever get used to that sound. A human being makes a very distinct shriek when they are being ripped open, torn apart, and feasted upon. I am sure I don't have to tell you. If you're reading this, you've survived long enough to have heard it a hundred, if not a thousand, times. It is like no other sound in the world.

The good news is that the weather seems to be clearing up again. We are hoping to move on tomorrow. Good thing...I'm getting a little stir crazy. If I try to sharpen my blades again, or re-organize my cart, I think Eric will smack me.

Wednesday, February 10

We're spending the night in a little colony. We met one of their scouting parties early this morning. This group is surprisingly well-supplied, armed, and organized for as out in the open as they seem to live.

Oh...did I mention that the oldest person in this group is seventeen?

This place used to be some sort of small Christian school back in the day. All of the children here—and I only use the term technically as they all seem quite grown up—were at a "lock in" at the church to support a drug-free life or something. They were all praying or whatever people did at those sorts of things. However, one of the "bad" kids had managed to sneak in a radio. He heard the first big news report and told the others. Of course they didn't believe him. When morning came and the bus driver didn't show up to take the kids home, they started trying to reach their parents. The youth group leader was the first to reach somebody. That person said the same thing that any of the children who actually managed to get through to somebody heard: STAY PUT! We'll come for you as soon as we can.

Nobody ever came.

Well, at least not anybody still living. They saw their first zombie that day. Fear was their biggest ally. Several of the children witnessed the youth group leader ripped apart...then, moments later, get back up. It's an old story by now, isn't it? Some of the parents tried to get to them, but that didn't go well either. They spent the next several days hiding in one of the bathrooms after they'd barricaded the doors with everything they could find.

Somehow, they've managed. I guess they normally kill adults on sight these days. (They had a very bad experience that none of them will go into detail on. I can only guess.) It seems that me being a female, plus the cute puppy factor that Sam rocks so effortlessly, they decided to take a chance. Chalk one up for the big goofy dog.

These kids have their stuff together. We ate steaming hot venison stew and some very coarse bread. But I am so impressed. They have wood stoves and an underground room for cold storage. There is a hand-pumped well (they boil all their water just to be safe) and even a well-stocked safe room. To their credit, they wouldn't let us see it after one of the little ones blurted out its existence. Who can blame them?

They have an array of long spears up on the roof just in case the building gets surrounded. They have hundreds of arrows for the dozens of bows just sitting around everywhere. Also, there is a field out back. A structure sits right in the middle. It looks like a giant sawhorse, only the crossbeam is about ten feet off the ground. It's at least twenty feet long. Currently there are five corpses hanging from it. Each has a sign around the neck. Three say "pedophile" one says "murderer" and the last says "thief".

Like I said, these kids don't play around. They certainly don't need anything from us. My guess is that they will be fine long after Eric and I (along with Sam-the-Wonder-dog) have gone on our way. Some of the girls are very timid, even around me, but many reminded me of what I remember reading about Amazon warriors. Nobody stays still here very long either. I've noticed a constant state of energy that is kinda tiring to be around. Also, it has made it impossible to get a real head count of how many are here. I think the number is close to thirty.

We made it clear that we will be moving on come morning. Don't get me wrong, it was nice being here for this brief stay. It made me miss Jenifer just a bit. I hope she is doing okay.

Thursday, February 11

Didn't go far today. We are in a giant U-Pull-It yard. The metal fence has collapsed in a bunch of spots, but Eric insisted that we stop here. He says that this place is a "goldmine" of potential supplies. The good news is that the zombies don't seem all that interested in wandering around in here. If this were the movies, they'd be lurking in every shadow. However, without any snacky-snacks holed up in here trying to survive, they've got no reason.

***

Eric has me hiding in the cab of an eighteen-wheeler. Now I know what he was all excited about. The kids apparently don't know much about how to test for a viable alternator. He found, tested, and removed a dozen. Then, he jogged off into the darkness after telling me to stay put and that he would be back by sunset. Sam is snoozing in the back of the cab while I sit here waiting.

I can't really bitch…I mean he's doing a very selfless thing. I just wish he would've clued me in instead of wandering around this place for an hour with all its blind spots. I don't care if he did have Sam beside him as an alarm…I hated not knowing what the hell was up.

Oh well.

Part of me wants to do a little exploring of my own, but I'm not that foolish. It feels weird just sitting around doing nothing. I have no idea why I couldn't tag along. I mean, Eric doesn't strike me as a glory hound. I don't believe that he did this for some sort of special recognition...I just...

Crap! I just started my period.

Friday, February 12

Catching a break in the weather today. It is sunny and, while I wouldn't call it warm, it is tolerable. That is one of the beauties of the Pacific Northwest. If you don't like the weather...wait five minutes.

Eric got back last night just *after* sunset. So, of course, I gave him a little old fashioned Meredith ass chewing. (Yay hormones!) Then we ate dinner and turned in. On the plus, he tried to make things up to me by whipping up some of his yummy venison stew.

We had a long stretch of open road to travel. However, the signs are giving us ominous messages like: Sandy 12mi.

Around midafternoon, we stumbled upon the Sandy School for the Blind. I saw the campus through the trees. Initially I thought it was a small college. Since it was getting late and the last sign warned that we would reach Sandy in three miles, the school seemed like a good place to camp for the night.

It was a nightmare!

I can't imagine the horror that the students here must've felt. Oh...and blindness *does* have a cure: zombieism. There was no difference in how the walking dead from that school pursued us versus any other zombie I've encountered since this ordeal began.

We slipped through the trees, coming in to the...campus? ...from the rear. We didn't even know it was a school for the blind at first. That discovery came when we circled the place to get a better look. The remnants of the sign out front revealed this place's identity. Perhaps that is why we thought we could slip in and see if there was anything worth taking. An institutional cafeteria is always worth a peek.

We didn't have to break in. The main doors in front are gone. Perhaps that should've been the first warning. The halls were littered with garbage, the walls smeared with what had to be blood. There were even some places where the ceiling was splattered.

The echo of the moans and groans of the undead quickly had Sam's hackles up and our weapons drawn. I went with my scimitars; Eric chose a long-handled hatchet. Finding the school's cafeteria wasn't a problem. It was what we discovered inside that changed everything.

Neither of us thought much about how many guide dogs there might be. Nor did we know that this place had its own guide dog training facility. My conservative guess puts the dog population here at about a hundred. They were in clusters, just sprawled on each other. All of them were horribly torn and mangled. Some missing a leg...or two...or more.

I can't get that image out of my head. It looked like several of the students had come here; many with their dogs, but there were so many that there has to be more to the story. It looks like the dogs were infected first. There weren't any students in the cafeteria...zombie or otherwise. The floor was littered with parts. Oh! There were a few heads. That will give you the willies I'm tellin' ya. Some were on their sides; a few had a neck stub to rest on. Still, when those eyes roll your way... Eww! Amongst the body parts were lots of cleanly stripped bones.

Good thing for us that zombified dogs are no faster than their human counterparts. We sealed the door, closing it with an audible click that sounded like a gunshot to me.

Then, we ran. We continued along Highway 26, and it was late afternoon when we found a quaint little church beside the road. We had to dispatch a few of the inhabitants before we could close the place up and seal it for the night.

I just have the feeling that tomorrow is gonna be a bitch.

Saturday, February 13

This brings back memories.

Eric, Sam, and I are hiding out in a multiplex. We are only a stone's throw away from a hospital-turned-fortress. The people there have figured a way to get in and out without being seen by the zombies. They have erected an impressive barricade around the parking lot using school busses, city busses, fire engines, and

RVs. Then there is the wall of cars parked bumper-to-bumper. After that—as if there was a need for more—there are coils of razor wire like the type you see atop the fences of prisons.

The folks at the hospital weren't outwardly hostile, but they weren't friendly either. When we spotted what I imagine were their sentries on the roof, I waved. They didn't. At least they didn't try to attack us or anything like that. However, they sure as hell didn't roll out the welcome mat.

We kept moving and came to a part of the highway that was so congested we had no choice but to cut through a parking lot of a strip mall. We didn't see the mob until they were right on top of us. I guess they had the shopping center surrounded. We had to cut through some trees to get off the highway. It was literally as simple as choosing the wrong side of the road. Had we gone to the other side, I think we slip by those bastards without them seeing us.

So…here's where things went wrong.

We emerged through the trees and Sam immediately starts growling. The worst part about being in an area with so many of the undead is the pervasiveness of the stench. It is so overpowering that it loses its ability to be a warning of sorts because you are flooded with the smell. Walking past cars with zombies trapped inside…just…they were freaking everywhere. Oh, and about the cars; the windows were so coated with filth that you couldn't see inside any of the sealed up ones unless you were directly in front of or behind the vehicle. Of course the cars with the windows down were a real treat. Every single one we passed seemed to have one of those bastards strapped inside. It would get to moaning as we crept by…like a new aged car alarm.

Anyways, Sam growls and about a hundred heads turn. The problem now is that we are pulling our harnessed carts. While great for all sorts of terrain, they suck when you are trying to do something fast. Eric and I collided with each other…and I fell. It was straight out of a *Three Stooges* routine. To add to the slapstick humor of the moment, I fell in a big, squishy mud puddle.

By the time I got up, Eric was engaged with three of those things. I fumbled around and managed to scoop up one of my scimitars just as the first one reached me. Since it is impossible to backpedal in the harness, I hit the quick-release and tossed the harness into the cart. Eric was already disappearing back through the trees we'd just come through. We both know that in situations like this, it is every man or woman for themselves. No hard feelings.

By the time I emerged back and beside the highway, Eric was weaving through a gap in the vehicles. He disappeared behind a black pick-up truck. Sam was standing in that gap staring at me. When I almost reached him, he bolted away again. He stopped at every opening between cars and waited for me to almost catch up before taking off again. I don't know if he was actually following Eric, or just leading me away from the oncoming horde of zombies.

We emerged about a half mile up the road. Some of the zombies managed to stay on my tail, which flustered the hell out of me. I was forced to push the cart by now, and my body was drenched with sweat.

I know that you might be wondering how I couldn't elude the slow moving undead out in the open. First, there were all the cars. You try getting a cart to twist and turn in a space where I can barley fit it, much less turn it. I had to turn when there was room…that meant long bursts of straight ahead.

When I got to the other side of the highway, I saw Eric climbing through a ticket window of a huge theater. He had already killed off a few zombies, unloaded his cart, broke his cart down, and shoved it through the box office window. Then, Eric went through the hole. He was nice enough to help me once I finally made it to him.

We didn't have any way to block the wall of glass doors at the entrance—some of which were already broken—so we made a hasty retreat in to one of the pitch black theaters. We had to pull out one of our flashlights with the red lenses in order to see anything as we hurried down the aisle. We were gonna duck out back and keep running, but when we managed to force the exit door open, we found ourselves in a long—perhaps thirty feet or so—corridor. We decided that it was as good of a buffer as we were likely to find. We wedged the entry door to this particular theater shut and have decided to wait things out a while in here.

We know that there are survivors in the area. That means that it is likely that any of the zombies that have been drawn by us will eventually be drawn away by other distractions. Seriously, zombies have the memory of a goldfish…at best.

The hornet's nest we have kicked around these parts will die down. In the few hours we have been here, the pounding and other noises that go along with a zombie horde have dwindled significantly. Twice I have gone out to that corridor and listened at the doors at either end. It is silent. While I can't be totally sure, I am fairly certain those doors lead outside. Probably open out to a side or rear parking lot.

Well…I've had enough of Eric's dirty looks as I run down the batteries on one of our flashlights. I will stop writing for now.

Sunday, February 14

I thought we might be screwed, but we finally got out of Sandy. Well…the main part of it anyways. We are now shacked up in this really posh house outside of town. It sits at the edge of a gigantic farm. Hard to tell what used to grow here, the military took a position on this land complete with what look like holding pens and massive trench burial sites. There are lots of blackened bones scattered around from the burning piles. (It takes a lot of heat to burn a body down to just ash. Bonfires wouldn't be enough to do the trick.)

We are up on this hill that offers a perfect view of the highway. A forest flanks us on three sides. As nice as this place is, it has been absolutely gutted. It is worse than a *Who* house after the *Grinch* picked it clean on Christmas Eve night.

We are in the rear of the place with a nice fire going in the sunken tub of what used to be the master bedroom. Eric nailed a few fluffy, white bunnies for us to eat.

I can't recall being so tired in a long time. We've been ducking and dodging for the past thirty or so hours. It is a blessing to be able to lay back and relax. Plus, I doubt we'll be moving from this spot any time soon. It's snowing again…hard.

It has been a while since I've seen so many of those things scattered around and lurking at every corner. Between the singles, roamers, and the always dangerous creepers under seemingly every vehicle…I've probably put down over two hundred of them in the past day and a half.

I kept hearing the voice of *Doctor Who*—the dreamy David Tennant version—saying, "Run!" We even had to ditch our carts for a while and go back for them. I was really glad mine didn't get stolen by some passing survivor, and there seem to be a peculiarly high number around these parts. We just got so tangled up with fighting and evading, we had no choice.

At one point, we were hiding out in an overgrown cemetery. I'm not sure, but I believe that there are still people out there who think that the dead will claw their way from the grave. Those people have never read *Behind the Formaldehyde Curtain*. Mouths are sewn shut, organs are removed—including the brain—and the body is pumped full of chemicals. I get that zombies are not normal…Wait. Let me rephrase that. Zombies didn't *used* to be normal.

Nowadays, *we* are the anomaly.

Early this morning or late last night—can't tell which—we made it back to where we'd ditched our carts. We hitched up feeling pretty safe, but made sure to lead the ones we gathered just in that short time back to the movie house. We used the woods to get to this place once we spotted it to keep any zombies off our trail.

We were moving along the single-lane road that runs parallel to the highway when the first great big snowflakes began to fall. These didn't drift gracefully. Nope, they plummeted to earth.

The best thing about this place as opposed to a lot of the houses in the area is that it has all its doors and windows intact. So, now, a million dollar home is nothing more than a flop house for a pair of vagrants and a dog.

Monday, February 15

Wow! There's at least three feet of snow on the ground outside. We are so totally stuck. There is absolutely no way that we can leave. It snowed all night and has been coming down steady all day. We can hang here for a while, I guess. I know that we will have to deal with snow in the mountains, but we ain't there yet. I won't ever say this out loud in front of Eric, but perhaps we should've waited one more month before heading out.

I can't help it; I wanted to get out of that confined, mundane, prison-like environment. I felt as if I were dying a slow death. I can't explain it anymore beyond that. At least Eric hasn't said anything. I don't believe it matters to him one way or the other. I have to say it again; I couldn't be making this trip with a better person.

Friday, February 20

The storm has passed and we've had a sunny day to enjoy…at least from inside. It is freezing out there. Still, there is this square of sunlight coming through a window that is blissful. Oh, and Eric bagged a deer. He called it a spike; I call it yummy. We have feasted the past two days.

From our position overlooking the highway, we haven't seen much movement of any kind—zombie or otherwise. And have I mentioned the glare? It never once crossed my mind until Eric handed me these dark goggles. He thought it was amusing that I would even consider going up into the mountains with no eye protection. To my credit, I didn't stick my tongue out at him until *after* his back was turned.

Wednesday, February 24

It was nice to be on the move again. Because of the downpour of rain the past two days, much of the snow has been washed away. There are still some mounds here and there, but the road is fairly deserted and easy to travel along.

So, about these mounds or "snow drifts" that are scattered about; some of them contain nasty surprises. I'd all but forgotten that zombie that I'd seen fall in the street and eventually stop trying to stand again on the slick ice. It'd frozen in place then gotten covered with snow. Today we learned quick to avoid anything that even remotely resembles a lump, bulge, or drift.

We were passing this gigantic truck stop just after sunrise. There were dozens of rigs with names that would mean nothing to the next generation. We'd decided to poke around since we'd spotted a Pepsi and a Lays truck. There were a few roamers that we could see, and we considered skipping past, but Eric wanted a Pepsi.

I didn't see too many of those things to handle and decided that it couldn't hurt. I wasn't going to deny my travel buddy something that seemed so simple. It was when we stepped up to the rear of the trailer with the big, open cargo doors that we almost suffered a terrible loss. Eric went to kick the ice-crusted pile of snow that was kinda in the way. He didn't expect to discover a solid center. The look on his face would've been funny when he tripped, if not for the zombie.

A big hand with fingers like kielbasa sausages burst from the mound and wrapped around his ankle. If that big old trucker—or what was left of him—still had any of his lower jaw left, there would've been a remarkably different outcome to that encounter. The top teeth scraped Eric's pant leg, but didn't get through to skin or anything like that.

I drove one of my scimitars into the side of its head and kicked it away. After catching our breath, we returned to the task we'd initially embarked on. Swinging the cargo doors the rest of the way open proved to be a huge disappointment. The roof was nothing but brown stalactites from where the Pepsi bottles had burst and sprayed the ceiling.

We did find a few twenty-ouncers that hadn't exploded, but it was an unsatisfactory haul. We also salvaged some sour cream and onion chips. After our snack break, we sat there not talking about that mound incident.

We got back on the road and passed a roadside diner that was nothing but a charred husk, but right after this dog-leg turn, we happened upon a school building. It was tiny, not even a cafeteria, and situated in a perfect place. We had a great view back the way we came for a good distance, along with a wide open look ahead.

I don't believe in fate, luck, or divine providence. That said, we could've easily kept on going and pulled up at a place a mile or two up the road. I do think that we were both still a little spooked by that snowdrift incident at the rear of the Pepsi truck. Whatever the reason, we chose this place to stop for the night.

They came from the north. It started about an hour ago. Sam's growling alerted us. Lit up by the setting sun, we can see them by the hundreds…maybe thousands: a horde.

Thursday, February 25

Got up early this morning to see the damage.

The field that they cut across was enormous. The horde emptied into the clearing across the highway. There were four houses spaced out in this area. All of them would've made ideal spots to stop for the night. Only one is still standing.

From what we can tell, they stomped straight through. However, when they reached the south end of the clearing, it narrows and eventually gives back over to the forest. It was probably like water hitting a barricade. There was a thin row of trees on the east "wall" of the clearing. That's right, I said "was." Perhaps it was because the ground was so wet, but several of those pines were toppled like a bulldozer had gotten to them.

We didn't stick around long. The trees and terrain acted as a diffuser and scattered the horde. Several pockets of them are sorta hanging out like they got lost or something. The one remaining house that is still standing is surrounded ten deep. A few houses up the road a ways have a handful swirling about. I hope there isn't anybody trapped in any of them; not that we could do anything for them if there were.

Then, there are some houses not in the path that the horde took. These are simply on the other side of the road. Not a single zombie is in the vicinity. This is a perfect example of their single-mindedness.

The road here has a slight roll to it as we get closer to the big mountain. We crested a ridge on this particularly long, straight stretch. That is where we discovered 'SE Paha Loop Drive.' We followed it into the trees and discovered an old bed and breakfast. Thankfully, it was long since empty.

Friday, February 26

Made good distance today. Wow! It gets noticeably colder the moment that the sun ducks behind the horizon. I'm talking face-numbing, toe-stinging, don't-want-to-pee-because-your-hoo hoo-freezes cold!

Eric says that we are lucky. The weather, by his reckoning, is rather mild for this time of year. I told him…well…never mind what I told him. The lack of zombie problems have been replaced by an eternity of pine trees coated with white, sparkling snow. It looked so pretty in pictures. Make no mistake…this sucks!

We found a place to stay. The sign beside the highway said 'SE Weber Rd.' A little ways in, we found a house. My guess is that either neighbors or family—perhaps running from the city—brought the horrors here. At least five of the eleven people here were small children. I say "at least" because I am quite certain that there were infants here. There just isn't anything left of them to find to prove their existence.

In one of the photos on the wall, there is a picture of a woman holding an infant. It is one of those artistic skin-on-skin black and whites with soft diffused borders. I put my blade into the woman personally. She was even wearing the same diamond necklace from the picture.

We cleaned out the house and dragged the bodies out back. Eric says we'll probably have to stay here a few days. His spider-senses say that there is another storm coming. We aren't too worried about the zeds right now. That means a big roaring fire in the fireplace and even a few oil lamps! Absolute luxury!

Eric slipped out for a couple of hours and came back with a deer over his shoulders already stripped. I guess two years of not being hunted has made them plentiful. Zombies have no interest in them. Either that or they are too slow—the zombies, not the deer—to catch them.

Monday, March 1

Here's a great idea. Trek through the mountains at the apex of winter. Meredith Gainey…you are a DUMBASS!

Wednesday, March 3

When exactly is spring? I don't actually recall. But if I see one more snowflake, I'm gonna scream.

***

AARRRRGGHHHHH!!!!!

Saturday, March 6

Rain! Sweet, blessed enemy of the snow! Come and wash your frozen brethren from my sight. Oh…and I'm getting REALLY bored with venison. (All I hear is my mother's voice saying, "Meredith Gainey…eat your dinner! There are people in China going hungry." I never understood that logic.)

Sunday, March 7

Spent the day outside. We walked (hiked) out to the highway. The snow is washing away. Eric says we should be able to resume our trek in a day or two if this keeps up. I think there is less than a foot of the stuff still on the ground.

Oh yeah, Eric says we will probably have to deal with this sort of erratic weather for the next month at least.

Monday, March 8

Holy Crap!

Okay, remember the whole thing about dogs turning? (But not cats, that is still so weird.) Well, wolves are related to dogs. AND, if you leave rotting meat outside—for instance, rotting zombie corpses—wolves will come back and pick over the remains.

We woke in the dark of night, the fire down to glowing embers, to something *wrong.* At first I thought it was the cold that woke me. Then I realized I wasn't the slightest bit cold. And Sam was growling. I reached for Eric, but no surprise, he was already awake.

There was a scratching at the door. Zombie-wolves have a yowl that you only need to hear once to remember forever. It made my hair stand up on my arms (and legs…no, I haven't shaved in a while. What's it to ya?). Also, I peed just a little.

We got up and put on all our gear: lined gloves, goggles, leather coat, and modified welder's leathers over our denim. What can I say? We've gotten a little bit lazy having been so long without seeing a single soul…living or undead. The house has kept us toasty with the huge fireplace and two woodstoves going twenty-four/seven.

Weapons ready, we had to wait another hour for dawn. What? Did you really think that we would venture out to fight zombie-wolves in the dark? As soon as it was light enough, we snuck out a side window after making a bunch of noise at the front door to lure them to one spot.

I am thankful that those things are no more agile or limber than their human counterparts. The fight was…different. Actually, if anything, those zombie-wolves were even clumsier than humans. They staggered and stumbled a lot. Perhaps it is because of the four-legged thing.

The scariest thing is that you couldn't tell that the wolves had turned until you got a good look at their eyes. Since they'd eaten contaminated flesh, there were no injuries to give them away. Their eyes, however, are even creepier than a human's. It is just so sinister looking.

We dispatched them quickly, but it seems to have really bothered Eric. I've seen him take out a lot of zombies of the two-legged variety without wincing (even the little ones, which most folks are VERY squeamish about). In fact, I'd say he is the only person I've met who, like me, is very dethatched when it comes to taking down zombies. But this—the wolves really appear to have upset him.

Tuesday, March 9

Finally! We are back on the move. Only, if you trade one house you've cleared for another that you haven't, is it really a good thing? The best thing about this place is the river practically right outside the back door. I have no idea which one it is, and when I asked Eric, he said, "Pick a name and that is what it shall be." Personally, I think he is still moping about the wolves.

At first I didn't know what the hell Eric was doing when he just turned off the highway and we started walking along this branch-strewn road that was quickly being supplanted by the forest. I could hear the trickling of a nearby stream as we walked deeper into the gloom.

Maybe he knew this place existed. I've been nosing around while he went out to hunt some sort of furry critter. I mostly flipped through dusty photo albums. I guess I thought that I would miraculously find a picture with him in it. No such luck.

Still, this place is nice. We had to take out a lady today who looked as if she'd dressed for an extravagant dinner party. Well…if you take out the fact that she was missing an arm and a chunk of her throat big enough to cause her head to tilt. She was in the bathroom. From the looks of things, her husband came home as one of *them*. He got her in the hallway.

Of course the blood has long since dried, but there are smears and stains on the walls leading away from a huge stain on the hardwood floor in the living room. A well-gnawed bone that is probably her missing arm—part of it at least—was there (stuck to the floor by the congealed and dried blood). It was only part, which made me wonder where the rest is, and where her hand might be.

I took down the husband while Eric, followed by Sam, took out the wife. Oh, and in case you're wondering, there is a huge portrait over the fireplace that definitely pegs these two as our couple. We put both bodies in the bathtub and covered them with a sheet. Now they are at rest together forever.

There is a loft here. That is where the master bedroom is. Also, there is a pair of smaller bedrooms on the main floor. One of them had its windows broken by a fallen branch. I wanted to put the bodies in that room, but Eric said it might bring more wolves. He said they—the living variety— could jump through those windows without a problem. Good enough for me.

Wednesday, March 10

Heavy rains and wind today. We are staying put. No sense rushing out to be in such miserable weather. I thought we heard screams last night.

Staying alert.

Friday, March 12

Back on the move. It's clear, but very cold again. This weather is freakin' bi-polar. At least the home we are crashing in tonight was empty when we arrived.

No sights or sounds since that noise that we are both certain was a human scream the other night. Not a single wandering zombie up here. I can see where this area made for a great location to run to when this whole thing started. The only drawbacks are the weather—which could be as lethal…if not more so than zombies—and lack of readily available food. I do not know how I would be doing if I'd made this journey alone. Not that I'm not a capable person, I most certainly am. It's just that if you go into a slump, you starve. And the larger the group—had I travelled with several people instead of only Eric—the bigger the supply issue becomes.

Being a duo, this is monumentally easier. In fact, we have more than we need. We end up wasting a lot of food. I feel only a little guilty about that.

Last night, I was watching the rain come down as the shadows of night were swallowing up the surrounding landscape. I thought long and hard about what I expect to find in Las Vegas. Here's the kicker: I couldn't come up with a single thing. At least not one that holds up to scrutiny. This is all about being selfish. I've been let loose in Willy Wonka's chocolate factory and plan on seeing everything. I realize that my goals aren't very lofty at this point, but Europe might as well be another planet. This is just the first step. I mean it could've just as easily been Disneyland.

But that would've been silly.

Saturday, March 13

We found a small inn...and a lot of dead people. Not zombies, but honest-to-goodness dead folks. There is a church across the road with a dozen more bodies hanging from nooses. Most are frozen solid, but one is merely cold. This place is giving off seriously creepy vibes.

Checking out the inn (that is fun to say out loud); it looks like most of the people were beaten to death. Heads were crushed, but Eric got all *CSI* and pointed out the shattered arms on every single body. These people were trying to fend off an attacker or attackers. Looking even closer—which meant scraping off dried blood or pouring a little water on the body—we found no bite marks or scratches.

The most heartbreaking scene involved a woman who was still clutching the hand of a little girl no older than eight or nine. The rest of the arm and the body it was attached to were several feet away in a mangled heap. Axes were used here as well as blunt weaponry.

Of course we couldn't stay at the inn. We decided on the church across the way instead. I don't understand. Not one thing here makes sense. Hangings. Brutal mass slayings. WTF!

Eric and I will sleep in shifts tonight. We intend to be on the road as soon as we've both gotten a few hours of shuteye.

Tuesday, March 16

I can't believe I ever considered making this trip alone. Thank God for Eric. I doubt I would be alive right now if not for him. This is like the mountain version of *Deliverance*.

I guess there are little pockets of locals out here; and they don't take kindly to strangers. These folks are no joke. They know this area well, are outdoor types—most are decked out in layers of furs—and remind me of the pictures that I saw in high school history books. You might remember the ones I'm talking about; the ones that are all grainy, black and white, showing the trappers and gold diggers from the olden days. We ran into the first one when we were leaving the church a few days ago. Literally ran in to him.

We were harnessed up and making for the highway. A noise from the direction of the inn started us jogging. (Seriously, I can not convey how creepy the vibe in that area was.) This guy stumbled out of some trees, crashing into Eric and knocking him over. Thinking it was a zombie, I hit my quick-release buckle and came in with my scimitars flashing. Well, it was kinda dark so they weren't really flashing, but you get my point. I connected solid with a body shot intended to distract the zombie and keep it from biting Eric. Then the zombie screamed. Too late, I recognized the stink coming off this thing to be of the booze, urine, shit, and vomit variety.

Eric shoved the body aside, wrenching his own knife from the eye socket and sending a spray of blood that turned the snow black in the pre-dawn gloom. I asked him if he was hurt and he said no. We got moving in a hurry, Sam leading the way as he trotted along like nothing was wrong and we hadn't just killed a living person. Sam is well trained to sniff out zombies, to be alert for their presence. He would be absolutely useless for the next few days. Living people don't come up on his radar.

We decided to duck into the trees and travel parallel to the road as much as we could. No sooner had we vanished into the pines when some sort of gang passed by on the highway. They were carrying torches...and something else. At first I thought it was a deer hanging from the pole hoisted between two of the group. I can't even say men because they are so bundled that it was impossible to tell. Then the light from a nearby torch flickered just right and I could see the naked human body bound to it. Whatever it was, there were too many for Eric and I, so we retreated further into the woods.

That is where we discovered 'Camp Despair.' Mostly comprised of tents, but with a few log cabins; that place was like an old pioneer outpost. It is walled off by ten-foot high poles made from the abundance of pine trees. We didn't go in. Eric climbed a tree and scouted it out. He reported twenty men, women, and children inside the walls. There is a huge fire pit in the center of camp. Also, there is a pair of huge stakes with a zombie chained to each one. We moved on, but our level of awareness is probably back up to where it belongs.

We had no choice but to put our sub-zero gear to the real test. We found a dense copse of trees and made camp. No fire tonight. As the sun sets, I can hear the wolves howling. At least I know that they are living. Sam doesn't care for it at all.

Wednesday, March 17

Met a small group of locals. On. Accident.

We'd broke camp and were moving along, just off the highway. By the way, big chunks of pavement are buckled or missing as the weather and lack of any department of transportation to tend it have let the road fall into a state of serious disrepair. Anyways, we were moving along when Eric gave me the signal to freeze. Ironic since I was already teeth-chattering cold.

I don't know if I am just oblivious or what. However, these people stepped out of the trees—skinny ones not nearly big enough to hide behind in my opinion. They all had axes, blades, and hammers dangling from their furry outfits—many from places that I never considered hanging a weapon.

The woman was scraggly looking with at least half of her teeth missing. One of the men was gigantic. I'm talking Tom Langston big, and that man was the largest person I'd ever seen in my life. The third man looked like the kinda guy who've had to register with the local police and isn't allowed within five hundred yards of a school or playground. Hey…what can I say? I'm a big fan of first impressions.

Of course I was wrong on about every level. The woman, Lisa, was just as sweet as she could be. The two men rescued her from a nasty little gang. Her missing teeth were the result of multiple punches to the face (along with her captors' lack of concern for the hygiene of their victims).

Ryan, the human mountain, worked with the elderly. He held out with a dozen senior citizens at a nursing home for eight whole months! Once each of the elderly folks under his care and protection had died a natural death, he moved on. That's when he found Benjamin.

Benjamin Cruikshank, DDS, had to fight and kill his own wife after she turned. He also had to put down all five—yikes! five!—daughters. Not at once, mind you. That might've been somewhat merciful. No. He had to do it over a period of eight months. Benjamin is amazingly sweet, but timid. He had nothing but compliments for me and Eric on our dental care. He even gave Sam a check-up and suggested that we get something hard for him to gnaw on.

They told us that they were headed north to Canada and perhaps even on to Alaska. They are originally from Santa Fe. They also remarked that this area is very *Old West* in its atmosphere. There are a few tribes—or communes if you prefer—scattered about. There are trading posts as well. The thing about the trading posts is that there are gangs or groups of thugs who lurk in the area and rob folks after they've made their purchase or trade. If you go back shortly thereafter, the stolen goods are back on display for sale.

I guess the Mount Hood resort, Timberline Lodge, is like a huge community; sorta the New York City of the area. Lisa, Ryan, and Benjamin stayed there for the past three months. According to them, there are jobs, an entire economy. Gads! What is it with everybody? Why is everybody so intent on bringing back the old ways? Oh well…not my problem.

We shared a lunch with them and got back on the move after awkward hugs and goodbyes. It was nice visiting with strangers. It was nice being around somebody who didn't want to kill you or cause you harm.

Thursday, March 18

It was actually freakishly warm today. Eric says at least fifty degrees! Felt tropical. We found the community of Welches. It *looks* like a town from the Old West. Actually, it goes by the name of 'Fort Bingham' now, but the old signs still say 'Welches'.

They've adopted the walled fort look here as well. And they have horses! Great big shaggy ones. The largest structure inside the walls is a church. We met Matt Bingham—he didn't laugh or even smile when I said, "Hey, did you know they named a fort after you?"—and we're treated like foreigners entering a country. A man asked our names, purpose, and how long we intended to stay.

At first, we were going to press on, but Eric suddenly announced that we would be staying for two days! I tried to keep my chin from bouncing off the ground, especially considering how muddy it is. We had to pay five cans of food as well as the last of the meat we had wrapped up on Eric's cart.

Personally I thought it was a bit steep; especially since we were given one room in a trailer that has been partitioned into three very Spartan rooms. I can't say anything for the other two, but I'm guessing they looked like the one we were given.

I had kept Sam beside me after a half dozen offers from people interested in buying him. And they weren't looking for a pet. I will let Eric do whatever it is that he's so keen on here, but we leave within two days or I tell him to catch up to me on the road.

Friday, March 19

A travel-wagon rolled in today. It wasn't exactly like the old pioneer Prairie Schooners...but fairly close. Just imagine the wagon mounted on shocks with tires that were almost as tall as me. What bothered me was that it was hauled by a team of twelve...men. And it didn't look like they were doing it happily. I don't care...I'm leaving tomorrow. No matter what.

Saturday, March 20

So, I guess Eric saw somebody he knows. He called the man "a native brother" or something like that. I feel only a little bad in hurrying him out of here. However, when I asked why he didn't ask his friend to join us, he told me that they have different journeys to take. I asked what he meant, but that was apparently the end of the conversation.

Tonight, we're in perhaps the strangest commune I've encountered: All women. Nothing fancy here to differentiate it from Fort Bingham. Same walled-in motif. There has been no effort to change the name from Zigzag...but then, why would you want to?

Not only have they converted a small school into living quarters, but the nearby campground has a fence as well, and evidence of cultivated fields. The health here seems above average. And...make no mistake; these women will put the smackdown on you in a heartbeat.

There are dogs here. Huskies and a pair of Great Danes. Sam didn't care for it at all. Our 'fee' for spending the night was feeding the dogs and cleaning the kennel. Also, we had to help haul water from the river. I didn't mind a bit. None of the creepy vibe here. I don't know how, but these women are handling their business.

This is Girl Power!

Monday, March 22

Whether it is the sheer remoteness of this place or the weather—it is snowing again—I don't know, but I haven't seen any zombies for a few days. We've left Zigzag, even though we were invited to stay another day or two to see what the weather was going to do. We're actually camped beside this river or creek—whatever the hell you want to call it—with a decent fire going.

Sam is great for the possibility of any zombies that may approach. Eric and I take turns on watch. The only bummer is that Eric says there are no signs of deer in the area. He thinks they know that they have all of Mount Hood National Forest to wander about. The tiny communities of men (or women) are invasive enough to keep the deer away. He says that there is actually more population and human activity here now than before the zombies. (Before…it was passers-through, not entire settlements.) Towns of twenty or fifty are now villages of over a hundred.

One thing…we did meet the sheriffs or whatever they call themselves. A troop of five men and women from the various settlements that travel on a circuit and administer what passes for justice in these parts. Their "pay" is free room and board as well as certain 'social' amenities. I wonder if the two women in the group are given the same opportunities in other communities.

They were surprisingly only moderately interested in us. I gave them only the briefest outline of my and Eric's plans. In fact, I didn't even mention Las Vegas. I simply admitted to heading south. It is beautiful out here. And after a few days around people, it is nice to be out in the wilderness…alone.

Friday, March 26

Cold, tired, and angry does not make for a pleasant Meredith to be around. I'm currently hiding out in the woods near Rhododendron. Funny how each of these communities is only a few miles apart, but none of them is remotely the same.

We actually had no intention of staying in 'Camp Archie', the name hanging above the large entry gate. Our only reason for even stepping foot inside was because we knew it would be a few days before we'd likely see any other such outposts. The next would be Government Camp. We thought we might check the shops; see if there were any supplies.

Just a note, we've passed a few independent traders' huts, all outside of the various communities we've visited, and it was easy to spot the vultures. They're worse than carnival barkers the way they try to lure you to their shops.

So we stopped at Camp Archie and…well, it's my fault. I was the one who saw the sign that announced: BAR. Eric wasn't all that interested, but I whined and pouted about how nice it would be to have a drink or two.

The two goons wouldn't leave me alone or take no for an answer. I didn't ask for him to save me. It's not like I can't deal. When the fight broke out, I was all of a sudden fighting off three bimbos who were accusing me of putting the moves on their men. AS IF! Eric went down under a bum's rush of yahoos and that was the last I saw of him. Being thrown out—*through* is more correct, but hey—a window is what probably saved me from being "arrested" by the locals.

Sam was barking and I had had enough of getting my ass kicked. I lucked out with the main gate being open and bolted. I'm fortunate that nobody was actually chasing me and managed to grab my cart. I strolled out with Sam as four men on horses were coming in. I had to beeline for the woods. It wasn't that I wanted to leave Eric; it's just that when things get chaotic, you have to clear yourself before you can do anything for anybody else. It does nobody any good if we *both* get nabbed.

I'm waiting for that sheriff's group to make an appearance. The only thing that I know for sure is they took Eric to one of the buildings. All I can guess is that it is their version of jail. That means living out in the woods, staying hidden from the comers and goers. I have been able to keep supplied with water from a nearby stream…but I've relied solely on our supplies for food.

Sam is helpful inasmuch that I don't worry about zombies creeping up on me. However, I do have to stay vigilant for the living. This was just not supposed to happen. We only wanted to have a drink and then resume our trip.

Saturday, March 27

The law patrol arrived yesterday afternoon. Wow…this place is freaky. The only thing missing was a pair of mirrored sunglasses and the potbellied cop saying, "Y'all's in a mess a trouble." They weren't at all interested in anything resembling the truth.

I shudder to think of how this could've played out if I hadn't thought things through with my normal suspicious mind. I opted to stash my cart and even left all my weapons except for a machete and a spiked-tipped pole.

Our so-called fine for disturbing the peace was Eric's cart with everything on it and permanent barring of entry into Camp Archie. They didn't take any of Eric's weapons, but still, it was a total shakedown. If I ever come back this way, I just might burn this dump to the ground. Oh…and the yokels that jumped us? The equivalent of community service. The goons were sentenced to "two weeks on the gate." Awesome, we get out stuff taken, and they have to open and close the entry gates to the camp.

So, I am waiting for Eric. He's been allowed to use the public shower. Staying in the holding cell is truly quite nasty. I could actually smell him when they brought him into the makeshift courtroom.

***

I take it back. We got a hefty fine, but they didn't let the Joe-Bobs off the hook after all. Two weeks "on the gate" is a literal punishment. I thought those guys were just hamming it up for our benefit when the verdict was read and the sentence pronounced.

We left—a little less burdened—as soon as Eric was clean and dressed. He still reeked. His clothes are filthy. On the way out, we saw the three troublemakers locked in the stockade atop the fence. A sign is above them: Assault and Public Nuisance. Wow…maybe they'll bring back witch trials, too.

As I sit beside the fire watching Eric scrub his clothes in the creek, I'm even more aware than before how crazy we are as a species. Our sentence seemed harsh. But those guys basically got a death sentence. I mean, I wanted them punished, but if the exposure doesn't kill them, any sort of zombie attack could be very bad. I didn't see any means of protection in place for them. If anything, they're *bait*. Yeah, they were jerks, but being a jerk wasn't reason for the death penalty last I checked. Could you imagine if that'd been the case back in the olden days?

Sunday March 28

Finally…something I can understand. Sam's growls woke me just before sunrise. A creeper was dragging itself from the thick undergrowth. This one had been dead for a while. I couldn't determine if it'd been male or female. Clumps of hair remain in a few patches on the skull, but most was gone. The nose had been torn off, one eye was missing, and it was practically flayed from dragging itself along the ground. It really looked like little more than a creeping slab of rotten meat.

I didn't think anything about it as I woke up, grabbed my poker and ended it. The thing was not even remotely threatening. Then it hit me like a fist in the gut.

Eric!

He was on watch. Or…he was *supposed* to be on watch. I started looking everywhere. Then I found him. He was leaned against a big tree. Thank goodness he's geared up. The big lug had fallen asleep. I guess he was more tired than he realized.

I've actually moved the fire closer and covered him up. He needs his sleep and I can't afford him to slip like that once we get out of the mountains and return to an environment where zombies are plentiful. Of course when he wakes up, I will chew his ass. He should've told me. And he does me no good if he is so exhausted that he can't stand his watch. I wonder if he slept at all while he was incarcerated. I shudder to think that I might've actually had it better than him while I was hiding out in the woods…bitching and complaining about how tired, cold, and angry I was. Hmm. Maybe I'll make a tasty midday meal of canned beets, beef stew, and fruit cocktail for him.

Thursday, April 1

We are scheduled to leave Government Camp tomorrow. I say "scheduled" because the weather has turned once more and decided to get in its last jabs before spring. This past week we have seen just how overmatched we are by Mother Nature. I guess—according to the signs and the burning in my lungs—that we are at over four thousand feet. And if you think that making this hike on foot allows you to acclimate…you are so very, very wrong.

As the route got just a bit steeper and we climbed steadily upwards, the world seemed to change. It was as if there were an imaginary line where the snow begins and gets deep fast. Here at Government Camp there is a two hundred and thirty-six inch base! Yes! Of snow!

So, we earned a pair of snowshoes during our stay. At the bottom of the mountain there is an outpost that is run by settlers where we can turn them in for trade before continuing on our journey. Yeah, when I said "earned," I meant we earned the means to rent them.

The cart works well on runners by the way. Good thing, too. This was one hell of a field test. So, tomorrow, when the caravan scheduled to leave here to go down the south side of the mountain departs, we will be going with it. I don't like the idea of travelling with a group, but that is how they do things here and I don't get a vote.

We've been told that the trip takes five days. When we reach the bottom and arrive at Government Base, we will be required to go through an exam. The military is long gone, but it seems that the civilians decided to maintain the protocol. I guess it helps them keep folks from bringing the infection up or down the hill. Plus, the Native Americans won't allow anybody to travel through their territory without appropriate medical approval.

Oh yeah, did I forget to mention that the Natives have exercised total sovereignty over the Warm Springs Reservation land? Well they have. I guess there is some sort of government liaison or detachment of officials that set up at the base of where Highway 26 begins to climb up Mount Hood. They tried to fall back into Warm Springs when a zombie horde came, but the tribal council of Kah-Nee-Tah denied them access unless they agreed to certain terms. The OIC wouldn't even listen to what the emissary had to say. That OIC and his detachment went the way of Custer.

The local civilians were far more reasonable. Now it seems that the Warm Springs Indian Reservation is now called Confederated Kah-Nee-Tah. They have a much stricter immigration policy than the United States ever imagined; even from the farthest right wing. I think it is something about not trusting the White Devil.

Once more I will be grateful that Eric is with me. Otherwise, I would be forced to go all the way around their land. It seems that, while they do business with those on the border, they absolutely will not allow non-Natives to pass through their land unescorted.

How do I know all this? Eric has spoken with the liaison here at Government Camp. It seems that there is an embassy system in place. Eric is very excited by it all. I guess he hasn't seen many of his "people" since this nightmare began. It never occurred to me what that might feel like. I mean, Eric is slightly darker complexioned. He looks like he is rocking a decent tan...even in the winter. But...how do I say this? He looks ...normal. That isn't the right word. But he isn't Black or Hispanic. I guess I really never saw him as anything but...Eric.

Sure, he has a cool last name, but I don't go around saying, "Hey, Grayfeather! What's up?" He is simply Eric. Perhaps, in a couple of days, I'll get a taste of how he's felt this whole time. I am going into his people's land. I'll be the only "white man" around.

Friday, April 2

I feel like 'Polly Pioneer' as I travel with this caravan. The word is that we probably won't see any zombies for at least the first two days. The eighteen mile journey to Government Base will take four days provided that there are no problems.

Saturday, April 3

White! Everything is white. I don't care if I never see another snowflake again. I used to love watching snow drift down from the sky. I am SO over that.

Sunday, April 4

Rain. Blessed and glorious rain!

Monday, April 5

A few of the escorts had to take out the odd lone shambler from time to time, but it's official, we've relegated zombies to the Old World equivalent of the rat. We hate them. We kill them. We no longer fear them.

Tuesday, April 6

We are in Government Base. Well…'in' is a relative term. We are in the medieval lockdown ward. Each of us has been examined for bites (or signs of healed bites as there is apparently great medical interest in those showing immunity).

Now we must endure four days of isolation. It sucks, but them's the rules. Sam was even taken to a secure kennel. I signed a form saying that if he proved clean, I would permit him to be exposed to a female in heat should the situation arise. Hey, just because I'm living the life of a nun when it comes to sex doesn't mean Sammy has to.

Saturday, April 10

I picked up my journal several times, but never had anything to say. I thought I might wax poetic or go all philosophical…get into the whole retrospective thing.

Nope.

I slept. Ate. Slept some more.

Today I am free to wander the base. Eric is busy making whatever diplomatic arrangements need to be made so that I can travel the Confederation Territory. Can you believe that there is a sign warning: "All non-Native persons trespassing on Confederated Territory will be considered an enemy of the Peoples of the Kah-Nee-Tah tribe and its affiliates and will be shot on sight."

Whatever.

Oh, and it seems that several other Northwestern tribes are in on this. I know zilch about Native American history—half the time I slip up and call them Indians…nobody says anything, but I sense the disdain—much less the politics. I guess several of these tribes have had problems with the local tribe, blah, blah, blah. Tribes are doing this all over the country.

I heard rumor—actually Eric did and relayed it to me—that the entire state of Oklahoma is being claimed. Tribes from all over are sending delegates to arrange for something like a walled nation. They are talking about fencing off the entire state! I don't know if it's true, but he sure seemed to believe it. I did ask him what would/did happen to any survivors of the non-Native variety that might be there. He very calmly said they were probably escorted to the border…or killed if they resisted.

Like I said, I don't know much about history, but I know enough to recall our government really screwed them at every turn. I guess they are enjoying some get back now. I don't think I blame them.

Wednesday, April 14

Today we arrived in Warm Springs. The local tribe—Eric calls them "Springers"—is very hospitable. Granted, I am under approved escort at all times. Still, I expected there to be cold looks, or even a challenge here and there. Everybody I've met has been amazingly polite.

Eric says that there are tribes from all over the Pacific Northwest congregated here. Also, some of the delegates, or whatever they call themselves, from the Oklahoma region are present. So it *is* true; the Native American population is withdrawing to Oklahoma and sealing it off. I don't see how they can hope to accomplish such a thing, but it ain't my problem. As for if it is possible…who would have believed in actual zombies overwhelming society except for the fringe types who read that crap?

The best part is that we're out of the cold and snow. It is really nice here and there is so much food. Eric seems to be really happy. If I didn't need his escort out of this place, I'd consider slipping away and leaving him here amongst his people.

Thursday, April 15

We're on the move again.

A security detail took us by horseback all the way to what they consider to be the border. We are about five miles north of the city of Madras, Oregon.

Eric really stocked us up with food. We shouldn't need to worry for quite a while in that regard. I could tell he was torn about leaving. It's the most emotion I've seen from him…ever. We are camped just inside the reservation. There are regular patrols along the fence on horseback. I have to admit that I'm super impressed that they have erected a fence all the way around their territory. It must've been quite an undertaking.

Tomorrow…The Wilderness.

Friday, April 16

Damn! Damn! Damn!

Sam and I are in an overhead crawlspace of some Mom & Pop sporting goods store. I don't know exactly where Eric is. One day away from his people and I practically get him killed.

If I ever see him again, I'm gonna have some serious butt kissing to do. That, and about a gazillion "I'm sorry, Eric, please don't hate me!" mantras to start on.

Saturday, April 17

It was too dark to write anymore yesterday, so I had to quit. In case you're wondering…I'm still hiding in the same spot. I did crawl down once to look for water. I had to scramble my ass right back. Did I mention that there are THOUSANDS of those things milling about? Oh…and that it is totally my fault.

Here is where yours truly screwed the pooch. (Eric says that a lot and I've sorta adopted the phrase.)

We were moving down into Madras late Friday afternoon. Most of the city is toasted. It looks like there were some nasty battles here. Many of the buildings were torched, bombed, or bullet-ridden. All the way around this one field was a fence constructed of that corrugated metal. We couldn't see over the wall, but we didn't have to in order to know what was inside.

From what we could tell, there were a few roamers scattered about. It was quickly obvious that we wouldn't be doing much scavenging around here. While it was possible that we might find a few odds and ends, this town was wrecked.

Eric suggested that we push through and make camp on the south side of town. We had at least a two day journey to Prineville—the next real town on our map. I'd been a bit cooped up the past couple of weeks and wanted to have a look. I *knew* there wasn't likely to be anything here worth the trouble. Then…I saw the armored RV with the heavy machinegun mounted on top.

I had flashbacks of the trip from Irony to Portland with my All-Girl Army. It'd been one hell of a *Road Warrior*-esque adventure. Sure, it ended badly, but there were some moments. I wanted to check the vehicle out. I could tell that Eric wasn't excited about the idea, but he apparently decided to let the crazy white woman have her fun.

I recall walking up the hill to the abandoned RV. The closer we got, the more obvious that it was unlikely that we'd find anything. For some reason, my brain refused to process that bit of information. All the signs were right in front of my face: hundreds of bullet holes, the rusty machinegun, the long-since-dried gore on the inside obscuring the ability to look in the windows that remained intact.

I opened the door and the smell that rolled out was almost a physical presence. Sam actually skittered away and refused to come any closer than about thirty feet. I pulled out my mask and climbed in. There were a dozen dead soldiers (at least a dozen) strewn about the spacious interior. I could tell they'd fallen back to the rear of the RV where an equal number of zombies lay in a pile signaling the site of the last stand.

I was curiously drawn to the scene; trying for some reason to decipher how it all went down. I was also checking the bodies for weapons. It was becoming clear that they had used up everything in this final skirmish. The guns were empty, slides open and locked. Many had been converted to bludgeons—the grips caked with gunk and strands of hair.

From all the useless electronic gear, it was clear that this place was some sort of rolling command post. I moved forward to check the driver's area. The angle that we were parked, it made things a little more difficult than you might think. The driver's and front passenger's seat were occupied. Both looked like they'd chosen to eat a bullet rather than change. Each had multiple bites on their arms.

It was here that I'd found what might've been my validation for this little diversion. While they were firmly gripped in dead hands, both pistols looked like all they needed was a little spit and polish...and some oiling. On the driver's belt was a pouch holding a pair of magazines, and at his feet, a box of bullets for the Colt .45s.

I had to tilt the steering wheel up to get at the pouch, and was prying/tearing the pistol from stiff fingers when I heard it: a baby's cry. It was from close by. I looked up, and that's when I noticed the head of the person in the passenger's seat turned my way.

The mouth was a mess. Eating a bullet will do that. However, if not done correctly, all that is accomplished is that the would-be suicide comes back as a zombie with just another nasty wound. The bullet exited, taking most of the right ear...and that's it.

He...it...was reaching for me with filthy hands. One had a pistol dangling from it. I still shudder to think of what might've happened had I chosen to loot that body first.

Anyways, I reacted fairly normal to the sudden surprise. I screamed—not cool at all—and I threw myself backwards from the threat. It really doesn't matter if it couldn't have reached me from where it was strapped.

I guess I hit the emergency brake. At first, nothing happened. And had I not been throwing myself around like an idiot to get away from something that couldn't actually hurt me, not to mention the fact that I was now certain the corpse in the driver's seat was also a zombie, things probably turn out different.

The vehicle began to move. I finally got loose and tumbled to the floor. My head smacked a damn toolbox or something and made all the pretty lights flash in my brain. By the time I was aware that Eric was dragging me, we were moving at a pretty good clip.

He drag-pulled me to the side entrance and dove out of the moving vehicle with me in his arms. I was getting to my feet—about to yell at Eric for trying to kill us by jumping out of a moving RV—when I heard the crash. I looked in the direction of the sound and saw the RV jutting from that big metal fence.

For a moment, I wondered why it had come to a stop. After all, it had been moving fast as it careened down that steep slope. What happened next was like watching dominoes fall. Section by section, the fence began to topple. All those zombies that had been inside burst forth like pus from a boil being squeezed on your gross Aunt Maddy's back.

I was ready to run when I realized that Eric was still on the ground. He was making funny noises from having the wind knocked out of him. We had plenty of space between us and the approaching mob, but it was taking Eric way too long to get to his feet. Finally, after an eternity, he was up. By now, Sam was bounding towards us, obviously anxious to get the blazes out of here.

I helped Eric get up, but he wasn't moving that well at all. We rounded a corner and some of the roamers had come to investigate. And still Eric wasn't moving well. He kept making these gasping attempts to get air in his lungs. It sounded like he was a giant frog.

Sam could've taken off, but I guess Eric trained him well because he stayed right beside us. Sure, he growled and woofed, but he never ran. Then we reached the intersection where I was faced with the choice of fight or flee. I let go of Eric—who melted to the ground like a candle tossed into a kiln—and rushed to take out the leading zombies.

One of them actually made me pause. They say that everybody in the world has a twin. I am certain that I found Calista Flockhart…or her twin. This skinny little waif couldn't withstand a serious breeze. I have no idea what the zombie that bit her must've thought when it bit into that scrawny arm and chipped a tooth on the bone.

By the time I'd taken down all three, I'd migrated about a half of a block up the street. Fighting is not a stationary event. When I turned back, Eric was moving up the street in the opposite direction. Sam had stayed put, but was crouched down and backing in my general direction.

"Go!" Eric croaked. "We'll split up here and try to meet up as soon as we can!'

Then I saw what had spurred his recovery and sent him weaving up the street. The horde was on us. I recall seeing the wall of debris and dirty water moving down that road. I remember Indonesia when that awful tsunami hit several years back. Well, if you can remember that image…just swap it with zombies. I noticed how some in the leading edge fell and vanished under the army of churning feet that would not be slowed.

I whistled for Sam and ran. I didn't even bother to kill the zombies I passed as I sprinted by. And in no time…I was absolutely lost.

I finally decided on this place. A ransacked sporting goods store. It had a second floor which was good. But even better was this crawlspace. I'm sitting in this air duct by a vent that I've bent some of the slats on so I can look down to the street below. I can see them. This town is now crawling with all the zombies that had been put in that pen. It's like the beginning all over again.

It's strange…gunshots are a rarity. But I've heard some. Oh…which reminds me; in all that madness, I dropped the gun I'd found when I started all of this. This means that I not only endangered myself and Eric, but anybody that had been using this area…for nothing.

Who knows, maybe there is somebody in this town, Madras, sitting someplace with a journal or diary. They are probably cursing me right this very moment. Me. Meredith Gainey. The woman who unleashed an entire town population's worth of zombies because she was careless.

And now…my canteen is almost empty. I've been sharing my water with Sam and must find more soon. If I don't catch a break in the near future, I'll lower Sam down. He could probably find water in no time. No sense in making him die of thirst just because I am. Also, and this is selfish, but his running off might clear the area for a minute.

Sunday, April 18

Weird.

I woke this morning to loud music being blared someplace nearby. I'm no classical music genius, but I know enough to be certain that it was Mozart's *Eine Kleine Nachtmusik* Da. Da-da. Da-duh-duh-duh-duh-duh. Dee. Dee-dee. Dee-dee-dee-de-dee-dee. Bum. Bum. Bum-bu-bum-badda bum.

So that has been in my head ALL DAY! Don't get me wrong. I love music. Buy you know what it's like to get a song stuck in your head? And I even used my old standard. The song I use to get those songs out of my head: the theme from *The Brady Bunch*. Nope. Now I'm singing *The Brady Bunch Theme* to the tune of the Mozart song.

Aaargh!

Monday, April 19

I put Sam on the floor. For a while he just stared up at the hole in the ceiling waiting for me to join him. I think thirst got the better of him. He ran off. It's been just a few hours and he hasn't come back. I watched him emerge onto the road. When the zombies in the area noticed, he bolted.

Good doggy. But I'll miss the company.

Tuesday April 20

I'm thirsty.

Water is officially all gone. I forget. How long can a person go without liquids?

Cripes! This is the school gymnasium all over again. Only, I'm not pregnant.

There's something to be thankful for. I did hear barking a while ago. I don't think it was Sam. He almost never barks.

Wednesday, April 21

Dizzy. Don't feel good. Where the hell is the rain everybody used to identify the Pacific Northwest with?

I'm sorry.

Saturday, April 24

Have I mentioned what a good dog Sam is? I totally owe my life to that goofy dog.

We are a couple of miles outside of Madras now. Me. Eric. And that stupid, wonderful dog!

I guess he just wandered around until he found Eric. Then, he led him straight to me. I feel like such a doofus. Those zombies I saw wandering the streets? Yeah, well there weren't more than two dozen out there. They were all just rambling in and out of the shops along this street.

Leave it to me not to pay attention that there was a fenced dead end to this street about two buildings past the one I was in. Zombies would wander in…and then circle back. Yes, the town is crawling with the undead, but not in any condensed way. They've spread out all over Madras.

After a bit of water, Eric helped me down and we slipped out under the cover of night. It seems a bit cowardly in retrospect. I mean, I can't pretend I didn't hear multiple sources of noise from living, breathing people. I haven't said anything yet to Eric. He seems the exact same as he always does.

Whatever.

Tonight, I'm going to sleep in this empty house and try not to concentrate on the fact that I almost cost us everything while Eric re-packs the harness cart that he was smart enough to go back for and stock with a few cans he scavenged while waiting patiently to find the crazy white girl.

Saturday April 25

We found one of those shiny silver trailers on an overgrown lot all by itself today. It was just sitting there. There wasn't anything special about it. Not one single, solitary thing.

So…I have no idea how Eric knew.

Inside was a mummified family. A father. A mother. Two children: both girls. Each had a bullet hole in the head. The father obviously went last. He was still holding the small caliber pistol in his hand. (I didn't get close enough to take a look.) Eric made me wait outside. He didn't actually go in either. He stood in the open door and got a good look…to confirm his theory, I guess.

Then, he asked me to go wait at the highway. I didn't even think of arguing or asking questions. I could tell there was something going on here. He seemed to look around in the bushes for a little while, plucking up different plants. Once he had what he wanted, he set them on the top step and lit them on fire.

I've never actually heard a real-live Indian…Native American song…you know what I mean. Anyways, I've never heard one chant or sing. I didn't understand one single syllable. But I've never heard anything that made me feel so sad—and your're dealing with a girl who cried for six months after seeing *Titanic* every time that Celine Dion song would come on the radio.

Eric knelt in the dirt and raised his hands to the sky and just started. He went on for twenty minutes at least. I had to kill four roamers that came wandering out of the high brush that dominates the landscape here. I guess he just trusted that I'd take care of it. But part of me thinks he would've done the same thing if were all alone. He hasn't spoken since.

Monday April 26

Great. Prineville is a wreck. But…we are learning that multiplexes are great places to camp out. Even more specific, the bathrooms. We have a fire going in the sink. It isn't a roaring blaze, but it allows us to see and prepare food; so it's all good.

This little complex we are using has a few other bonuses. There is a small emergency clinic and a few restaurants. Of course the restaurants were mostly busts, but we found a few things. As for the clinics, it's funny. Obviously the place has been looted, but by people looking for drugs. We scored a few bottles of iodine, hydrogen peroxide, and even a couple of bottles of isopropyl alcohol. Not to mention bandages and other useful first aid knick knacks.

Just up from here is a huge park. It shows signs of having hastily built fencing. But I was interested in the three burned out husks of what were obviously military helicopters. There are a lot of dried out corpses littering the ground. It's clear that birds and other things have picked them fairly clean. I shudder to think of how bad this nightmare would be if birds turned into zombies. But…would they be able to fly? I don't know if they'd have the ability to keep themselves airborne. Still…yucky!

Tuesday, April 27

Thankfully there is plenty of brush to use as a screen. We didn't feel like scavenging in Prineville. Too crowded. We're back on the desolate and empty road. We're on some back road that cuts through absolutely nowhere and nothing. Zombies probably won't be a problem…but boredom might prove to be fatal.

Wednesday, April 28

The good thing about being in the middle of nowhere is the chance to get your head straight. I finally spoke with Eric about Madras. I told him how sorry I was, and about how I would try hard not to do such stupid things.

Eric's response?

"Meredith, it would not be good for you to change your nature. It is what makes you all that you are." Then he told me some story about a frog giving a scorpion a ride on its back across a stream. The scorpion ends up stinging the frog, killing them both. Ooo-kaaay. So…am I the scorpion?

Sheesh!

Thursday, April 29

Hiding in a leaky barn. It opened up today. I mean the sky just started dumping and there's been thunder and lightning almost non-stop. So…we're cold, wet, and miserable. But Eric shouldn't mind…he's a frog. Right?

Sunday, May 2

We've been forced to travel at night the past couple of days. That sounds funny...but anyways...

A fairly large band of people have apparently laid claim to this area. We found the first signs of them when we set out after that wicked storm.

A man was strung up by his feet from a road sign. He'd turned and was squirming, but what was upsetting was the child, no more than five, sitting on the ground. The somewhat fresh blood caking her mouth, coupled with the smallish bites on the man's arms...and face...told the gruesome story.

The child had been a zombie for quite a while. That added another layer of "what the fuck?" to the scene. It must've been done during the storm, because we should've heard the screams. *That* is how recent this was. Also, the ground was a pretty obvious giveaway. There was a lot of foot activity in the mud around the sign. The good news is that it looks as if the mystery group headed west. We are going east.

Yay!

Monday, May 3

I thought I knew what desolation was. Nope! My God, there is NOTHING out here.

Tuesday, May 4

We're hiding in a drainage pipe while a sandstorm howls out on this flat, godforsaken stretch of the world. I'd been noticing long sections of the highway that looked like they had been washed away or something. Now I know...it's simply covered with inches or feet of blown dirt and sand. Oregon has an actual desert. Who knew?

Wednesday, May 5

Woo-hoo! *Cinco de Mayo.* All we're missing is the chips, salsa, tequila, and one of those big hats to dance around. Lord knows we've got plenty of hot sun beating down on us, making us go through our water waaay faster than normal.

We saw a little action today. A creeper. It literally burst out of this mound of sand. It was like a desert version of when zombies get covered with ice and snow. It was so dried out that we couldn't tell if it'd been male or female...but that wasn't the problem.

I drove my spear through its head, but it looked like it was still moving. My concern was that, for some reason, destroying the brain didn't cut it any more. Then this cluster of scorpions came scurrying out of its hollowed out abdomen.

I'm trying super-hard not to giggle as I write this, because then Eric will know that I am writing how he screamed and ran...faster *and* higher-pitched than I did. It was probably reckless, but we hauled butt down the highway.

Also, we've seen signs of other survivors today. A campfire was still smoldering, and there were a few empty cans at one spot beside a stretch where you could actually differentiate between the road and the flat, barren, brown landscape.

We couldn't really find an honest-to-goodness shelter for the night, so we're sleeping under the stars. I'm taking first shift. Eric insists that he heard an engine at one point. I didn't hear anything, and Sam's ears didn't as much as twitch. I guess it's possible, but it doesn't seem likely.

Vehicles are little more than dinosaurs. Most folks abandon them because they'd bring zombies from miles away. Plus, it's not like there's any reason to be in a hurry these days.

Thursday, May 6

We've walked down this empty stretch of road for what seems to be forever.

It was almost midday when Eric pulled me up. In the distance, the sun was reflecting off of something. The closer we got, we began to notice other details like the chest-high fence. What we initially mistook as a small car wreck proved to be more of a makeshift barricade.

Here, in the middle of the Oregon high desert, there exists a small community. I wouldn't put their numbers above fifty. They have a creek that runs through and everything. It seems that all their needs are provided for. We were briefly questioned and asked our intentions. Nobody tried to insist on anything. Not even a body inspection. Then I noticed all the dogs. There are dozens—five to every human at least—just wandering free.

We dropped in to check out their trading post and I picked up a set of military-issue boots that fit perfectly. The price was steep—three cans of food and a pair of thick, wool socks—but since I'm on the move, I'll probably have no problem replacing what I traded away.

Of course, I could have *found* a pair of boots. It was more about the interaction with the lady that runs the shop. Oh…and naturally…Eric got absolute nothing.

As we headed out, a sign caught my eye: Joe's Diner.

It wasn't much to look at. The sign was basically scrawled on the ripped off hood of a car in very faded, white paint. The 'restaurant' was one of those silver, bullet-shaped trailers with one side cut off and a plastic tarp extended over some rickety card tables and rusty lawn chairs. There was a counter where the woman took the order and gave them to a cook behind a window.

It was when we got up to the counter that things started to not look quite right. The waitress was missing most of her teeth. Her skin was…sickly is the best description I could give you. She had sores and huge bruises all over that you could actually see through her pinkish threadbare blouse. Her hair was thin and wispy, completely gone in patches.

She gave me a dirty look when we made eye contact. I can't blame her, I'm pretty certain that my revulsion was clearly visible on my face. As for Eric, not even a twitch around the corners of his eyes.

I'd already decided that it was a mistake and we wouldn't be eating here. Still, the post-apocalyptic 'Flo' placed a laminated sheet in front of us. Written on it were the two choices that this place had: Snake Soup and Judge's Stew.

As the waitress-from-hell was getting us our complimentary glass of water—just as the sheet promised at the bottom in writing in what looked like the only thing that didn't get changed daily—I took a look at the other patrons. They all seemed far too interested in Sam. I noticed one gaunt man in particular. He stuck out because of all the folds of skin hanging around his torso. Currently the guy looked to weigh no more than one hundred fifty pounds tops. However, he must have easily weighed over three hundred pounds before. (I think I now know why Jared from Subway never did bathing suit ads.) Somebody who loses that much fat that quickly doesn't lose the stretched out skin.

When I turned back, our water was being set before us. I tried to ignore the beige hue. Then Eric asked the sixty-thousand-dollar question.

"What is Judge's Stew?"

"Trial two days ago for a pair of fellas that got a bit too rough with one of Madam Judy's working girls. Judge found them guilty and sentenced them to hangin'."

"You mean…?" I tried to ask, but couldn't say the words.

"Can't be wastin' perfectly good meat these days, little Missy," she croaked.

Okay. I probably come off a bit snooty with a statement like "she croaked." So, I'll leave it to you. Did you ever know a chain-smoker? I'm talking lighting the next one with the one still dangling from their lips. *That* kind of chain-smoker. Okay. So the chain-smoker's voice would sound as smooth as Sinatra if compared to this waitress.

Still think I'm being a bitch?

Now, you'd think that'd been enough. You'd think that Eric would have taken my glare, raised eyebrows, and not so subtle tilt of my head towards the road out front that would take us away from this roadside circle of Dante's *Inferno*.

Nope. The big dummy ordered the Snake Soup. Personally, I think he did it on purpose to screw with me.

Saturday, May 8

Her name is Tricia Maio (pronounced like mayo short for mayonnaise). She used to be a dancer. Judging by her body, I bet she made a fortune off of desperate, middle-aged men. Seriously, I'm very hetero, but she made my tummy tingle. Oh…and Eric? Not so much as a batted eyelash.

Anyways, we met Tricia at a ransacked old gas station sitting off the well-covered-by-sand highway. There was an intact off ramp that we decided was as good as any to search for the possibility of camping out for the night. Imagine our surprise when we peeked through the busted out front windows to discover a naked lady hanging her clothes over a small fire concealed behind the checkout counter.

She'd been in a nasty fight with a small pack of zombies earlier in the day. She'd washed the worst of the gore from her clothes in an old, yellow, plastic mop bucket that she'd found in a closet.

When I'd asked about the water, she told me that there was a small spring just out back that drains into a pond that has two large concrete pipes at the lowest end. She's pretty certain that they lead to a nearby reservoir a few miles away.

I lent her some of my clothes so that she wouldn't have to stand around naked in front of strangers. I'm not sure who I was trying to make feel better. Still, that led to the obvious question.

"Where the hell is the rest of your stuff?"

She said that a small herd of a couple hundred zombies caught her off guard. She was camped out in some random apartments. She had to leave her backpack and could only bring what she could carry in the pockets of her heavy field jacket. She escaped by climbing up on the roof—which couldn't have been that easy considering that she had to use a piece of metal pipe to bust a hole through it when she climbed into the overhead crawl space. By getting most of the zombies down to one end, she was able to run to the other and jump.

She eluded most of them, but then ended up having to fend off a fair amount. Hence being such a mess and needing to clean up.

I asked her where she was heading. She said that some travelers heading south told her about a safe zone on Mount Hood. I filled her in on the details, including the situation regarding the Warm Springs Reservation. I also hinted where we were headed.

Tricia is coming from Utah and didn't have any info about Nevada. I asked about Utah, mostly just curious to hear if it was as bad as every other place I've been. I never considered how a heavily religious region might react and respond to an event like this. She said that the zombies were almost less of a concern when compared to some of the zealot extremists. Oddly, the main body of the Mormons wasn't a problem. It was the off-shoots that continued to lurk in the shadows. It seems that there is a very male-centric core that views women as subjects, serv-ants, and vessels to carry their offspring.

Some sort of Holy War erupted and a lot of people were killed by the lunatic fringe. I guess, right up to the end, the el-ders of the central body were condemning the extremists…all the way up to the point when an eighteen-wheeled car bomb was rolled into their main cathedral in downtown Salt Lake City.

Sunday, May 9

Tricia was gone when we woke.

My clothes were neatly folded and sitting on the counter. I think she did Eric last night when I was sleeping. He seems to be in a strangely cheerful mood.

Whatever.

Monday, May 10

We should be reaching Burns, Oregon soon. Eric says that we might be able to replenish supplies there. The population was scarce and spread out. There really wasn't that much to Burns before. At least that's what Eric says.

Eric explains that we need to be on guard. Burns being so rural, there is a high probability that some of the yokels may have survived. Towns like Burns had a heavy gun-to-person ra-tio. I remember the carnage on the streets of some of the small towns we've been through.

We haven't seen a zombie all day. And in some respects, that actually seems kinda creepy. A lack of undead can mean a lot of things. Not all of them are good.

Tuesday, May 11

At the best of times, children were something I was always thankful for NOT having to deal with. I mean, it was always nice to visit friends or family with rugrats of their own...and leave when they got tiresome. (My personal best being about two hours.) If they cried and wouldn't stop...hand them to mommy. Dirty diaper?...point, hold my nose, and leave the room. See? Simple.

And yeah, I'm aware I've given birth to a child. However, I knew myself well enough to know it was a bad match. I am not a good candidate for parenthood. I am saying all this so that I can also clarify that I've never wished harm on children. (Also, in case you are wondering, yes, I do still think about my daughter. I still feel like I made the right choice of parents. I gave her to a good couple, and The Warehouse is probably the safest place I know.)

So why am I blathering on about all this? Well, it has been a rough day. We were moving along, Sam trotting ahead marking every shrub, clump of grass, or abandoned vehicle we passed. Then we heard *the* scream. It was coming from beyond a ridge off to our right.

Needless to say, we ran to find out what the hell was going on. We had to keep Sam back. Eric held him by the scruff of his neck while I moved ahead to check out the situation. You might criticize us for taking too long to respond to an obvious emergency, but rushing blindly into anything these days will just get everybody killed.

I was in no way prepared for what I saw.

Five girls—ages fifteen to (maybe) twenty—were up on an abandoned RV. It was that kind that isn't much bigger than a pick-up truck. Dangling from the rear was a man. Naked. About a dozen creepers were flailing and squirming, trying their best to get ahold of the man. I could see that one of his arms was dripping blood. It was obvious that he'd been snacked on already.

As for the girls, the taunts and jeers coming from their mouths were...heinous comes to mind. They were actually laughing while they jerked on the ropes that they had tied to each of the man's ankles. The curious and bizarre thing about the scene was that the girls were each wearing nothing more than their bra and panties.

I slipped back down the hill and relayed things to Eric. He seemed to puzzle over it for a minute, and then said, "Not our problem."

I couldn't believe what I was hearing. As I argued my point, I heard another scream. This one was much longer and louder than the first. It ended in a sudden and liquid-sounding yelp. Then…there was the distinct cacophony of rabid cheering.

Eric seemed to be much more concerned about leaving. Since I really had no idea what was happening, it was very difficult for me to agree to leave. However, I was still self-conscious about the trouble I'd gotten us into a few days ago by nosing around. Therefore…against my character, I agreed without an argument.

We were almost to the road when we heard a voice. A girl was calling for us to wait up. When I turned around, I was only mildly surprised to see a girl in her bra and panties running after us. She looked even more surprised at *me* when I turned to face her. I guess with all the gear on—leathers, boots, gloves, and a baseball cap pulled low over my eyes—I could be mistaken for a guy.

The story—as they told it—is that these girls are escapees from some compound in the area. They've been at 'war' with the men of this compound for about five weeks. They use one of their own as bait. Apparently the men are stupid enough to keep falling for it. She didn't even hide her glare at Eric as she talked.

I didn't feel like spending my day talking to this girl, but I needed to ask: What's the situation in Burns? She looked at me like I'd just fallen off the moon.

"Walled up, locked down and they don't allow in strangers."

She elaborated by saying that if you weren't born in, or a resident of, Burns for a year or more *before* the dead started walking, you received the same mercy that they showed the zombies…none. They keep mounted patrols, *most* of which give you a warning that you aren't welcome before they open fire.

The "wall" that they've built encloses about three times the area that was formerly known as Burns, Oregon. They are most protective of the river just south of town, and have towers that allow their watches to see for a few miles in every direction. They mostly worry about zombies and don't seem to mind folks filling water containers as long as they are downstream.

We're about two days or so from Burns. There will be a small airfield when we come out of the pass that opens up on the farmland community surrounding this city-fortress. We are supposed to keep heading south along SR-205…a highway that will take us to a big lake. From there, we can head east again until we hook up with OR-78/Steens Highway. Eventually, that will dump us onto US-95, which will take us to Nevada.

I realize that we had to wait to cross the Mount Hood section of our journey because, as it was, the weather made for a tough trip. I think that crossing Nevada during the summer may actually be worse. Finding a car wouldn't be tough. Finding one that would work—one that the gasoline hasn't gone bad—would be practically impossible. What we need are bicycles. Good ones.

Even if we have to push the bikes for parts of the trip when we hit hills, we would move so much quicker when we rode over long stretches of the flat desert terrain ahead. If we don't find bikes, we may not survive the summer. It's almost funny; the walking dead are less of a concern than Mother Nature.

Eric was a good boy and didn't let it slip as to where we are headed. However, I think that the girl had inkling. After all, she not only told us how to get around Burns, she also told us when and where to get back on the highway headed south to Vegas.

Once our little chat ended, she turned on her heel and strutted off. For somebody so young, she was awfully comfortable with her body. At that age, I didn't let my boyfriend slip his hand under my shirt if the light was on. I guess we are reverting to our more raw natures…the way we were before society had its way with our moral compass.

I think it is different in many ways this time, though. Women who have survived this long are probably a strong bunch. We won't be second-class citizens this time. And, judging by those girls we left behind today, men had better watch themselves.

It's definitely a New World Order.

Wednesday, May 12

Rain.

No…wait…scratch that. The skies have opened up in a waterfall-like torrent. There is not one single part of me that is dry. We are sitting in this abandoned car to avoid the worst of it. Well, at least as best we can. I say that because one of the windows on the passenger side of the car is gone and most of the rubber seals on the rest have froze and melted so many times, to the point that there is no watertight integrity here. Water pours in from every seam, crease, and crack. Still, this is better than being outside.

I'm sitting in the middle of the front seat, Eric is in the back. Sam is curled up beside me. He was shivering in that way doggies do when they are cold and wet. I have him wrapped up in one of my sweatshirts. Now he only shivers in little fits every few minutes.

We have all our empty containers outside collecting water. That is one true blessing from all this. I've watched three lone shamblers and one mini-herd of twenty or so go past. I got a little worried about the herd, but they were in the other lane and never even made a move our direction. All of them were headed *away* from Burns.

During the brief conversation I managed to coax from Eric today, I laid out my plan for a bicycle. He nodded and asked me why I waited so long to make that call. I gave it some thought…then told him to shut up.

Okay, Meredith…why *did* you wait so long?

Thursday, May 13

The road is probably not going to be here much longer. We've passed entire sections that are buried or washed away. It keeps getting worse.

We came out into this large opening, a valley that cuts between the hills on either side of the highway. The remnants of large, circular farm plots can still be seen.

Then there is this charred husk of a fighter jet that is jutting from deep in the fields on the south. I wanted to go check it out, but once again Eric was against it. Sam sorta backed Eric in a way. He kept sniffing towards the chest-high growth that has laid claim to the area and growling with real purpose. It could've been the wind...or not...but there was a lot of rustling in the grass or whatever it is that makes up that mini-jungle along the southern border of the highway.

Tonight we are camped on a rocky outcropping that looks down into the valley. As the sun sets, the bowl fills with shadows which quickly become an inky blackness. Sure enough, every once in a while Sam's ears will perk up. Sometimes, I think I can hear them, too. Just as the citizens of Burns have staked their claim, so too have the undead...in this valley.

Friday, May 14

The sounds of distant gunfire woke us today. Not from the valley below...or Burns to the east. This came from the hills above us. Eric told me to stay put. When I woke, he was already awake and strapping on his gear.

I tried to protest, but he told me that I needed to listen to him "just this once." He said that Sam and I should find a spot on the next ridge where we could keep a good eye on the highway in both directions. He wouldn't answer any of my questions. Then, just like that, he was gone into the darkness. I don't know if it is a Native American thing or what, but he vanished from sight before he even hit the shadows.

Since he's been gone, I've moved like he asked. I can't really see into the valley/jungle below, but I don't think that Eric was all that concerned about zombies. I am keeping my eyes on the highway like Eric said...and I haven't seen a thing.

Something feels very wrong. I don't know exactly what, but there is a definite *wrongness*. Sam feels it, too. But it isn't from the road below. There is something in the hills. I may not trust *myself* sometimes, but my dog?

Saturday, May 15

Screams.
Lots and lots of screams.

It is impossible to tell if it is male or female. It has been going on all day long. I hate it. Oh, and Sam doesn't like it either. He's actually been hiding between my legs most of the day. And when I stand up, he presses against me.

Funny thing about however many zombies are in that little valley below. They don't seem inclined to roam. They don't venture out of the tall grass. I see a lot of movement, but I've seen very few actual zombies wandering these parts.

Monday, May 17

I'm in a mostly burned out motel near what can only have been an airfield. I can see the town of Burns, or, more aptly put, I can see the wall. It is a mix of cars, trucks, concrete, and razor wire.

Leave it to rural America, but this town has their shit together. There is no place to approach without crossing a few hundred yards of open, scorched ground. I can see a huge trench that I can only assume circles the entire town. There are towers every quarter mile or so. They're only ten feet high—the barricade is maybe five—and each is manned. It all makes sense, I guess. Zombies aren't known to be climbers. Also, there are bridge-like catwalks that span the trench. It is genius. They control where the zombies cross. Then they use hand-held weapons to dispose with the ones that reach the barricade. All of this is speculation, but it makes perfect sense if you actually see their setup.

I've seen horse patrols come and go. One even rode out this way. They came close enough so that I could see them clearly as they waved. They know I'm here, and made it a point to let me know that they know. Whoever they were, they pointed to town, and then looked back at the window I was peeking from while trying *not* to expose myself. They made a big production out of shaking their heads "no." The message is clear: I am not welcome here.

As for Eric, he is sleeping in a nest of our gear on a filthy bed that you don't need to shine a black light on in order to see just how vile it is. He came back late Sunday night. He was covered in blood; none of it was his. He refused to talk about whatever was going on in the hills. It begs the question: With all we've seen these past couple of years, what could be so bad that he won't even talk about it?

When he got back, he simply told me to grab our gear. We started walking in the dark; something that we never do. Eric says it is foolish to take such a risk like traveling in the dark. That holds true even on a clear night with a bright moon. Funny how things change.

I've traveled with people who prefer night and those who prefer day. It is all pretty much the same to me. However, I did come close to breaking my ankles when we moved down out of the hills. Also, the ruined roads are no treat either.

When we spotted the airfield and this place beside it, we found one of the few rooms with intact windows and a door. Eric didn't even bother to clean up. He curled up into a ball and crashed.

Sam won't go near him. I couldn't help myself; I checked his body very thoroughly for bites or scratches. He *looked* clean, although it was hard to be certain with all that blood. As you might have guessed, I won't be sleeping. I will be watching Eric. Every hour or so, I peel his eyelids up and look for black tracers.

So far, so good.

Tuesday, May 18

Eric is awake. He still won't talk about what went on up in those hills, but at least he went outside and cleaned up. We were blessed with rain again today. Nothing like the other day; just a nice steady downpour for a while. When it blew over early this afternoon, there was a beautiful rainbow that was brighter than anything I've ever seen. It made me understand where that old "pot of gold" myth started. We could see where the rainbow ended in the fields south of us. The ground looked like it was glowing.

Some time in the night, a delegation from Burns left us a note on the door. It is seriously creepy that neither of us heard a thing—more so with Eric than with me. The note was simple:

> *We hope you enjoyed your stay.*
> *Checkout time is tomorrow morning.*

I guess we're leaving tomorrow morning.

Thursday, May 20

I'd almost forgotten how scary situations can be when those things get you in their sights. Slow doesn't mean a damned thing when there are a couple hundred.

Eric and I were cutting through some fields on the route that girl suggested. The sun was high overhead and it was getting too hot for traveling. We were engrossed in one of the first real conversations that we'd had since he came back. Well, actually we were arguing. That's why we didn't see them.

I was insistent on doing all our moving early in the morning and finding someplace out of the sun during the worst part of the day. Eric was insisting that it didn't matter if we sweated out the day in some dreary shelter or dark cave…hot was hot. It was clear that he did not want to travel at night.

Then we heard the first one let loose with that baby cry. I have no idea if Sam was trying to warn us or not, but when that thing cried, he tore away from us and charged the approaching herd of zombies. Of course those stupid walking strips of jerky started falling all over each other trying to get at the noisy, bouncing dog. It was like watching a twisted version of the Keystone Kops.

We both knew that there was no way we could take on that many. If your weapon gets stuck once, you're through. The biggest problem besides there being so many was that there wasn't any place to run. We were out in the middle of nowhere amidst gullies, arroyos, and gently rolling—for the most part—hills. Oh…and did I mention that it was hot.

We started at an easy jog. Every hill that we put between us and them gave us a moment or two to catch our breath and alter our course, taking us further and further from the main body. It took almost the entire day to swing wide enough, but we eventually managed to give them the slip. Sam was blessedly quiet while we ran.

It didn't seem like we would ever actually shake them. By the time the sun was at our back, I began to think that we might not escape this one intact. Then we found what I'm pretty sure was a wheat field. It had grown into something else. All those vines and plants that I would call weeds were in a battle to reclaim the land. The actual rows were hard to find, but we were able to weasel our way through.

When we found the great big John Deere, Eric came up with a brilliant plan. So now we're sitting in this huge storage section. We even have a bed of decomposing stalks to rest on. It smells like rotten leaves, and there are a lot of bugs, but it is better than being eaten by zombies. We've heard them pass by for the last couple of hours and the sun will be setting soon.

The smell ain't the greatest, but I've smelled worse. I'm not exactly sure where we are, and we won't know until tomorrow if our little plan worked. The hope is that when we peek over the lip of this long, metal bin…the coast will be clear. We'll resume heading east until we rejoin the highway. Our gas station map says that we shouldn't run into much more than pencil-dot towns until we cross into Nevada.

Hard to say what we will find in the small towns, but I'm actually a little tingly when I think about reaching Winnemucca. Not only will it represent the best chance at scavenging, it should provide a challenge…some real fighting. What the hell is wrong with me?

Sunday, May 23

Nothing. That is all there is to see for miles in every direction. To the south, I can see the uneven horizon of a distant mountain range. The landscape will funnel us to the remnants of the highway…eventually. But for now, there is just nothing here.

To the southwest we've seen tendrils of smoke from multiple small fires. Eric is convinced that there is a small community over there; probably on the shores of Malheur Lake.

There are a surprising number of streams and creeks to be found. I don't know what exactly I expected, but after miles of high desert, this is like a whole other world. We've discovered an abundance of edible plants, and even rabbits. Lots of rabbits. Either the zombies aren't interested, or they just can't catch them.

Monday, May 24

Thunder. Lightning. Rain.

Tuesday, May 25

The reddish-brown clay or dirt, or whatever the hell you call the crap that is so dominant around these parts, is sticking to everything. Every hour or so, we have to stop in order to scrape the stuff off the tires of our carts and the soles of our boots. It would be a disaster if we have to move with any sort of urgency. We are finding that more and more of the highway is gone.

Also, we ran across something that made us stop for the day: a military caravan. Tanks, Jeeps, troop transports, the whole ball of wax are here. There isn't a sign of a living soul having been through here in…ever. Even though we don't expect to find anything too exciting—that is still functional—we will search everything thoroughly in the morning. Tonight, I'm sleeping in an honest-to-goodness tank. Alone. You never realize how much you miss your privacy until you never have any.

Wednesday, May 26

Swapped out into some nicer boots. I'm fairly certain he won't miss them. More and more I am finding that I have low-ered my standards on what is acceptable. For instance, the young man whom I discovered inside a tank with his brains blown out from a self-inflicted gunshot wound to the face; it wasn't until just now that I gave a thought to the fact that I peeled his boots off his feet. Or that they are now snuggly fitting on my own.

Tonight we're in a tiny one stoplight town called Lawen. There is nothing to see. However, there was a bottle of disinfect-ant on the shelf of this little market. After ransacking a few residences—mostly trailers—I also happened across some ultra-thick socks. Eric hit the real jackpot, though. He found a never-been-opened three-pack of tightie-whities. In his size!

Thursday, May 27

All day long we had a lone shambler on our tail. We've been walking along Highway 78 all this time, and today we settled into a groove along this stretch of empty, void-of-any-life, washed out road. At some point, I glanced over my shoulder and saw it. It was just a dark shape moving through the shimmering waves of heat rising off the ground on the horizon. I mentioned it to Eric and, in typical fashion, he shrugged and continued walking.

About midday, I asked him if we should double-back and kill it. He explained that it didn't seem to be drawing a crowd, so what was the problem. I didn't really have an answer. We found an abandoned farm house on the edge of a cluster of circular crops and made camp. Just before sunset, the zombie staggered up to the porch. It was a woman. You could hear the skin crackle as she moved, and there were nests of insects moving about inside her ripped open and long-since-dried abdomen. A couple of splintered ribs poked through the parchment that was her skin. Also, I'd say she's taken a few dozen bullets; one that shattered her lower jaw.

I ended her existence by planting my axe in her forehead. Afterwards, Eric and I sat down for a bitter—but strangely good—dandelion salad with a dash of apple vinegar and a pair of roasted rabbits.

Is this really all there is? I am beginning to wonder why I'm doing this. Don't get me wrong, I do not doubt my choices, nor will I be going out and tossing myself into a ravenous herd of zombies any time soon. I am simply trying to figure out what possessed me to do this. And to take that question one step further; why did Eric join me?

What do I really hope to find in Vegas? And let's say that the lights are on. Will I settle down and call it home? Why would I think I will be any happier there than at The Compound, Sunset Fortress...or Irony, USA for that matter?

All I'm truly doing is roaming a dead world. What would all the shrinks—who seemed to have a label for everything back in the pre-apocalyptic world—say about me? Was I always like this? Or, did the situation mold me into who I am now. I mean, I've met some wonderful people, and I've met some monsters disguised as human beings. Did this event bring out the "real" person lurking inside each of us? Did it break us all in some way, and this is the Phoenix that rose from the individual ashes?

I can hear the low, distant rumble of thunder. The smell of rain is floating on the night breeze. A chill is in the air just like any other night in the desert and I'm sensing…something.

There is that wrongness out there in the darkness again. When I close my eyes, I can feel it closing in. Not just on me. On everybody.

Saturday, May 29

We didn't travel far these past couple of days. We found a small town. Unfortunately it has been mostly burned to the ground. However, there were a few places to rummage through.

We looked for bikes, but didn't find anything worth a damn. It looks like survivors were here and tried to make a stand. Something went wrong at the small airfield. That's where the fire seems to have started.

One thing I've learned in all of this is to trust my instincts. I feel like we're being watched. I've been keeping my eye on Eric, but he doesn't seem concerned, cautious, or anything out of the ordinary. As for Sam, other than hiking his leg every ten seconds, nothing. Seriously, who or what can possibly pee that much.

Sunday, May 30

Something is definitely watching us. Eric finally said, "I can feel something piercing my skin like tiny needles."

Well thanks for finally joining the party. Sam still appears clueless and continues his cycle of sniff and pee…sniff and pee.

There is a lake to the west of us—on our right as we are now headed directly south—and clusters of those circular crops so prevalent in this region. I think there is a cluster of survivors set up off in that direction. Campfires have a very distinct look. These were pretty big. That means that whoever they are, they aren't scared of revealing their location.

But back to whatever is following us. Obviously it isn't a zombie. Zombies don't stalk their prey. They just stumble out and hope for the best. Not that zombies feel hope…who knows what I mean.

Something is out there. It is hiding in the shadows as darkness spreads its blanket over the world again. And whatever it is, I would swear that I feel its misery…pain…anger.

Monday, May 31

His name is Cody. He turned sixteen yesterday. It took most of the afternoon to get those two pieces of information from him. Not that he actually told us. We learned it when we finally got the book pried from his hands.

Cody was carrying one of those baby books that new parents buy and fill in diligently for about the first three months. He was also carrying a wicked looking blade and the mother of all slingshots. (Eric tried it out and put one of those little steel balls that Cody has in a pouch hanging from his belt through a car door.)

Cody has been bitten. More than once. He is missing two fingers on his left hand—which he seems to favor nonetheless— and his right cheek and lower lip are mostly scar tissue. It is safe to assume that he is immune.

We didn't find him so much as he found Sam. Or…Sam got close enough for the boy to grab hold. When I heard the yelp from a nearby gulley, I took off expecting to see my dog being turned into zombie chow. What I saw initially seemed to confirm my fears. I was bringing up my crossbow when Eric touched my arm and made me stop.

The filthy creature wasn't trying to eat my dog. Instead, he was hugging him and scratching the exposed belly. Honestly, I couldn't even tell that it was a boy. His face was so caked in dirt that I didn't see the soft, downy hair on his chin.

The boy paid absolutely no attention to either me or Eric. He just sat in the dust, holding Sam and petting him while making these strange cooing sounds. Eric whispered that I should keep an eye on him while he nabbed us a meal.

An hour later, we had a pair of rabbits on the spit over an open fire. The filthy mess eyed us like he expected us to turn into zombies at any moment. He didn't warm up to me or Eric when we offered food. However, once he had a full stomach, it wasn't long before his eyes began to droop.

As soon as they closed, Eric pounced. It was actually a fairly even fight. That kid managed to open up a nasty gash on Eric's forehead with his bony little knuckles. Once he was secured, Eric toted the trussed and angry boy to a nearby stream for a bath.

While that little war raged—causing Sam no end of grief; I haven't seen the dog that agitated, ever—I flipped through the book that was bundled up in plastic garbage bags. What I saw was almost enough to make me cry.

There was a family photo on the first page, titled "Our New Family" in carefully hand-etched calligraphy. The mother, Marie according to the caption, was clutching the tightly bundled infant in her arms with a smile that only new mothers are capable of. Standing behind her, with his hands resting on her shoulder and waist, is the father, Chad.

There are a dozen or so other photos, but it is something about that first one that is so heartbreakingly sad. I actually began to feel guilty flipping through the pages of this young man's life. I made certain to replace it exactly as I found it.

Once Eric finished cleaning Cody up, the boy curled into the fetal position and went to sleep. That's when Eric told me about the rest of the bodily injuries. Apparently, along with his lower lip, Cody is missing most of his tongue.

I'm not sure about what will happen now. We haven't asked him to join us, and I'm not sure he will want to even if we did.

One more thing; that feeling of disquiet I've had? It isn't gone. Whatever has been gnawing at my nerves...it isn't this boy.

Tuesday, June 1

At Eric's insistence, we got up this morning, ate a light breakfast, left some for the boy, and then started on our way. Stupid Sam didn't want to leave Cody behind and I actually had to use his leash. The road curled slightly in an eastern direction and took us into a gouged out valley.

A twisting creek is winding along beside us as we go. In a few spots it has cut away the ever-deteriorating highway. However, it would seem that there are plenty of fish. We were cooking a lunch of trout over a small campfire when Cody strolled up and nonchalantly sat down across from Eric and me.

Naturally, Sam padded over and plopped down beside the boy. We ate in silence and then resumed our journey until we came upon a half-collapsed roadside motel.

Up ahead, the mountains look ominous. I think I understand the mindset of ancient civilizations better. Those mountains look so dark and forbidding. And with the clouds stacked up against them, there is a feeling of mystery. The world is silent save for an occasional flash in those distant clouds followed by the low, sonorous rumble of thunder.

Friday, June 4

I'll say this much…Cody can handle his business in a fight.

The steady climb into the Steens Mountains was much more arduous than I remember Mount Hood being. We were moving slow, and my calves felt like rubber bands that had been stretched to the point of nearly snapping by midday. And that was on the *first* day.

It was on the second day that the squeaking rumble woke us about an hour before sunrise. We were well off of the road, camped up on a large, flat ledge that gave us a good view of the pass below in both directions. In the direction we were moving, there was a curve in the road about a mile off. It was from around that corner that we saw the strangely modified truck come rolling along.

It was one of those big ones with two rear axels and chrome sideboards running along the elongated bed. The cab had been transformed into a cage like one of those cars in the old county fair *Zipper* rides. Inside was a man. A big, fat, bald man with the hairiest body I have ever seen on a human. He had a handlebar mustache that sported curlicues at the ends like a cartoon villain that went great with the two-pronged goatee he was sporting.

A long, metal bar extended from where the engine used to be. Chained to each crossbar that had been welded to it were a mixture of two living humans and fourteen zombies. The living folks were in front to urge the zombies forward in a twisted parody of carrot-and-the-stick. The driver was using some sort of elaborate braking lever to keep the vehicle from trundling out of control down the hill.

When Cody took off down the rocky embankment, I might've briefly considered leaving him to his own fate. No, I didn't like what I was seeing, but in my defense, I'd just woke up and my legs were killing me. My calves actually feel like somebody is flaying them right now. Then Sam bounded off after the boy and I wasn't left with any other choice.

There was some sort of narrow slit in the side of the cage where the driver sat. I'll never know how Cody did it, but he fired a shot from his wrist rocket that found that small opening. I don't know where he hit the driver, only that he did. That was bad news for the two living souls in front of the long metal pole. The manual brake must need to be held down, because after a pained gurgle, the truck began to pick up speed. It built quite a head of steam before it veered into the solid rock that bordered one side of where the road should be.

We were so fixated on the spectacle that, by the time any of us recognized the sound, five three-wheeled choppers came around the bend and were bearing down on us. We had no choice but to fight. Any thoughts to the contrary evaporated with the boom of a double-barreled shotgun that reverberated through the entire carved out pass.

Eric went down like a sack of rocks. Things were a little blurry after that. I had enough time to fire my crossbow once, then draw an axe and hurl it. Cody, on the other hand, managed three shots with his wrist rocket before any of the riders were able to locate us and fire another round. I moved in on those he'd injured with my blades drawn to make sure nobody got back up.

As for Eric...he's fine. Mostly. His chest is badly bruised from the rubber balls. I guess those guys prefer to take their victims alive.

We are fairly certain that their camp is not far away. I have no desire to search for it.

As for Cody, I chewed his ass good for charging into a fight like an idiot. He didn't look all that chastised when I was finished. Eric was silent through the whole thing. Whether out of pain or something else, I have no idea.

Here is my problem: Why did I bitch out that kid for something I would've done myself not more than a year ago? The only real difference being that I would've done it in a way that tried to save those poor souls chained in the front of that truck.

We'll camp for a few days before moving on. We found a really sturdy old National Forest Visitor's Center. It was on a mostly overgrown access road that led into the tall pines. The dust in here is thick enough that it is obvious nobody has been here for a long time. That makes this the ideal place to rest up while Eric recovers. He wouldn't have asked, but his pain is obvious.

Saturday, June 5

Holy crap! Bears!

Today we watched a large, brownish bear sit in the shade of the trees while its cubs played in the open, sun lit field. Seeing a grizzly (Eric said it was a young, female grizzly) in the wild is a big difference from seeing one in the zoo.

I am told it is a big deal. Not that I would know, but I guess it has been generations since grizzlies walked wild in these parts.

Sam was a handful. That stupid dog wanted to go outside and check out the visitors. Eventually I got him corralled in a closet where I left him until our visitors wandered off to do whatever it is that bears do in the woods. Today was the first time that my dog was completely out of control. Sam hates bears more than zombies...good to know.

We did find a few things around here that we could use: kerosene, two bottles of hydrogen peroxide, some fishing gear, and a rugged looking radio that came with a pair of nine-volt batteries that tested good in their little display pack battery tester.

Of course we didn't pick up any signals, but it will be nice to have and make periodic checks with; especially when we get closer to Vegas. (I know that I need to see it for myself and it doesn't matter if anybody is still alive there or not.) I also like that we can see if there is anybody else out there transmitting. I picked up that initial Vegas signal from northeastern Oregon with a clunky old normal radio. Perhaps we'll find other places to see after Vegas with this baby.

I say "we" but I do not count on anybody making these trips with me. One post-apocalyptic walkabout is probably all Eric has in his tank.

Wednesday, June 9

I should learn to trust my intuition. After all, it has kept me alive this long. Now, I'm alone in the middle of nowhere and basically stripped of all but the most basic and meager supplies. I have two filtration canteens, my crossbow with seventeen bolts, my spike-tipped walking stick, a long knife, machete, and an empty backpack; empty save for the journals.

Oh yeah…and my dog.

The day after the bears, Eric and Cody were down at the creek trying out the new fishing gear. I was impatient to resume our trip, but didn't feel right asking Eric to travel yet. He was obviously still in a great deal of discomfort. Also, he and Cody were bonding. To be perfectly honest, I think that I was a teensy bit jealous of them. I've known Eric for quite some time, but we've never been what I'd call close. As for Cody, well, we'd just met him, but it was clear that he preferred Sam's or Eric's company over mine.

I decided to take advantage of their absence to enjoy a little 'me' time. Guys are so funny about that sort of thing. They think that they have the market cornered. Back in the Old Days, men would be surprised to know how often we ladies had to finish the job they started after they rolled over and went to sleep.

Anyways, I was just finishing up and debating on whether or not I would mosey down to the creek to see if I could embarrass the boys by taking a bath. (If I am being totally honest, I think I was suffering from the lack of attention…and horniness. I don't think that I would've ever considered sex with Eric, but it would've been nice to know if I could at least raise his eyebrows.)

That's when I heard *the scream*.

Coming from Eric made it all the more terrifying. To my credit, I buckled on my gear and grabbed my crossbow. I know better than to rush into a fight without my stuff. Plus, most of what I carried was still hanging on belts or straps attached to my clothes. When I threw open the door and stepped outside, I knew that there was nothing that I could do.

A wall of undead was pouring through the trees. It was a massive horde. There had to literally be thousands. It took me several seconds of standing there like an idiot to fully process what I was seeing. Here. In the middle of nowhere. The biggest herd I'd ever seen with my own two eyes. I say that because, from where I stood, they stretched on in either direction for as far as I could see.

Sam's barking is probably what saved me in the end. My faithful companion was sprinting across the field. Turning my head to the left, I saw one of the advance stragglers step around the corner of the building. She'd been a big girl in real life. Not fat…I mean WNBA big. She was well over six feet tall.

The screams had already ceased. I doubted that there would be enough left of Eric or Cody to come back considering the size of this pack. I would never learn how this herd came up on Eric and caught him by surprise. Then it dawned on me…I hadn't heard a sound. Not a moan, groan, or baby cry.

My walking stick was actually leaning by the doorway out on the porch. I grabbed it and jabbed it through the freakishly tall female zombie's chin and up into her head where it burst out through the top of the skull. I let the body fall off the porch and free up my walking stick.

I grabbed the canteens and the backpack from just inside the door. I knew that there was no time to pack anything. Going inside would likely seal my fate. I wouldn't make it if I didn't run. So, that's what I did. I ran. Just like Rose and the Doctor…Sam and I ran.

We made our way back to the wide swathe where Highway 78 used to be—it is so washed out through here that it really looks like nothing more than a very wide trail. All that day I kept up a fast walk or slow jog. Sam trotted alongside me with his tongue lolling out of his mouth like everything was just fine and dandy.

We passed cars and trucks. Some empty. Some not. But we never stopped. Every time I looked over my shoulder, I saw them. At some point, I actually stopped looking. But as the shadows of the early evening began to grow long, and a chilly breeze began drying the sweat that still clung to my body, I looked to find…nothing. It was as if it had all been an illusion.

That was when I realized that the area around me was changing. The trees were gone. Just before it got dark, I passed a sign that said something about lava fields.

We actually backtracked and found a place to camp for the night where we still had trees to hide amongst. Sometime in the middle of the night, that herd must've stumbled upon the camp or base of the guys that we had it out with the other day. The sounds of distant gunfire and those awful screams came. It sorta reminded me of microwave popcorn. It started slow, and then there was a flurry, then a few aftershocks of noise…then silence.

My desire to continue on was hampered by the fact that I was exhausted. I didn't feel I would be able to push through a day under the sun if I didn't get some rest. Also, Sam didn't look like he could go on much more. His head had drooped at some point and he was barely getting his feet off the ground by the time that we stopped. The last factor was that we would be out of water soon. I didn't want to miss even the tiniest creek.

The rest of the night, I slipped in and out of sleep. I woke to a pale sky without even the slightest wisp of a cloud. There wouldn't be any relief from the sun. And it was already showing signs of getting warm. The only good news that day was the lack of any signs or sounds of zombies…or survivors from that camp or compound that got overrun.

Thursday, June 10

Being completely on my own seems weird. I can't actually remember being alone like this since this whole thing started. Sure, there have been moments; periods of time when I was all by myself. But right now, for the first time, I am totally alone.

I woke this morning and crawled out of the bushes that I'd chosen to hide in while I slept…and discovered that Sam is gone. I've called him. I've looked around.

Nothing.

I am in the middle of nowhere.

Alone.

I haven't moved from this spot in the hopes that my stupid dog will come back. I can't stay for long because I have less than a quarter of a canteen left as of right now and haven't found any water. I won't die of thirst. I can backtrack if need be in order to refill at one of those mountain streams.

Tomorrow, I will press on and give myself a full day to find more water. But today…today…I'm just gonna sit here.

And cry.

Saturday, June 12

No dog. No zombies. Nothing. Although I am nestled in on this rock that has a clump of scrubby looking bushes sticking out from the—wall? No, that isn't right, but it will have to do. I am above a creek that is tiny enough to step over. Oh yeah, and I'm roasting a pair of rabbits that I nailed with my crossbow.

I got all my tears out yesterday. I don't think that all of them were for my dog. Even as quiet as he was, I miss having Eric around. He was something special.

Sunday, June 13

Reached a three-way intersection this morning. The military will never make sense to me. They had a large presence here.

There is a giant, fenced perimeter with about a hundred zombies milling behind the ten foot high barricade. All of them are wearing the remnants of their uniforms.

I saw a few things in there that looked very tempting. But there is no realistic way that I could've gone in and made it out alive. If I were the heroine in an action film—I'm looking at you Mila Jojovich—I'd have gotten in with no problems.

Anyways, south of that junction I came across an old graveyard. The stone wall around it was still intact, so that is where I am camped for the night. Of all things, there is a burned out restaurant in front.

Sometimes you stumble upon something that makes you scratch your head. "Hey, waitress, could we get a window seat? We are here to visit grandma's grave and might as well do that over the meatloaf special."

South. My trail leads me directly south. I know that if I keep heading that way, eventually I will reach Vegas. The only thing that sucks—besides the million other normal things associated with everyday life—is that when I grabbed my backpack and ran, I lost that nifty radio. Also, the gas station maps with our route highlighted were in Eric's bag. My one consolation is that both Sam's journal and mine were in my pack. I believe I would've risked going back if I'd left them behind. I just wish I'd had a little food and that radio in my pack.

Thinking back, I realize just how sloppy I have gotten. I'd been relying on Eric. I won't make that mistake again. *Always be ready to run.* That is Rule Number One when you are out in the wilderness. My backpack should always be stocked so that if I have to grab it and run, I'll have all I need for a few days at least.

Monday, June 14

My only happiness in a while came today. I was actually kicking this rock and not doing anything more than convincing myself to keep putting one foot in front of another. Then my rock went under this RV. It wasn't anything fancy. In fact, it looked far worse than could be accounted for with simple neglect, age, and weathering. This vehicle looked bad.

There were brown stains all over the side door—old blood obviously. A body that had dried out to almost nothing but the skeleton was still in the driver's seat. A wash of icky stuff was spayed all over the inside of the window from where the guy had eaten a bullet.

I had to go in and take a look just in case there was something in there worth taking. Mostly I was hoping for food. I set down my pack and decided that my long knife would be my best weapon in such close quarters. I'd climbed up on the front bumper for a look inside, but just because I didn't see anything didn't mean it was safe.

I pulled open the side door and was greeted by an old death smell. Not the nasty rot or zombie funk, just the bitter stench of old death. Nothing tumbled out or anything, so I went inside.

This RV used to belong to a group of guys about my age—mid-twenties. They were a band. A folded up banner revealed a wordy if not intriguing name: *James Dean Kindle and the Eastern Oregon Playboys*. Guitar cases, keyboards, drums, and a variety of instruments that I could not identify were strewn about. The photos that I found in a scrapbook show the four of them performing. I only found two bodies. One of them was locked in the bathroom with an empty bottle of booze and a bunch of pill containers. That couldn't have been pleasant.

There is a lot of blood, long since dried and turned into a series of dark stains. Also, I found a hand with a bite out of it that had been chopped off and thrown in the sink. Poor bastard.

As for food, I found a jar of rancid peanut butter, a lump of moldy cheese—at least I think it was cheese—and two tins of smoked sardines. I ate the fish and drank lukewarm water from my canteen while I enjoyed my real find: an iPod. It has all kinds of artists that I have never heard of before.

Alexa Wiley...Laura Gibson...and of course JDK and the Eastern Oregon Playboys.

The battery only lasted a little over an hour. Surprisingly, there was enough juice in the auxiliary battery of the RV for a full recharge. But it was neat listening to music. I probably would have never heard any of these people in the Old World. And the sad part is just how good they are. It almost seems like a crime that talentless, over-processed hacks like Britney and that

Simpson girl got airplay while folks like this languished in ano-nymity.

Then there were the pictures. You could tell that these boys had fun performing and playing music. And you could've walked right past them in the grocery store and not known how talented they were.

I'm keeping the iPod in hopes of finding more opportunities to charge it. It would be nice to listen to them again. I didn't travel far today. But it's not like I have a schedule to keep.

Tuesday, June 15

I woke up this morning to a loner pawing at the side of the RV. Imagine my surprise when I threw open the side door—after taking a look out of all the windows to ensure it was just the one—and came face-to-face with the owner of the hand I'd found in the sink.

As hard as it is to believe, one of the Playboys...or maybe JDK, hell, I don't know...was standing there. He was barely recognizable from the pictures I'd seen yesterday. Funny thing is that I didn't recognize his face so much as the remnants of the tattered shirt he was wearing. It was the same one I'd seen on the tall, skinny guitar player in several of the photos. I almost felt...something. Maybe like I was doing this thing a favor by ending its miserable undead existence when I stuck the knife in its temple. It was my way of saying, "Thanks for the music."

Then I did something very much not like me. As I sit beside this stream and watch the sun set, I still don't know why. I dragged the body inside the RV with the other two and torched the thing. I punctured the gas tank and used a flare from the emergency roadside kit I found under the passenger's seat.

I can still see the dark smudge in the sky.

Thursday, June 17

People.

I've come across a tent city built along what I assume was once an airstrip. There is literally nothing remarkable about this place. No fences, no barricades, nothing.

The people here are friendly enough. I had a fantastic meal of rabbit stew and flat bread. They have gardens scattered about with a variety of things growing. They even have homemade soap! This nice lady gave me some—and encouraged me to "enjoy" it right away. I had a bath down at the stream that runs through just south of camp.

They are a very religious group. But not religious in the crazy Genesis Brotherhood way…or any of the other wacky fringe types. These folks are actually very nice. They even invited me to church and didn't flip out when I paused long enough for them to see that I wasn't thrilled with the prospect.

I can hear them over in the tent right now. They're singing and sound legitimately happy. I catch snatches of the preacher's sermon. He isn't yelling or telling everybody how much they need to change. Actually, it sounds like he is just reading the bible.

There is a little girl here. I've seen her two or three times. Just glimpses really. She is immune. One of her arms is scar tissue from elbow to wrist. She has a long, blonde braid and sparkly eyes. Each time that I see her, she is laughing.

These people are frighteningly normal.

Saturday, June 19

Back on the road. Don't get me wrong, the people were great, and it was nice to have conversations with somebody other than myself for a change. Not to mention the luxury of not having to worry about food, or becoming food if you nap too soundly. It just felt…crowded.

Crazy. Right? Here I am, trying to reach a city like Las Vegas that might be secure enough to have electrical power, and I'm all buggy about a few dozen people living in a tent city.

Honestly, I'm not sure what the hell I'm doing anymore. Even worse, those folks told me that I am two or three days from the border town of McDermitt. It is thick with zombies, but reportedly has a good amount of scavengeable goods. Whole stores are intact. Imagine…aisles of canned goods…hygiene products. (That is good, because I'm due for a visit from Aunt Irma any day now, and what little I had in feminine products were left behind at the forestry center where Eric died.) There might even be some firepower to be had.

I asked why it is that nobody has made a run on the place if it is so well stocked. It seems that the good people of McDermitt did the same thing as the folks at Burns. Only, the infection was already inside the walls. People have tried, but it never ends well. I guess you know where I am headed.

Tuesday, June 22

It has been a long, boring climb into these mountains. The good news is how cool it has been temperature-wise. I've been lucky. The bad part has been how cold the nights are. I had to sleep out in the open last night because I couldn't find a vehicle or shack of any sort.

Tonight, I am safe and sound in a firewatcher's tower. It doesn't have any windows, but it is off of the ground. There are telltale signs that other survivors have stayed here. The ground is littered with empty cans with labels faded into unreadability. Also, there is an arm. Well…that's not entirely accurate. There are the skeletal remains of an arm; complete with missing pinky which was obviously bitten off.

Unfortunately, there wasn't a single thing to drink. I had to bring my water from about two miles away. It wasn't terrible, but it is inconvenient. I imagine that is why nobody stayed here permanently.

The best find—besides this sturdy, secure tower—is all the blackberries. I used an empty plastic jug that I found and washed it out to gather a bunch. I easily ate more than I picked, which is why it took so long to eventually come up with a full jug to snack on when I start hiking again.

There is a lot of wildlife in the area. Just sitting here snacking on blackberries, I've seen a pair of wolves, a deer, an elk (at least I think it was an elk), and a REALLY big bird that I think was an eagle. Oh…and bugs. Lots and lots of bugs.

Tonight, I shall dine like a queen. The deer I mentioned? Yeah…it is dressed and a haunch is currently roasting over my fire. I dragged all the icky stuff down by the stream I mentioned that is a couple miles away in hopes that it will keep any wandering beasties far from my camp.

Wednesday, June 23

Wow! Last night, from up in the tower, I spotted over a dozen other fires scattered throughout these hills. A few were in clusters. This is perhaps the largest signs of life I have encountered since being in Portland. Of course, in Portland, you heard more than saw other people.

I guess it makes sense. The zombie presence is minimal if not non-existent. There is an obvious abundance of wild game and fuel in the form of the wood. I imagine that farming is possible. Plus, there are lots of edible plants if you know what to look for (like Eric did). I wish I'd paid better attention when he came to me with all those leaves and roots.

I'll move on tomorrow.

Thursday, June 24

I am camped out in a completely looted, vile-smelling farmhouse. I had to backtrack here to camp for the night and get some good sleep. The walled town is only a few miles down the road. I want to get there just before sunrise to ensure the most time possible for exploring.

I'll get as much rest tonight as possible, but I have seen a few roaming stragglers. Just on my return trip to this place I had to put down a pair of zombies. They were holding hands! That's the first time that I've seen something like that. My original thought as I was approaching was that perhaps they were stuck that way. I checked…the fingers were actually laced.

Weird.

Saturday, June 26

Zombies are only a part of the problem. I'm in the high school locker room catching my breath from yesterday. And it wasn't a zombie that almost did me in. Somebody has managed to exist here amidst at least a few hundred of the undead. What's worse, they've set up booby-traps using the zombies! Or at least parts of them.

I found the first such trap right after scaling the northern wall. I was near a building that I was fairly certain used to be a bank. All the windows were painted black, but the doors were gone. I peeked in and a pair of dead hands snagged me by my hair. A creeper was suspended upside-down just above the main doorway. When I stepped inside, I triggered a release mechanism that dropped the thing right on top of me.

To make things more entertaining in this little slice of Hell, I think at least half the zombies are wearing helmets. Somebody has way too much time on their hands.

Since then, I've walked around blind corners to find a dozen still-animated heads suspended from wires, more creepers—many obviously made that way intentionally—than I have ever seen before in one place at one time. There are also regular traps designed to maim or kill. Even the rooftops have been rigged in places.

My shoulders are sore from all the killing I did today. And while I haven't seen this mystery person, I know that he or she is out there somewhere…watching me. Two of the traps that I triggered intentionally have been reset.

Okay, I get it. This is "your" turf. But aren't you being just a bit greedy? There is enough here for several people to live off of for another year or so easily. Using that time, gardens could be planted; the hills are teeming with animals that would keep an abundance of meat on the table.

Oh well, this isn't my problem. I just want to load up with enough essentials to last a while and be on my way. I'll try to do this without going heads-up with the resident of this dead town. I've gathered a few things; womanly things, a sleeping bag, a stone and steel for blade sharpening,

Today I wandered the halls of this school. I half-expected the person to be hiding out here. The building is well-barricaded with a reinforced fence that goes all the way around. There is a courtyard with a barbecue pit that had warm, smoldering coals in it.

Tomorrow, the plan is to grab a few things; perhaps fishing gear and some canned goods from one of the grocery stores. Instant coffee wouldn't suck, either. Now there's a sentence that I never thought I'd utter.

One last thing...I will get a map of Nevada. I'd love an atlas, but I'll settle for one of those foldy things. As long as the resident or residents of this place leave me be, I will be gone tomorrow.

Sunday, June 27

I met the Keeper of McDermitt. He's not at all what I expected. His name is Michael DeNoma, and his story is...

I can't explain it. He and I have an indirect tie. He was in the prison in Pendleton where Sam and the others stayed briefly after their capture. I was floored when that bomb dropped. But I am getting ahead of myself.

I was leaving. It was around noon when I had my things on a line and had thrown the end over the wall when I heard a quiet voice tell me to "be careful, there's a few roaming around outside today." I almost broke my neck, it whipped around so fast.

When I laid eyes on him, I almost laughed. This was no action hero or *Road Warrior* wanna-be. What I saw was an incredibly overweight young man with crazy orange hair and the scraggliest wildman beard—also orange—that I've ever seen in my life.

His more-than-ample belly sagged over the folded down waist of his jean shorts. His skin was ghostly white except for his glorious farmer's tan.

When I didn't speak right away, he brought up the sword he carried in his left hand. His expression switched to that of concern, like perhaps he thought that I would attack him. One thing that I learned over the next few hours was that this guy could never sit down at a poker table and hope to win.

I thanked him for the warning and turned to go. That's when he called out.

"Wait."

Just a single word, but there was so much in it; pleading, longing, loneliness, sorrow. All the worst feelings that a person can feel existed in that single word. So...I turned back to face him.

After a brief exchange, we decided to go back to the high school. We started talking while he pulled out his secret stash of junk food. (At least it explained the obesity.) He showed me how a lot of the stuff still hadn't even reached the expiration date. Ah, the marvels of science.

We ate, drinking a bottle of Dr. Pepper that had a funky aftertaste, and talked. Actually, he did most of the talking. That's when I discovered that he'd been in prison. When the inmates took over, he was one of the "freaks" who survived. When the opportunity came and people were given the option to stay or go, he left. He wanted to save his mother. He didn't.

After that, he travelled. Sometimes alone and sometimes with others. He heard the Las Vegas broadcast one night and started heading that way. When he reached McDermitt, he expected the same reaction he'd gotten in Burns. That's when he heard the screams coming from within the walls. He cursed his poor physical fitness because, by the time he was over the wall, the screaming had stopped. It only took him a moment to discover the source…a crowd of those things hunched over a body pulling out strands of insides and ripping off hunks of meat.

Something in that moment broke him. He didn't have the nerve to simply offer himself over to the mob, but he made up his mind that he was done with running. He searched every residence and business for survivors. After three weeks, he was certain that he was alone.

Everything fell into a routine after that. He called it his daily cat-and-mouse game. The booby-traps came after that first winter. Three men showed up and just started to ransack the place. He didn't have the nerve to confront them, but they broke into the town's iconic White Horse Inn. They drank too much, too fast. The former citizens took care of the problem from there.

He went to work the next day rigging traps. He was often surprised at what he came up with. Everything evolved to what it is now from that day.

I'll leave in the morning. I asked Michael if he wanted to come along. He said no. His only reason was that he just didn't see the point. Did it matter if he died on the road, or in this dead town? At least here he would be relatively comfortable and never worry about food. I guess he doesn't expect to outlive his resources. Looking at him, I'd say that is a good guess, but he has defied the odds so far.

Monday, June 28

Back on the road.

As I head south, the left side of this sometimes invisible highway is dotted with more than the occasional body hanging from the big power line structures. Many of them are still moving. However, several of the bodies finally succumbed to the strain. There are piles of bodies, and even the assorted head or two, strewn about. It's gross.

There are signs written in a strange language along the way. It took me most of the day to remember where I'd seen that type of writing before. It's the Natives. I saw the same sort of stuff when I was at Warm Springs with Eric.

I stopped around midday at some ransacked, old casino. You might say that I hit the jackpot. It had shade! The sun is blazing. I've drank a lot of water. Since I'm alone, I will be changing my travel times from morning to late afternoon and early morning. The heat is just too brutal for travel.

Thursday, July 1

Cody survived! And my stupid dog is back. My stupid, wonderful dog.

From what I gather, (Cody scribbled this down for me on a few scraps of paper) he escaped because of the actions of Eric. The big idiot sacrificed himself so that this young man could have a chance. Cody was able to run, and followed the stream until he lost his footing on a slippery, flat rock. His ankle made a loud popping sound that he could hear above the noises of the water, moaning zombies, and Eric's screams.

He tried to stand, but couldn't. All he could do was drag himself with his hands—the one missing two fingers sure didn't help—down the stream. Twice, he went over small waterfalls. Both times were incredibly painful; the second time, Cody lost consciousness. He has no idea how he didn't drown or end up eaten.

By that night, his foot was almost black and swollen so bad that he had to cut off his shoe. He couldn't walk, and kept hearing zombies groaning, crying, and crashing through the brush. He managed to climb up in a tree where he stayed for two days.

Then he got sick. He doesn't remember much over those next couple of days. The next thing he *does* remember is Sam curled up beside him. That explains where my dog went, but I don't know whether to be proud of him…or jealous.

When he recovered, Cody said he started off in search of me, and it was Sam who led him in the correct direction. Sam walked and Cody followed because he didn't have anything better to do and he liked having a dog around. Talk about making a girl feel special.

He didn't enter McDermitt. Sam skirted it and wandered around most of the day until he picked up my trail again.

So…here we are…one big, happy family.

Friday, July 2

Reached the empty—for the most part, but I will get to that in a minute—and surprisingly intact town of Orovada. This place was worth a day long stop. Had I known we were so close, I would have pushed through yesterday. I guess I don't even think about it anymore, but remember all those signs that used to tell you how far to the next town? Most of those are gone. For whatever reason, they are basically extinct.

This place couldn't have been home to very many people before. There are a couple of small schools and a lot of farm equipment. Also, a family of five.

Yes, today we met Jack Billings, his wife Candela, and their children, Enzo, Monica, and Lupe. They were not only friendly, and insisted that we stay for a few days and refresh ourselves, they requested that Sam be allowed to hook up with a pair of his bitches that are due to go into heat any day now. Jack said he was starting to get concerned about the gene pool of his dogs. (If there are less than fifty running around this town, I'll pitch a tent and call it home.)

Everywhere you look, dogs of all shapes and sizes are sprawled in the shade. Looking around, it didn't take me long to come up with a million questions. But I settled on two.

How in the hell are you surviving out here in the middle of nowhere? Take your pick, zombies or raiders, you should be easy pickings.

Jack showed me an impressive array of booby-traps, but that still didn't really assure me of anything. He explained that the Santa Rosa Mountains on the east acted as one buffer, the inhospitable and empty terrain was helpful, but the military presence in Winnemucca to the south was likely the biggest factor.

I was so caught off guard by that statement that I didn't remember to ask my second question for a few minutes. To his credit, Jack just sat at the table with his hands folded neatly in front while I processed this news. Eventually I asked the second question, but only because I still needed a moment to deal with the answer of the first.

How do you keep all of these dogs fed? He told me something about plentiful game and that the dogs helped ensure that nothing ever went to waste. He mentioned some process with bone meal, but I wasn't hearing much of what he said.

Once he finished, I was prepared to dive in and find out about this military presence in Winnemucca. Before I could, he asked me where I was headed. I figured his honesty deserved mine.

Las Vegas.

He said that he figured as much. Then he went on to tell me that most of the military in Winnemucca escaped from Vegas about eight months ago. My ears perked up at the use of the word 'escape'. What I heard has me more curious than ever before.

The power was, in fact, on in Vegas. Another faction of our military is still there. It seems that two units falling back from California—one from Sacramento and one from Los Angeles—both retreated to Las Vegas. The one from Sacramento went through Reno where they initially planned to stay but were forced to retreat again. It was during that retreat that they ended up meeting the other unit.

Both were led by colonels who were activated by the National Guard in the first week of the outbreak. It didn't take long for a pissing contest to start. The Sacramento group's colonel was technically senior. However, the Los Angeles group had already secured Vegas to a certain point and had power running from the hydro-electric dam nearby. They'd established a secure perimeter and were actively expanding it. At some point, the pissing contest erupted into a fire fight. Several soldiers from both sides ran for it when one of the main walls was blown.

They quickly decided that none of them cared a lick about whose colonel was senior. They all stripped off their rank insignias and headed north. Cutting through the Nellis Air Force Range, they cleaned out every depot and kept going. Somebody suggested Winnemucca because it was fairly remote and had a water resource. It didn't hurt that there was an ample amount of farm land and a fair distance between there and Vegas.

By the time they arrived, most of the locals were gone, or dead, or deadish. They did find some survivors, and over the past several months have been securing the town.

Of course that begged the new question. Why were he and his family *here*?

There had been survivors trickling in to Winnemucca on a surprisingly regular basis. At one of the meetings held for all of the citizens, the idea of trying to start settling the surrounding areas came up. Nobody even considered Orovada, but Candela, Jack's wife, is from here. Good reason as any I guess.

The idea sounds okay, but there is a part of me that can't believe that this will end successfully. There are simply too many of the walking dead and not enough of the walking living. Compounding the problem, not all of those still alive are what can be considered 'good'. I give humanity a decade at the most.

My God. Is that why I, for all intents and purposes, abandoned my daughter? Did I do that because I know in my heart that she's doomed? What does that say about me as a person? Am I really the heartless bitch that so many people believe me to be? (Hush! That was rhetorical.)

Saturday, July 10

Today was bittersweet. I left Jack and his family in Orovada. I also left Cody. He wanted to stay. He wants to help the Billings family. Also, I think he has a bit of a crush on the thirteen-year-old, Monica. I can't blame him.

The good thing is that my trusty dog Sam came with me. He didn't even seem to look back as we hit the road. I gave Cody a hug, but I don't know why. I didn't feel any particular attachment to him. I think I may be losing my ability to care about anybody. After all, none of them are permanent fixtures in my life.

My Life.

What will it amount to? I've all but conceded that life is hopeless. The undead show no signs of falling over. I took out a couple in the past week that could've been around since this nightmare became real. They didn't smell much worse than some of the folk I've travelled with when we were forced to go for days and weeks without cleaning up. They were a little dried out, but still completely mobile. The ancient Egyptians couldn't preserve bodies this well! I may not know much about science—specifically Biology—but I do know that these things should have decomposed months ago into puddles of unmoving goo, or dried up like a corncob left in the sun. Simply put: they should not be!

Yet, there they are. I left one about a mile back in the middle of the washed out highway that I have been walking on all day. I couldn't tell if it was a little girl or a little boy. I also couldn't tell you how many bullet holes were in the body. I can say that most of its permanent teeth were broken and that it still had several baby teeth when it died. I know this because of how empty the mouth was. Funny, the things we observe now.

Sunday, July 11

I slept in a giant earthmover last night. I found it to be strangely comfortable. I watched a summer storm pass through, enjoying the lightshow while I played my iPod (thanks for the charge up, Jack). Laura Gibson goes well with thunder and lightning.

I was thinking back to when all the girls and I left Irony in search of our own adventure. Did we really stop at an adult bookstore to load up on vibrators and such? While I'm on the subject, I've been 'tending my own needs' for quite some time now. When I get to Winnemucca, I may have to get just a bit slutty.

Why do guys think that they have the market cornered on sexual urges…or playing with themselves for that matter? Fellas, let me tell you something, women love sex. And if more of you did it right, you'd be more aware of that little fact.

Monday, July 12

Well, I'm in Winnemucca. It's pretty much like Jack said. The outer-perimeter security is highly impressive. They've got fences and moats and towers (oh my!). There are a lot of civilians mixed in with all of the soldiers and everybody seems to be working and doing their share.

The best thing that this place has going for it besides the people is the wind and solar power setup. They don't use it for trivial things like lights. In fact, all the fixtures and such have been removed. What the power *is* used for is keeping the wells pumping. Everybody gets a warm, five-minute shower every other day. Also, some of the juice is used to keep the electrical fence hot. The biggest draw on the power comes from the five greenhouses (a dozen more are under construction) that keep these people well fed and something about a factory, but I didn't really pay attention.

This place has a police force, a fire department, and what has to be a first…a college. It's broken into six specialized trade schools. There is medicine, agriculture, construction, and military/security. The other two are a streamlined K-12 setup. They're segregated. Boys at one, girls at the other.

When I arrived, I was taken to a quarantine room and given a full visual lookover, then a physical that included all of the standard bodily fluids, pokes, and prods. I can't say I was treated roughly, but there certainly weren't any kind words or smiles.

I've been interviewed three times; twice on video and once on audio recording. There were various questions, but I noticed a core group that was repeated just using different words. If nothing else, this place is very thorough

When I made it clear that I do not plan on staying, nobody tried to convince me otherwise. I was told that I am welcome to stay for however long I wish, but must sign up for the work pool each day. The good news is that if I work for five days, I get a two day weekend. I was strangely impressed by that.

This place has actual entertainment. In fact, when I first came through the final security checkpoint I could see a softball game taking place off in one of the open fields. I've been told that there is a library, a movie bar—apparently there are several booths with big screen televisions and you can check out a movie.

Of course, I'd be lying if I didn't admit that I am watching everything with a suspicious eye to the point where I refused to let them isolate me from my dog. I told the nice soldier that we were a package deal. If one of us were infected, both were. Some gruff-sounding sergeant told the guy escorting me that it was okay. So, I've been present for all of Sam's checkups as well. Tomorrow I will be allowed out. I was even given a work detail.

Sanitation…hmmm…

Tuesday, July 13

Today I swept floors, hauled trash to a burn site, sorted trash that could be sent to the compost yard, mowed lawns with a push mower, and hung clothes to dry. I met a lot of people, but couldn't tell you the names of most. There was one girl, Ronni. She is sixteen, and perhaps even more of a hard ass than I am.

I guess she was swept up with the army unit that bugged out from Sacramento and tried to hold Reno. She is the only survivor in her family and had the unpleasant task of putting down her mom, sister, brother, an aunt, and two nieces one by one over the past year. I noticed that she didn't mention a dad, but when she was flipping through pictures, I did notice two with a man in them. There was no mistaking the eyes.

Anyways, when they handed out work details this evening for tomorrow, I was kinda happy to discover that she and I will be working together at the greenhouse construction site.

Other than that…this place is frighteningly normal. Maybe I was too pessimistic. Maybe we can survive…the unconquerable human spirit and all that.

Wednesday, July 14

I talked to my supervisor today. I can actually "buy" a quality mountain bike and a rugged little trailer. There is no restriction on me. I can leave any time I choose. I'm also welcome to stay as long as I like. If I live here a year, I get to move from my hotel room to one of the private residences. It's all very structured here.

This evening, I was visited by Betty Childs, the governor. Winnemucca has a governor. And get this, none of the military are eligible. She called it a "conflict of interest" and something about avoiding a police state. They *really* have it going on here.

Betty's visit wasn't strictly social, though she did say that she made it a point to stop in on every new arrival to the community. Her main reason was that she'd read Sam's journal and wanted to have a copy made for the library. I was happy to oblige. She also wanted to talk to me about my intended trip to Vegas.

I totally forgot about that being in there. I knew it was in mine, but I don't remember every single thing I wrote or when.

Here's the deal: Betty didn't ask me any specifics about my plan. She simply said that if I didn't like what I saw there, that a team of her people was in Indian Springs and that they would want to meet with me. She didn't tell me how I could find them or anything. Just that there were some folks there. I wasn't really able to ask her too many questions, and she was very good at leading me away from subjects that she didn't want to discuss. She repeated a few times how much she enjoyed Sam's journal and that I must've been through "quite an experience."

People are already on a waiting list to read one of the five copies they made. I think it's just because the book is new.

Other than that, I've been given my work detail for tomorrow: food processing. I'm a little bummed that Ronni wasn't on the same list. She was assigned to foraging. She leaves with an armed escort team for one of the nearby towns and will be gone for two days. When she gets back, she gets four days off instead of the usual two. I guess that you have to be nominated to make one of those runs by a member of the military unit after you complete a series of courses that they offer at the military/security school.

Thursday, July 15

Pringles were made here. Who knew?

Today I learned that interesting tidbit of trivia and was able to work in the converted facility that now processes the non-meat food for the community.

The Pringles factory has been modified and set up to handle more than just potatoes. Also, it is the major draw on electrical power. It houses a considerable amount of food reserves. This place has it all figured out.

Sunday, July 18

Hung out with Ronni today. After talking with the folks, I decided to stay put until August. That will give me time to earn enough in credits—bonuses that can be used for luxuries—to get my bike. Also, July is the hottest month of the year, and in these parts…that's really saying something.

Today we went down to the park and watched a double-header at the softball field. The agricultural school beat the military team both times. They served frozen fruit-juice Popsicles, popcorn, and as an added treat, water with ice cubes!

The kicker was some bootleg vodka made on one of the potato farms. Alcohol isn't forbidden, but it is discouraged. Apparently the same holds true for pot. I caught a few whiffs of it today at the park, and nobody was trying to hide it. I guess there are bigger problems in the world now. The police here walk foot patrols all the time. I've seen one arrest so far; the crime…the person was skipping work. The sentence? Two weeks on ditch digging with no bonus credits and no weekends off. (Ronni said that that is the standard penalty.)

Today I also met somebody who is, how shall I put this, interesting.

In between the two games of the double-header, I went to get us another round of ice waters. When I came back, there was a woman in her late thirties sitting on my blanket and talking to Ronni. Her name is Chelsea Jones. I hate her.

She was trying to 'recruit' Ronni for a job. Winnemucca has a brothel. At sixteen, apparently Ronni is of legal 'working' age.

At last! I found the dark, seedy underbelly of the New Civilization. I was only moderately surprised to discover that if she was medically certified as a virgin, her 'first customer' is chosen through what amounts to be nothing more than a perverse auction. The 'benefit' is that Ronni would receive all of the bonus credits in the transaction. However, she would have to sign a one year contract to work the brothel.

I'm certainly not the morality police, but I found the whole thing to be obscene. I was able to keep my mouth shut because it was none of my business and Ronni was doing fine on her own telling Miss Jones how she wasn't interested.

The woman made her real mistake when he asked *me* if I'd ever considered working in the world's oldest profession. I made it very clear that if she ever spoke to me again she would find out how such a "tiny thing" like me has managed to survive on her own for so long.

To her credit, Miss Jones left without another word. I imagine she has been told no by meaner bitches than me. Still, the whole bidding on someone's virginity gives me the creeps.

After all of that, do I sound like a hypocrite when I say that I hooked up with one of the guys on the winning softball team later and had a nasty little roll in the sack after the post game barbeque? And I don't mind saying that I was extremely unladylike. However, I do feel much better.

Friday, July 23

Governor Betty and a few of the soldiers came to see me today. I guess I'd be foolish and naïve to think that everything was roses and puppy dogs. They asked me if I still intend to leave. I said that I would be rolling out of town—literally—on August 4th. (Hey, I will have earned my weekend by then, may as well use it.)

I've been asked to stop in Fernley, a small town south of here. They want me to deliver a little package. In exchange, I'll be getting some spare parts for my bicycle as well as some additional supplies. I didn't originally plan on taking the interstate, feeling that it might be a bit too crowded and busy with all manner of undesirables—living and dead—but I guess it really doesn't matter. Plus, this will make having a bicycle more worthwhile.

Saturday, July 24

Today I worked with Ronni in one of the produce fields. We talked a lot about her and her life. I felt comfortable enough asking her about Miss Jones and that situation. I guess she asks every woman in town, but to her credit, she does in fact take no for an answer.

I asked her if she was interested in maybe coming with me. We built a nice beginning to a friendship. I guess I wasn't too surprised when she said no. She wants to stay right here. She explained that, while she didn't hold any 'concrete' hope that he may find her; she feels that staying in one place gives her the best chance of meeting up with her dad. Her feelings are that if she remains in one place, at least there is some chance.

I guess anything is possible. Like the old saying goes, "Stranger things have happened." We did agree to hang out together for my last week here. So there's that.

Monday, July 26

Hung out at the river today. There is a particular spot that is open. They've taken every precaution. There is a heavy-duty grate at each end of this one mile stretch to ensure no zombie bits come floating along. The story is that they learned the hard way last summer when a head came along and clamped on some poor swimmer's foot.

The big excitement of the day was the arrival of a five-person group. They're all in quarantine now. I expected Ronni to show some interest, and I finally had to ask if she planned to enquire if her dad may be amongst the survivors. She said that she used to ask every time. A list of names gets posted now and she checks it at the first of every month.

"Hoping and expecting are two different things," she said, then rolled over to even out her tan.

Tuesday, July 27

A team of soldiers rolled out today. One of the scouting patrols located a herd off to the west. I guess the plan is to either lure them away, or do whatever it takes to eliminate them. Rumor has it that this herd numbers in the thousands. Nobody seems even the slightest bit concerned. In my opinion, that is a real problem. Any time you start to take things for granted or become too complacent, you get your ass kicked.

Far be it from me to tell these people anything about how to act. Still, in this world, all you need to do is screw up once for it to bring everything to an ugly halt.

Today, I worked at one of the clinics. I was basically a janitor, but it felt strange seeing people come in with bumps and bruises and funny rashes. When did those start mattering again?

Wednesday, July 28

Heard distant rumbles off and on today. Sounded like thunder, but there isn't a cloud in the sky in any direction. It is ungodly hot outside…and inside. Air conditioning doesn't fall under the 'necessity' category. I don't know why. I'm sweating in places I've never sweated and my shower day isn't until tomorrow. I will go to the stream in a little while, but it isn't the same.

Thursday, July 29

My bicycle and the little trailer were delivered today! They really did me up nicely. It has mirrors and an awesome headlight that runs off of power generated while I pedal. Even more awesome, there is a small power converter kit and a rechargeable setup for my iPod. I can be fully charged at the end of a day's ride. Not only that, but I can jack into it and have music while I ride if I so choose.

I don't know if that is such a good idea out in zombie country, but it's nice to know that I can if I want to. This did give me another glimpse at how complacent they may be living in this place.

When Betty got ready to leave, she seemed to linger for a moment like she had something to say, but couldn't broach the subject. Maybe it was just me being paranoid. I've been living good for a while…that's usually an indication that a storm is a-brewin' on the horizon.

Maybe I'm just itching to be back out in the wild again. However, I must admit that there's a certain allure to plentiful food and water along with an honest-to-goodness bed to sleep in. I'm sure I'll go through withdrawals the first few days.

Saturday, July 31

I haven't seen Ronni for the past couple of days. I've stopped by her place and there isn't an answer. I've asked around but nobody seems to be able to help. You'd think that it would be easy to find somebody when there are less than two thousand 'somebodies' to choose from.

Maybe she just doesn't want to do the whole goodbye thing. That doesn't make it suck any less. I even went to Miss Jones' place on the off chance. I felt terrible for even considering it.

My last work day was spent at the daycare facility. I held, fed, burped and changed babies today. It made me think of my daughter, Snoe. I think there was a motive behind them putting me in nursery on my last day.

One underlying theme here that I've managed to stay out of is the wariness and even dislike of the Vegas people. There is a palpable 'us vs. them' sentiment in existence. I've seen the good image here at Winnemucca so that when I get to Vegas, I won't say or do anything to put these people in danger. Oh…and as an added measure, "look at all our babies." *Surely* I wouldn't do anything to put those precious cherubs in more danger.

Of course, that could just be me and my natural paranoid nature at work.

Monday, August 2

Ronni wasn't hiding. She's been working quarantine detail the last few days. A dozen new arrivals came and one had to be put down. That wasn't a big deal, but there were five immunes in the group.

Five!

This group was from Kansas. There's news from the east that at least a half-dozen cities on the East Coast vanished in a series of mushroom clouds. Also, the amount of damage from the various nuclear power plants that didn't fare well after their human care takers stopped coming to work has made, at a minimum, the eastern third of this country uninhabitable...at least by the living. According to these people, the Gulf of Mexico burned for almost the first year after the zombie outbreak. The arc of land from Tallahassee to Houston is all scorched earth. The oil rigs and refineries...gone. And if you believe these folks, the Mississippi burned in places for several months. Supposedly.

The patrol returned this afternoon and reported that the horde had been neutralized. They didn't suffer a single casualty, but they still have to submit to quarantine.

Ronni gave me a bundle as a going away present. She said I couldn't open it until I made camp the first night. She's a sweet child, and I'll miss her. We hung out at the river for a while, then watched a softball game and sipped ice water. I guess the playoffs have started.

After she left, I went down to Miss Jones' place. Did I fail to mention that she doesn't just employ women? Hey...I had a few credits left on my ledger.

It wasn't terrible.

Tuesday, August 3

Didn't take long.

I got to the burned out remains of Imlay when I ran into my first zombie. Actually, it was more like a handful...five children.

I've gotten good at dehumanizing, but one of them made me pause. There was something about the way she hung back from the rest, like she was studying how I took out her 'friends'.

Sam was really helpful, he bounced around keeping them turning and twisting while I moved in with my spear. I'm still trying to decide if the whole ordeal is shaping itself in my mind according to what I *think* I saw.

When I moved in on that last girl, it took me three tries to plunge my spike-tipped spear into her face. I swear she dodged me twice. The place looks pretty picked over. Vehicles are stripped bare, siding torn off, even windows have been removed. Not broken, I'm talking carefully taken out. Not one of the buildings that remain—many have been burned down—have a window or a door. The stores have been gutted; even the shelving has been taken.

I did notice something interesting: mounted security cameras. Three that I spotted without making it obvious. I'm willing to bet that they are being monitored by the folks at Winnemucca. Maybe they just didn't see any reason to tell me. However, if my guess is correct, then that would mean that they have some sort of security center.

Good 'ol paranoia. Where would I be without you? Seriously though, why *would* they tell me? I was a passer-through. And if I didn't know what I was looking for, I might have never noticed them. Had it not been for my little encounter, I absolutely would have passed right on by without ever noticing. When you think about it, this would be one highly possible direction that a coordinated attack would come from.

I veered off to spend the night camped beside this big-ass reservoir. The water is cold and clean. My filtration canteens are filled (I have ten now—one that I carry and nine in the cart) I didn't even need my tent. There was some sort of forestry department shack. I brought everything in for the night, and now I'm sitting in the doorway listening to some distant wolves or something howl as the moon fills the sky with a yellow glow. I'll stomp out my campfire in a bit, but for now, I just want to enjoy this moment and the candy bar Ronni managed to find and send with me.

Wednesday, August 4

I'll have to backtrack to Imlay tomorrow. Oh, and I'll be tipping off whoever is monitoring those cameras.

I'm in Lovelock, and tonight I'm spending my evening on the sixth floor of the hospital. It was easy, and I will go down in the morning and finish off any of the roamers that might still be calling this place home.

I still can't get over how creepy it is to be walking around in a small town completely void of any living beings. While there are zombies present, they are so spread out that it almost seems too easy.

I was wary at first. As the day wore on, I began to wonder why in the hell there isn't anybody living here. It is smack dab in the middle of some very farmable-looking land.

The most gruesome discovery was the derailed passenger train at the south end of town. A few of the cars are nothing more than tombs for a bunch of living dead. One car in particular was on its side, one end has another car practically jammed into it. The other end is wedged up against a concrete stanchion. Inside are at least fifty undead, some bent into obscene shapes, awaiting anyone foolish enough to think their deformities make them any less dangerous.

But back to *my* reason for riding back to Imlay. I will put my handwritten sign in front of one of their cameras...and hope that it is the Winnemucca folks that are monitoring them.

The hospital I am in is a treasure trove. Obviously it was no place to be at one time, there are bits of pieces of bodies everywhere. The walls are smeared. Still, there are lockers and cabinets and storage rooms full of useful stuff.

While there are still zombies in this town, it is certainly worth the effort for the hospital stuff alone. I've noticed that most of the grocery stores and such look well-looted, but that could have happened way back when all of this started.

I've come to one other conclusion. For whatever reason, this town had entire neighborhoods put to the torch. There are sections that are burned to the ground, but it is done almost surgically like there were people on hand to ensure that the fire didn't jump to a house or building that wasn't specifically targeted.

It seems odd, sleeping in a town this size. I've probably checked the floor at least a dozen times, and each one of the emergency doors that lead to the stairwell at least a hundred. It seems secure.

The only thing I don't like about this floor is that it housed the maternity ward. The nursery is a mess. The dark smears and stains are so bad; this place must have been really busy at the end. The only saving grace—if you can call it that—is that the zombie swarm was big enough to ensure that there weren't any 'reminders' left behind. Not enough to come back anyway. I'm not sure if I could have stomached putting down a whole nursery full of baby zombies.

It's bad enough seeing the curled over pink and blue cards announcing that such-and-such had a boy or girl. I couldn't help but read those cards. The last one was born January 11th at 3:07 AM. Her name was Rosalita Mendez.

Thursday, August 5,

There and back again. I did something a little bit careless. Something I never would have considered a year ago. I'm worried that I may be losing my edge.

I rode back to Imlay…without my trailer of supplies. I figured Sam and I could cruise and make much better time without it. The ride there wasn't much of a problem. I placed my sign after jumping around and waving in hopes that I gained their attention, and then I turned around and headed back.

Lovelock was strangely busy when I rolled into town. Sam started growling as soon as we peeled off of Interstate 80 and coasted onto Frontage Road—according to the signs still hanging.

Almost immediately I had to stop my bike as a trio of these migrant-worker looking zombies stepped out into the street from a hotel that appeared like it might have been expensive in another lifetime. It got worse when a pack of zomdogs limped out from the dark, gaping hole that was once the hotel's main entrance.

Sam *really* hates zomdogs. I don't know if it is because he can tell that they used to be dogs like him and it freaks him out, or what. Whatever the case, he went from prowling and growling to whimpering and backing up beside me.

I moved slow and had my spear in hand after I put three of the five dogs down with my crossbow. As I waded in, I found myself itching for a fight. It seemed to be exactly what I needed. Moments later, the intersection was littered with bodies.

The dust up did draw some attention, so I decided to jog away and lead the mindless mini-mob in the opposite direction of my ultimate destination which was the hospital. It took a bit longer than what I would have liked, and I ended up with two empty canteens, which, in this heat, can be very bad for your health.

By the time I got up here to my top floor, I was feeling more than a little light-headed and had a thundering headache. Did I forget to mention that it is at least a hundred degrees, I'm wearing a leather coat, gloves with a fine mesh lining, boots, shin-guards, and a riot helmet with a modified face shield designed to minimize the hindrance of my peripheral vision?

When I'm on open roads with long, flat, empty stretches of nothing, I can strip down to my sports bra and bicycle shorts. However, the moment I spot any former civilization zones, or even the slightest congested section of what's left of the road, it is automatic that I suit up. Heat is no excuse.

Right now I'm watching the shadows claim the town as the sun sets. Also, I'm stark naked. Hey…who's gonna see me? Good thing, too. My legs and pits are sporting three full days of not being clean shaven. And to think…there used to be a time when I wouldn't leave the house without my most intimate parts being perfectly manicured. Now I look like I'm straight out of a vintage Seventies Playboy centerfold.

Friday, August 6

This valley that Interstate 80 cuts through is a mess. Between the landslides and damage from unchecked winters that have wedged the asphalt apart, I spent most of the day on foot. The bike is a huge hindrance right now.

Just before making camp, I heard that hair-raising baby cry sound. The poor bastard was geared up with an awesome back-pack, but the weight, coupled with the left leg not only being chewed up, but broken in several spots to the point that I don't know how it didn't just fall off, kept this zombie as helpless as a flipped over turtle.

After I put it out of its misery, I was thrilled to find an awesome stash of foil-packaged, dehydrated meals. He also had a small caliber pistol, but that was beyond repair.

I briefly considered veering off and following the train tracks. But if I encountered some long, dark tunnel…there's just no way in hell.

Saturday, August 7

I imagined that this is Winnemucca looked like a year or so ago. The perimeter fence is mostly in place, the town itself is clean, but more undead straggle in than the living types.

There's a fire that's been burning for three weeks if I am to believe the person that escorted me and Sam into quarantine. It seems that the undead from Reno keep trickling in

There is a huge difference in the folks from Fernley and the ones I left behind in Winnemucca.

God.

This is a religious settlement. They have services three times a day, *every* day. I was given a bible in quarantine. I said it wasn't necessary, but the young man who escorted me to my cell said "one never knows when God will reveal himself."

He wasn't Genesis Brotherhood crazy, and he didn't try to preach or force anything on me—although he would not take the bible back, apparently it is my own personal copy…my name is even written in it—he just seems…*religious*. I do not have any idea how to explain it. It is like he is…happy. That is an emotion that I haven't seen or felt in a long, long time. Even on the best day you still have that niggling feeling in the back of your mind that something is wrong. That is the new normal. Only, this guy seemed different.

Sunday, August 8

I was brought out to meet the town elders—Fernley's version of government, I guess—and be grilled on what I was delivering to Betty from the folks from Winnemucca. Maybe I should have peeked, but I figured that the envelope was sealed for a reason. Primarily as a way to say, "Meredith, this is none of your beeswax, keep your nose out of it!"

Something was said about returning a girl to her family. See? Start civilizing things and people start losing sight of the real problems. I go back to my prior estimate of humanity not surviving another decade.

I told two dozen different people that I had no idea what was written on the note, it wasn't my business, and no, I will not take a message back. I made it clear that my ass is heading out of town at daybreak.

For a little bit I was worried that I might have to fight my way out. Thankfully, it didn't come to that. I was, however, made to camp in this little park. No room indoors for Meredith.

All that being said, I will make this observation: I don't give *these* people six months. They don't have the farmland that the Winnemucca settlement has. From what little I've seen, there are too many people making decisions. Remember how impotent our congress had become? Well, these folks didn't pay attention. Also, their security is crap. I don't know if it can just be credited to this place being a newer settlement, but I personally saw three roamers—one that *I* put down—inside the perimeter. I'm near the center of town.

Did I mention that I am sleeping up on top of a concrete building that once acted as the public restrooms in the city park? Oh yeah, this place has got problems.

Monday, August 9

I could not get out of that place soon enough. It was just too damn bizarre. I am happy to be able to pedal my bicycle once again. However, I will have to be very careful. It seems as if the undead are really drawn to the human buffet that is Fernley.

I never knew Nevada was so mountainous. I guess I always pictured it a lot like New Mexico and Arizona. There is certainly plenty of desert, but there are also plenty of snow-capped mountains. The good side of this is all of the little streams and creeks that I keep running across.

Tonight I am camped out inside an RV that went off the road and ended up on its side. There was a well-preserved but very dead woman in the front passenger seat. She died from a nasty head injury. It looks like…well…her forehead is smashed flat at an angle that I would be willing to bet matches the dash of the RV. Of course she didn't turn because she died a normal death. I wonder where the driver went? There is no sign of a struggle, and no blood except a little bit around the dead woman's nose and ears. Did I mention that the woman is little more than a dried husk? I made no attempt to move her because I am certain that she would only crumble in my hands. Besides, I'm sleeping in the back.

Thursday, August 12

Vegas is still my destination, but it is officially on hold. I guess it was just a matter of time before I encountered some really bad people again. I am currently hiding out in a movie theater—what is it with me and theaters—waiting for it to get dark outside. Once it does, I'm gonna bring some serious pain down on the gang of sickos that slither around in this infested hole of a town.

If I die…you can bet I will be bringing a lot of them with me. I won't be carrying anything tonight except for my weapons. So if you are reading this and the rest of the pages are blank, then that means that I am dead. And if you see a zombie decked out in leather, bristling with weapons, with a 'Mean People Suck' sweatshirt underneath, please shoot me in the head.

The first sign that something was wrong came a mile out of the town proper. It was the sign: Entering Fallon…the town that God forgot. That last little bit was spray-painted on in red. Dangling from the sign was an armless, legless, female zombie with the word "whore" carved into her torso. When I got closer, it was obvious that she couldn't have been older than twelve or thirteen. She mewled and gurgled at me until I put my spear into her head.

As I crept into town, I had to put the leash on Sam because there were too many zombies around. It only took me about twenty minutes to realize that they were *all* female. I reached a city park that had reinforced fencing, and found more zombies—also all female—standing in clusters.

I was under a school bus trying to make sense of everything when a large cart being drawn by eight women, all naked and alive, came rolling down the street. They were escorted by at least two dozen men in everything from leathers to what looked like a baseball catcher's gear. The ones bringing up the rear were pulling along four boys from age eight to somewhere in the early teens. Once there, they manhandled them into a chute that emptied into the park/zombie pen. What they did next solidified my decision to stay and fight. They opened the cart, and then they began tossing bundles from one person to the next like you would sandbags to hold back a river. The last man at the end of the human conveyer tossed the bundle over the fence. These babies' cries were real.

A couple of the boys put up a really good fight, but it only served as a source of entertainment for the gang of men. One of the boys tried desperately to keep the swaddled infants away from the tearing jaws of death. Another managed to break free, climb the fence, and make it all the way to the sobbing females who had been leading the carts. He grabbed one and hugged her before being yanked away again and forced into the chute once more.

I was curious how come there wasn't more zombie traffic, and finally spotted the RVs pulled or pushed in place at the head of the three possible entry points to this street. The few that were in the area had been herded into some of the buildings lining the streets.

Back to the park scene. When the other end of that chute opened, the boys were forced into the park by the men with what looked like from here to be cattle prods. After that, it really didn't take long. The zombies are so numerous that there isn't enough left to come back. Sure, some of the boys lasted longer, running. But it was really a forgone conclusion, and none of them had a chance of escape.

The women were forced to watch. Some were even unharnessed and dragged to the fence for a closer look. During one particularly nasty moment, one of them was held down and brutally raped next to the fence where a young boy—apparently her son—was torn apart and feasted upon just inches away; the only thing separating them being that thin fence that may as well have been a mile-wide chasm.

Thinking back, I'm surprised I didn't cry. I believe that I was simply too horrified and shocked. I have no idea how we have come to this. I shudder to think of what went on in the minds of people that I walked by every day in the Old World. Considering what happened to me at the hands of my town's sheriff before I escaped and found Sam and his group that day…

Who were these men before? School teachers? Cops? Cashiers at the local grocery store?

The thing is, I've met good people, too. Decent folks who help the weak and care for others. But the bad…the evil…it seems to be amplified to a level that I could have never imagined human beings capable of, and it just rips out my heart.

Eventually, a few of the men went to one of the RV sealed ends of one of the streets and disappeared. Obviously their job was to lead away any of the zombies that had gathered. The women were hitched up to their harnesses again and away they went. Two men stayed behind for a few minutes to open the doors of all the buildings along the streets again to allow the undead captives to resume roaming free.

I wonder if the reason that the zombies stick around is because of this feeding event that I witnessed. Several hundred converged on the park once the men left, pressing against the fence where their zombie sisters stumbled about covered in fresh blood and gore. It actually allowed me an opportunity to escape from the area without incident.

I spent the next couple of hours trying to find that cart. You'd think it wouldn't be hard in a town with so few living. It turned out to be like finding a needle in a haystack. Fortunately, late in the afternoon, I found what I was looking for.

They had doubled back and taken a big circle to return to what is obviously their base. It sits atop a big, ugly, brown hill just past the northeast corner of town right next to the airfield.

They have it walled off pretty good. It is next to impossible to get an accurate idea of their numbers. For one, the wall is brick and about eight feet tall; for another, they all dress the same and I don't have any binoculars.

I spent all day and all night watching—and unfortunately listening—to the comings, goings, and carryings on of these bastards. I've developed a plan. The downside is that it will probably kill everybody, including the female captives. However, if it were me in there, and with what I've heard, I would welcome death over the alternative. The problem I'm gonna have is getting away.

Friday, August 13

No matter what, tonight is my "go" night. Last night, a caravan of strange looking, obviously heavily modified motorcycles rolled into town and straight to the encampment. Three of the motorcycles were hauling wheeled cages. I would guess that there were at least a dozen women and young girls crammed into each of them. This has to stop.

I'm not afraid to die. I am only afraid to fail.

One of the hardest things will be leaving this behind. By that, I mean these books. I hate the thought of losing these journals. I know that if something happens to me, there is no guarantee that these books will ever be found, or appreciated in the event that they are. However, if something goes wrong tonight and these were to fall into the hands of those animals, I am afraid that the pages would be used for nothing more than toilet paper or to start fires. There is no way that I could allow those assholes to ever lay a finger on these. I guess I never put any thought into how I would ensure that these were passed on.

Now, more than ever, I am grateful that at least there were copies of Sam's journal, and that a few people have a copy of my first one.

Monday, August 23

Of all of the places to be catching my breath…a cemetery. I've endured hunger, thirst, the kind of fatigue that makes you want to just curl up into a ball and die. I've traveled through a part of Nevada that looks—and feels—like a glimpse of what it must be like if there truly is a Hell. Oh yeah, and an earthquake. Something tells me that my days may be numbered and my luck has finally run out.

Once again I am down to less than the necessities. I had to leave my bicycle and trailer. The satchel that I am carrying has my blade sharpening kit, a spare canteen—empty—and my journals. I have my spear and a long knife on each hip. I am trying to save the last swallows of water left in my other canteen for as long as I can manage.

On the plus side, I don't think that there are any survivors left back in Fallon. Oh yeah, and then there is the guy lying dead on the ground ten feet away from me; he is probably the last of my pursuers.

It's still a bit of a blur, and I'm certain that I can't recall every single thing that happened, but I think that I can finally take the time to jot some of this down.

I waited until almost sunset and made my way back to that fenced in park. It wasn't like these guys had any reason to think that somebody would be fool enough to fiddle with their fence. All I had to do was flip a few latches and remove a pair of steel poles that were in place to keep the fence barred. From there, it was simply a matter of being a bit of a zombie Pied Piper while still managing to avoid the roamers remaining loose in town. Staying ahead of the one pack was easy; avoiding the others was a bit more of a chore.

I was only worried about my first phase of the attack when it came to the one bridge that I had to cross. Thankfully, the Keepers of Fallon were way overconfident and far too engrossed in their nasty habits to have anything resembling lookouts posted. Their idea of security consisted of the wall around their little compound and about fifty or so zombies on tethers designed more to keep the living away than anything else. Well, they didn't count on me…did they!

I'd crept close enough a couple of nights prior to putting my plan in motion so as to get a good look at their "intricate" security. Some were chained, others were held in place by strips of leather; nothing a good pair of bolt-cutters couldn't handle. The posts that held them in place were all about four feet tall, so reach wasn't going to be a problem.

The beam they used to bar their gate was no big deal, but the pair of double-wides mounted on wheels that took a gaggle of men to move would be a bigger challenge. That entrance would become a bit of a logjam, and I didn't know how many other exits they might have, but that was my objective.

When that first chain clattered to the ground, I knew that I was screwed. The door was more like a heavy grate. It looked like it had been stolen from a jail cell. I guess it made it easier to see things on the other side, but that goes both ways. I glanced over my shoulder; the leading edge of the zombie horde I'd led here was reaching the drawbridge-like crossing that I'd had almost no trouble sliding the three-foot wide plank over to allow access. So far...nothing was stirring inside the compound. Yep, those guys were disgustingly overconfident.

When the final chain fell, I heard my first indications of movement. It sounded like a door opening about twenty feet or so away. I looked around, and sure enough, directly across from me this guy steps out. He was carrying a lantern which lit up his face perfectly. Well, at least good enough to give a clear shot with my crossbow. He never saw it coming.

The propane lantern made way too much noise when it hit the ground. I was flipping up the bar that secured the door when I noticed more lanterns flaring up inside the other buildings, I shoved open the heavy gate and dropped a lit flare just inside and out of the entryway; sorta giving the zombies a target without risking the possibility that they veer away from the sputtering road flare. The dazzling white light gave the entire courtyard a peculiar glow.

Since I had buildings to both sides, I randomly selected right and ducked in between the building and the security wall. That is right about when the first zombie stumbled in. The flare actually helped to scatter the undead as they came in, each wandering away from the offensive light in a different direction. They were all over the place in seconds. That is something I couldn't have planned and had go that well.

I ran what seemed like a good distance and pulled the grappling hook from my belt to get on top of the wall. From there I had a good view of the compound's open area. I managed to get off a couple of shots with my crossbow. The lost bolts (there was no way I'd be getting them back) were a good trade. I shot to wound. In no time, the sounds of screaming filled the air. No matter how much of a bad-ass you think you are, being outnumbered fifty-to-one by the walking dead will not work out in your favor.

Then I spotted the big storage tank. I hadn't planned for it and had to improvise. That meant risking my chance of escape. I had to come off the wall and cross about fifty feet of open ground to get close enough for a shot that would stand a chance, then I'd have to lob a flare.

By now, the place was in chaos. I was really happy to *not* hear the sound of gunshots. While they continue to become more and more rare, they tilt the playing field drastically. If you don't believe me, think back to the guy with the fancy sword in *Raiders of the Lost Arc*. What girl didn't have a crush on Harrison Ford back then?

I lined up my shot and hoped. I really had no idea if my bolt would penetrate, or if there might even be any sort of fuel inside that thing. I was so excited when I heard the angry hiss of what I was certain had to be propane. I lit my flare, threw it, and hauled ass.

Nothing happened.

I was really bummed as I scrambled up my rope. All that risk for no results. Then some sap found my flare. He picked it up. That must've put it in line with whatever was coming out of that tank.

The next thing I knew, I was flying through the air backwards. I landed flat, which totally sucked. Had there been even one zombie in the area, I would have been screwed. I just lay sprawled in the brush and dirt trying and failing to get just one molecule of oxygen into my lungs. The tears filling my eyes blurred my vision so that all I could see was a bright smear filling the sky as the fireball rolled skyward, lighting up the night sky. At least it was a pretty orange smear.

Once I could finally move, I made my way to my hands and knees and looked around. I'd been blown *over* the moat. I could still hear shouting and screaming coming from inside the compound. I stayed down and started crawling.

I wanted to get away. I didn't have any real desire to witness my handiwork. Hell, I didn't even know how successful I'd been. All I knew for certain was that I'd caused considerable damage and put a nasty kink in the plans of those evil bastards.

The glow from the fire (or fires) let me see a good distance in every direction. The downside of that was that once I was clear of the compound, I had no night vision. I couldn't see five feet in front of myself. Once I reached the highway, I was basically blind.

I reached some sort of park or recreation area just outside of the main sprawl of Fallon. I climbed up on a wooden bathroom structure and caught my breath. I remember that, as I lay there, I was hoping that the damage was as bad as it looked from the outside.

That was also around the time that the adrenaline wore off. I could suddenly feel every lump, bump, and bruise. There were a lot of them. Also, I felt something wet and sticky on my back. That is when a new pain announced itself above all the others. A stick—about a finger's diameter—was jutting from my body. I had to reach back and grab it where it stuck out above my right hip. I might've screamed when I yanked it out...but since I passed out I can't be for sure.

When I came to, I realized that I had no choice but to return to town. First, that was where all my things were stashed. But more importantly, I had to try and break into someplace and find some hydrogen peroxide or rubbing alcohol. Also, I needed something to put over this seeping hole in my body. An infection these days is fatal.

The first time that I tried to sit up, my body refused. Pain was firmly entrenched in every muscle and joint. I cried out ...loudly.

That was most likely what brought the three zombies. However, I didn't see them right away. Thank God that Sam had picked up my trail and followed me. He was under a bush. When I heard his growl, then saw him creeping along the ground towards the approaching zombies, my eyes filled with tears.

I put my crossbow to good use then. Afterwards, I climbed down. Actually, that isn't really an accurate description of what happened. The pain came in a bolt; I lost my grip, and then fell on my ass. When I landed, I just stayed put for a few minutes gasping for breath while fighting back more tears. Sam, the big dummy, wouldn't stop licking my face.

Eventually I got up and started back to Fallon. A large, black plume was still rising. On the other side of that bald, ugly hill, I could see movement scattered everywhere.

I did my best to stay hidden when I could as I walked—limped is more like it—back. I slipped through some trees at one point and came face-to-face with an obscenely obese man. Zombies had ripped into his ample guts and all sorts of things dangled from the gaping hole they left behind. Also, his lower lip had been torn away and one meaty cheek hung down, flapping against his jowls as he lumbered along. Maybe I should've paid attention to the fact that the blood was still reddish—meaning it was still relatively fresh.

I speared him through the face. If you can score a hit to the eye socket, it is almost a guaranteed "kill shot" every time. After that, I was a bit more vigilant, as much as I could be through the pain. I'd been so worried about staying out of sight that I wasn't paying attention to what else might be wandering around in the shadows, or when I came out of blind spots.

Most of the houses in the area were already well-looted. It was fairly late in the morning, close to noon maybe, when I finally lucked into a bottle of hydrogen peroxide and some linens that were stacked neatly in the closet of an elderly couple's trailer. (I know they were elderly because the pictures were still hanging on the walls.)

This place hadn't been touched. The couple had obviously evacuated. Drawers were empty and still open; the bedroom closet was open and selectively picked through. The kitchen was a complete bust except for a Ziploc bag of pinto beans on a pantry shelf that I took.

I cleaned up as best as I could and found a shirt that actually fit. Then Sam and I made it back to my stuff. After giving him some water and taking a brief catnap, I was as ready to go as I could be.

After serious thought, I decided to leave the bicycle. I couldn't pedal it. Walking was painful, but sitting and pedaling was out of the question. Also, I needed to stay as concealed as possible. That would be impossible on the bike. There was a lot of activity in Fallon now; some of it far too fast to be a zombie. That meant some of the 'yay-hoos' probably escaped. I seriously doubted that any of the women made it out of there alive.

I felt better once I had Sam's and my journals back. I won't lie. I didn't realize until I'd spent that night away from them and doubting I would make it back, but they're like my security blanket. My therapy. Also, I realized for the first time that there is something in my ritual about noting the date. In just that one day away from those books, I'd forgotten what day it was.

Every morning when I wake up, even if I am not going to write anything, I make a tally mark in the book. Does the date matter anymore? Probably not. But, for me, it is just something I need. I always know what day and date it is.

I am certain that a shrink would have a lot to say about all of this. It has become my little OCD thing. How else can I explain the risk I went through to come back for them. All the times I have made certain I had the books even when I was forgetting things like food and weapons. And for what reason? Is my daughter ever going to read these? I'd say that the odds are against her ever seeing any of this. Hell…will anybody see it?

Still, my trusty mutt and I slipped out a couple hours before sunset and headed east. All I could remember was that I needed to find Route 361. My hope was that I could get away from Fallon without drawing any kind of attention to myself.

On that goal…I failed.

I was following US Route 50 and had just turned south. I was heading back into the mountains, and by the looks of things…a bit of a wasteland. It was dark, but the moon was a bright, silver disk in the night sky. I had enough ambient light to see—sort of.

When Sam stopped and suddenly turned around, sniffing the air and growling, I expected a zombie, or maybe even a few, to come shambling out of the shadows. When the dark figure broke into a run straight towards me, I was glad that I happened to be carrying my crossbow.

In movies, a person dies with one well placed shot. This one caught a bolt in the body close to the bottom of his ribcage. I bet it punctured his lung. What it didn't do was stop him. Sam took off and leaped at my living attacker. That is what gave me enough time to draw my big knife.

I think about those split seconds a lot. If I would have run at my attacker while drawing my blade. If my bolt would have been a few inches up and to the right hitting him in the heart. If. If. If.

My grandpa used to say, "If worms had guns birds wouldn't fuck with them."

I am sure there are a hundred "ifs" that would result in Sam still being alive. I got there just as I heard the yelp. I'd never heard my dog yelp before. He didn't seem to be afraid of anything. And...he was a good dog. Maybe I should have named him something else. Maybe that name is cursed.

When I got there, the man was on his knees with his back to me. I drove my knife into his back—the blade was long enough to stick out of his chest. He fell sideways, but I got a little scared when he tried to climb back to his feet. I have no idea how many times I stabbed him with my spear.

At some point, I stopped. Leaving the spear sticking up from the body, I went to my dog. My stupid mutt. I was still holding him and crying when the sun came up.

There was some sort of industrial-looking complex, and it might have even been an airport, but a nasty fire made it hard to tell. I carried Sam there and found a piece of metal that I could scoop up dirt with. That's where I buried Sam and covered the grave with a mound of rocks. I think it was noonish by the time I finished. The whole time, I cried off and on. A few times, I had to stop what I was doing in order to put down a roaming zombie or two.

I found a dark, empty, burned out building to hide in and catch a nap. I think God might still exist.

It was late in the afternoon when the earthquake struck. When I woke up, my first thought was that I had been discovered; either by the survivors of the place I blew up or by a herd of zombies. Things were falling and there was that sound. When

I realized what it was, I tried to get up, but kept falling down because the ground was rolling.

Finally, it stopped. That's when I discovered how close to death I had come. Just like that "little" earthquake in Portland, the zombies had fallen over and laid still. I'd guess their numbers to be close to a hundred. And it was obvious right away that they were all heading for the ruins of the building that I had ducked into.

That was another mistake I made that day. I didn't stop to think about what might have led them to me. I certainly didn't consider the possibility that one or more bad guys might be out there; much less hot on my trail. I didn't wait for the zombies to get up. I took off. I did stop off at a creek to fill my canteen sometime that evening around dusk.

When I finally found a place to stop, it was in the cab of a jackknifed semi. I was jut getting comfortable in the sleeper part when I heard something. In a dead world, the voices of the living really stand out, even when people speak in hushed tones. I made sure that my crossbow was ready and then set my big knife where I could grab it quick. If the owners of those voices tried to get in the truck, I'd get one good shot, after that, I would have to rely on my skills with the blade.

I was thankful when they passed. Then I heard that soft, feminine whisper, and the sound of a slap. There wasn't really a choice as to what I had to do. I waited long enough for the owners of those voices to get a little ways away from me before I climbed out of the truck and started after them.

I got close enough to make out three men and one woman. When they peeled off from the highway and cut into the brush and dirt headed towards the mountain, I almost let them go. After all, I can't save everybody.

Then they made camp.

These cowboys just picked a spot and flopped down. There wasn't anything special about it. A few minutes later, they had a little fire going. Then they did what I expected; they turned their attention to that poor woman.

The worst part was listening to what they were doing while I planned my attack. The way I figured it, I would have one shot with my crossbow. I could try for a second, but I needed to have my big blade ready. After taking a few deep breaths, I lined up my shot and took it. Finally a little luck came my way. The bolt was fired from a close enough range that it must have passed clean through. The big man collapsed, and his buddy obviously thought it was because he had just finished. As they were rousing their friend...or at least trying to...I got off a second shot. I risked it and aimed for the face of the man whose dirty grin I could see in the glow of the fire they'd built.

That's where the plan fell apart. The third guy jumped up and kicked away the fire. How was he to know that it was just l'il ole me? Then I heard an awful shriek and a gurgle.

"Hope you don't mind fucking a corpse!" the man yelled in the darkness.

I played it safe and stayed put a few minutes before I began creeping closer to where I remembered their camp to be. When I got there, I found three bodies. Feeling around revealed that the woman's throat had been slashed. Unfortunately, there was no sign of the third man.

Having no desire to stumble around in the dark looking for him, I crept back to the semi that I had been ready to bed down in. It took me a while to cycle down from the adrenaline rush, but when it did subside, I collapsed from exhaustion.

I slept way too long.

When I woke, I was bathed in sweat which added to the yucky feeling from the dirt and dried blood all over me. A pair of roamers were on the road coming my direction. I considered staying put and letting them pass, but if they caught even the slightest hint of me, they'd just turn around and follow.

When I came out of my cab, I waited until the closest one— a teenage girl and way too fresh to be anything other than hours old—made her approach. The strand of intestines slapping against her denim overalls still looked wet. I put her down and had enough time to reload for a point-blank shot at the other desiccated corpse that made a weird rasping sound that reminded me of a playing card in the spokes of a bicycle for some reason.

The first thing I did after that was drink my water and refill both canteens before getting back on the move. Of course I had my eyes peeled for any sort of movement or any sign of that third man's camp. And that is why I diverted my course and left the highway just as it started to cut through this mountain pass. I went north and it slowed me way down. But by nightfall, I was up high enough that I thought I might have a chance at seeing something if that guy made any sort of campfire.

What I wasn't prepared for was over a dozen!

Like a really spread out starfield, the pinpricks of light were scattered below me. In one spot there was a cluster of several. It caught me completely off guard. It made me wonder how many singles, or small, nomadic groups, I had passed by completely unaware during my travels. It also made me recall that young girl that I put down the day before. How similar to my story or Jenifer's, or even Gabrielle's was hers? Was she alone? Did she wander away from a larger group?

The only thing I now feel with a sense of certainty is the feeling of doom that hangs over humanity like the Sword of Damocles.

It wasn't that I felt any safer, but I did find a spot where I could curl up that night. I slept, for all intents and purposes, out in the open. Under the stars, above all the little fires that burned in the night. The strange thing was that in the morning when I woke and looked around, I couldn't see a sign of anything that indicated people were camping in the area. I knew the general locations of all of those fires, especially the big cluster, and there wasn't even a wisp of smoke that morning.

Down on the highway, I could see singles and small clusters of zombies. It's like they're drawn to any place where there are survivors. Even out here in the middle of godforsaken nowhere, they roam. I guess they're looking for those last living souls to feed on. Their biology makes no sense. They should have fallen over long ago…starved.

Staying in the hills all day as I walked probably slowed me way down. But I found myself in a funk and I couldn't shake it.

Then I saw him.

Even though I never got a look at the guy who escaped that night, I knew it was him. He was walking just as bold as you please down the middle of the highway with a naked woman on a leash. I guessed him to be, at most, a couple of miles ahead of me.

The first problem I ran into was coming down onto the highway. I lost sight of my target at some point, and by the time I was on the washed out remnants of the highway, I couldn't see him at all. As hot as it was, I did not want to jog. Then there was the inconvenience of putting down the occasional zombie.

I discovered real fast that tracking somebody is not as easy as it looked on television. Between the drag/step mark of the zombies and who ever else passed through these parts, I had no idea which set of tracks belonged to the man I was hunting. Then I reached a T-intersection with another highway heading straight south. Looking each direction it was like being given the choice of which doorway you'd like to use when entering Hell.

After taking out this particularly nasty creeping torso with only one arm that came of some brush beside the road—scaring me to the point that my bladder lost control just a teensy bit—I decided on south. The biggest benefit was the tiny stream that allowed me to stop and freshen up a bit while filling my canteens.

A few miles along, I began to think that I may be onto something. I started coming across an assortment of military vehicles. Late in the afternoon, I turned east off of the main road and found an old, abandoned air base.

The place obviously tried to set itself up as a safe zone of sorts. The fences all had makeshift towers scattered along the perimeter. Unfortunately, it also looks like a horde took down their fence. The good news is that this seems to have happened quite a while ago. There are literally hundreds of corpses—and parts of corpses—all dried out. It also looks like the animals came through for quite a buffet.

I couldn't pass up the chance to snoop around. After all, I did say that, before all of this zombie stuff, I'd never done much of anything. To go into a military airbase replete with: "RESTRICTED ZONE! DEADLY FORCE AUTHORIZED!" signs all over the place...you tell me you wouldn't go in and take a peek.

Liar.

I was never much on the UFO thing. I wouldn't know Area 51 from the Ronald Reagan International Airport, and any airbase I found out here could be something interesting. When I ducked through the gaping breach in the fence, I didn't have any idea what to expect. I think I was secretly hoping to find some hangar with a spaceship parked inside like in the movie *Independence Day*. Instead, I found a lot of planes, jets, helicopters, and big pieces of machinery that I had absolutely no idea as to their function.

I think I found some sort of workshop where missiles were put together or taken apart. The coolest find was this bunker with stacks and stacks of what are obviously bombs. They wouldn't do me one bit of good, but it was strangely cool to see them; stacks and stacks and rows and rows of bombs.

I imagine some of the empty rooms that I found were once full of guns and ammunition. And I imagine that if I were Angelina Jolie or some other female action hero in a movie I would have hit the weapons jackpot. No such luck for Meredith Gainey, child abandoning, angel-of-death to all she meets (especially if they were friends). I found zip. At least when it came to weapons. I did score one major find: MREs and cases of bottle water! That was what made me decide that I was being stupid chasing some 'Bad Guy' all around the Nevada desert. I'd already come to grips with the idea that I can't save everybody.

I'm a little ashamed to admit what happened next. Since I've decided I was going to hang out a bit and explore, I found a big basin. I don't know what it was used for in the past, but I filled it with some of that bottled water and took a bath. I couldn't do anything about my legs or armpits, much less the Enchanted Forest growing between my legs, but at least I could be clean. I found some liquid soap that smelled like melons and I gave myself a good scrubbing. Then I emptied the basin, refilled it, and just soaked in the lukewarm water.

Before you rush to judge my obvious waste of precious water, unless you've gone days or weeks without a proper cleaning, AND had to use ripped up t-shirts during your period, then just shush! It's not like this place looked to see any living inhabitants in at least a year. Besides, who else would be stupid enough to wonder around in this wasteland? Sure, I saw all those campfires scattered about, but strangely enough, I've only actually seen that one sign of a living, breathing person during the day.

And that is why it probably took me a while to realize that I was hearing a child's laughter. When I came out of the water and quick-changed back into my still-wet clothing that was hanging in the window to sun dry, my first thought was that the zombies had evolved. It would just figure that those bastards would learn how to make a new sound now that everybody pretty much knew about the baby cry noise.

I grabbed my crossbow, which due to recent events and my inability to do some searching, was down to eight bolts. Granted, you only need one, but that makes for a fairly useless weapon. Then I strapped on one knife and snuck down the stairs of the building that I had made camp in. If zombies were around, I wanted to put them down in a hurry before others came.

When I stepped outside, the last thing that I expected was a "family" of four. Of course it was obvious that the children were not from the two adults. Primarily because she was Black and he was Asian and the two little girls were White. Very tan, but white.

Alicia and Min were both from Texas. They were part of a much larger group of survivors which had dwindled down due to some folks simply going off on their own, others dying—of course—and some outright vanishing. They found the girls in Provo, Utah last year when they got stranded due to a fierce winter.

The two are like any married couple I have ever known. They bicker, finish each others sentences, and fret over 'their' children. It was Min's throwing knife that I had barely managed to duck as I stepped out of the doorway. I think the only reason he missed, is because Alicia screamed "Breather!" just as he threw. I think that because I have seen him throw a couple of times since. He doesn't miss. Ever.

Min and his family are headed north. I told them all that I could remember. After some discussion, he and Alicia decided that they would try to winter in Winnemucca before pushing on in the spring. They said that their ultimate goal was Alaska. A bit too cold for my taste, but I imagine that its small population, miles of empty space, and months of heavy snow has its appeal to some. In fact, they seemed more than a little dubious in regards to *my* plan of trying to get to Vegas. I guess they've heard some wicked stories. Still, I'm one of those people that, once she gets an idea in her head, have to see it through.

Of course I made their day when I showed them the cache of MREs and bottled water that I'd found. To their credit, neither said a word about my bathtub. Of course Alicia and the girls enjoyed it themselves. Min was fine with a sponge bath. When they joined me outside, they all looked and smelled much better.

I have no explanation for it, but for the next couple of days, the five of us just hung out around the now-defunct military base. Sometimes we went around together, and sometimes I would wake up and think that they had left. Then I would go downstairs and see their backpacks lined up against the wall. At some point the family would stroll in with a couple of odds and ends or knick knacks in their hands. The girls found a pair of model jets one day and played with them just like a couple of boys their age might. It was actually somewhat pleasant.

Once, I watched the girls so that Min and Alicia could "go for a walk". They came back looking like they had just run a marathon. Well...except for the ear-to-ear smiles on both their faces. Alicia probably thanked me fifty times.

Then, on a morning no different from any other, they said they needed to get moving. I actually felt a strange loss. Is this what it's like every time *I* tell folks that I'm leaving? I went up on the roof and watched them go. When the little girls looked back and waved...I cried. *What in the hell was that about?*

The next day I wandered around the base alone. When I came back to my little camp, I knew that it was time for me to get moving once again. I had ended up staying one day too long. I heard the sounds of breaking glass. That was what jarred me awake a couple of hours before sunrise. My first thought was kind of stupid: The family is back! Then my brain flipped a switch and more sounds of breaking glass had me up and grabbing my weapons. I don't know why, but something made me grab the bag that had my books and the MREs along with both of my canteens.

There was a voice in my head that was screaming for me to run. I ignored it and listened to the muffled voice that told me to go see what was happening.

In the shadow of one of the giant hangars that housed a pair of jets, I saw movement. The laughter gave them away as living. I stayed put as they cranked open the big doors. The hangar was dark, but those five morons had torches and lanterns. They were like kids who'd been let into Disneyland early and had it to themselves. They climbed all over the jets making quite a scene. Of course they had no idea what to do, so the jets were really nothing more than a pair of giant play structures.

I stayed back and kept quiet as the sun came up. Eventually I staked out a spot in one of the admin buildings. There was no reason to do anything. These guys weren't taking anything that I cared about. One of them had found a uniform and put it on. Another seemed content just to sit in the cockpit of one of the jets. The only real negative side of this situation was that I was stuck hiding and watching. I knew better than to show myself to a group of men.

As the sun began to set, they made camp in the hangar. I wasn't really paying attention any more. As long as they stayed inside that hangar, I could simply wait it out until it was completely dark, and then slip away. I must have been napping, because I was jolted to full alert at the sound of a scream. I was certain that somebody had been set on by a zombie.

I tried to move into a position to get a better look. I could still see a low fire burning in the hangar between the two jets. What I couldn't see were any of the men; or any signs of zombies. It went on for at least a minute. And let me tell you, when somebody is screaming in obvious pain, that is an eternity.

There was no way that I was going to snoop around in the dark for the source of those screams. Also, that meant I wasn't leaving. Something was going on in the darkness, and I had a nice, safe, defensible spot. I'd just wait till morning.

As the sun rose, bringing what I am positive was the hottest day I had endured in my life, it actually took me a couple of minutes to make sense of what I was seeing. Four of the five men were in the hangar huddled together. When one of them got up to do something, I spotted something large on a spit over the fire. It took a minute for it to dawn on me that it was a human torso. Things clicked. At least somewhat.

I considered making a break for it, but being in the middle of nowhere, it would take me over an hour just to get out of sight. I would be exposed for way too long. The only choice I had was to stay put. The worse part was the fact that the smell of roasting meat was making my mouth water. Try as I might to remind myself what I was smelling, I could not overcome the growling in my stomach or the saliva building up and occasionally dripping down my chin when I wasn't swallowing enough. I think, at first, I wouldn't swallow because I was protesting my bodily reaction to the smells versus the knowledge of where those smells originated.

Finally, late in the afternoon, they started gathering up their stuff and moving along. I waited for what felt like forever, but really couldn't have been more than an hour after they were gone before I came down. I couldn't help it, I had to go see. Finding the killing spot was easy. It was a big, dark stain in the sand. There were bones tossed about, and on a stick was the head. The boy couldn't have been any older than sixteen.

My guess goes something like this. They encountered this kid, maybe when they ran across another group. They probably enticed him away with stories of all the lawless fun to be had. I'm betting that this wasn't the first time that these guys had done this. It seemed too cleanly executed.

I waited until it was light enough for me to see a few feet in front of myself the next morning, and got moving. Of course I topped off on everything and stuffed a few days worth of the MREs in my satchel.

I was cutting across an airstrip when I heard a commotion from a squat building that sat at the end of a narrow path. It was right against the fence. I couldn't help myself; I had to go check it out. I was surprised to say the least at what I had discovered. The best I can figure is that maybe it's like prison. Some men go in and need sex so badly that they make do with whatever is available. Men who don't have a gay bone in their body, but just couldn't do without sex.

It was the same four from the boy-barbecue. I watched through a dirty window as they fought each other. It was definitely every man for himself. When the dust settled, two men were unconscious and two men were unbuckling their pants. I tried to wrap my mind around the whole concept.

"Sorry you lost the fight today, Pete. You know the rules. I will be butt-raping you now."

"It's cool, bro. I'll get you next time."

What I did next wasn't out of any sense of helping the two unconscious men. It had solely to do with the fact that these men were animals. They had succumbed to their most base level. They were barely a step above the slime that we supposedly evolved from.

Fortunately, these guys weren't worried about much. The door was shut, but a window that gave me a clear shot was open. I fired my crossbow catching one of the still conscious ones right between the shoulder blades. Have you ever noticed how close the sounds of sex and pain are? That is why I got off my second shot catching the other in about the same place. Two down and two to go. I figured I could go in and retrieve my precious bolts, then finish off the other pair with my blade or spear. I got two steps inside the door when the body underneath the first one I killed shoved the corpse off of him, rolled over, and came up with a blade that would make Crocodile Dundee jealous.

It never once occurred to me that one of the unconscious men might be playing possum. And trust me, as alert as he was, that was the only explanation. That brings a whole new series of thoughts and questions to mind, but all I had time to do was to turn and run. I don't know if you have ever tried to reload a crossbow on the run…I couldn't.

What I did do was duck inside a three-story building. I got up the stairs and kicked open the door at the top. It was probably all the noise I was making, but I wasn't prepared for the pair of zombies waiting on the other side of the door. I jumped back from the two sets of arms that came at me. That's when I dropped my crossbow. I felt a little sick when parts and pieces of it flew off as it bounced down the stairs.

I grabbed the first hand I could and did a yank-and-sling move that send it careening and tumbling down the concrete steps. I brought my knife up and drove it through the underside of the jaw of the remaining zombie, and then hip-tossed it downs the stairs as well.

I heard my pursuer burst in down below and looked for a place to hide. The sounds of a scuffle let me know that he went heads-up with the zombie I had thrown down the stairs. It sounded like they clashed on the second floor landing. By the time I heard booted footsteps coming up, I'd wedged myself in an alcove between two tall filing cabinets. My plan was simple. If he came in and looked for me, I was down low with my knife ready. I would thrust out and up.

Sure enough, the door slammed open and I could hear his heavy breathing. He called out, hoping that I would be some frightened girl who couldn't deal with the fear of being stalked. I heard him toss a few chairs out of the way, thinking that maybe I'd hidden under some desk. When he stopped in front of me…the idiot actually had his back to me. I must have hit a kidney, because when my knife plunged in, he barely made a sound. More like a hissing whimper. I scooped up the big-ass knife that he'd been carrying and drove it into his chest. The worst part was the fact that I did not feel one single thing while I looked into his eyes as the light dimmed, and then went out.

I wiped my knife off and headed for the stairs. My crossbow was in pieces. *That* was a bummer. I stepped outside and that's when I saw the other guy. We just looked at each other for a moment. Then…he leered, waved, and started heading my direction.

He was a big man and I didn't have any doubts as to who would win in a fight. Wait! Let me correct that. I didn't have any doubts about who would win in a *fair* fight. The first thing I did was run back into the cluster of main buildings. At the very first corner I reached, I took it so that I was temporarily out of sight. There were eight buildings to choose from.

The rest of the day was a glorified hide-and-seek game. In the movies, chases are so dramatic and rarely last beyond a few minutes. By nightfall, I'd been in at least a dozen different places, and hidden in every one of the buildings in this little cluster at least once at some point. At first, I considered trying to rig a trap. Those take much longer than a person realizes. I was really missing my crossbow. By late afternoon, I came up with an idea. He had set fire to the first building. All day I'd had to listen to this man's dialogue. He took great pleasure telling me about all the things he was going to do when he caught me.

When he ducked into a second building to light it on fire—by the way, I did kick myself for not realizing that he was preparing for this activity all day while we were playing our life or death version of hide-and-seek—I bolted for the structure that housed the bombs. I knew that, as far away as it was across open ground, he would see me. I had one canister of gas or kerosene; whatever it was that he had found as an igniting source for his fires, which were now burning in three buildings. There were a lot of wooden crates in addition to the metal ones in that storage facility. I didn't have any idea what was in those wooden crates.

I had enough of a lead that I could douse a few crates close to the rows of bombs. It really was a wing and a prayer. It didn't have the initial effect that I had hoped for. I tossed a rag that I lit after soaking it in the gas or whatever and then ran. There was a very small reaction as something cooked off and blew up…sorta. (Curse you Hollywood for filling our heads with so many ideas involving giant explosions.) It did do enough to have the man turn around and run the other direction…for a minute or two.

I managed to duck into another bunch of buildings and escape. For a couple of days, I hid in an air duct while my pursuer searched in vain. Then, the zombies started showing up. Some even wandered right into the building that I was hiding in.

Eventually, things settled down. I didn't hear anything living or undead. When I climbed down, I was surprised that things didn't look worse. The biggest bummer of a discovery was that the guy had torched the building with the water and MREs. I only had about a half of a canteen of water left.

I was walking northish, heading back to the highway. That was the only way I figured to get past the mountains to the east. That was when I stumbled, almost literally, on the cemetery. When I saw the pair of legs sticking out from behind a cracked and worn monument, I brought my spear up. His eyes opened just as I raised my arms to plunge the spiked-tipped spear into him. His head moved just enough to cause me to miss.

He swept my feet out from under me and I barely had enough of a chance to get my knife clear. His fist smashed into the side of my head, and just like that, the fight was over.

When I came to, I knew he had done a number of unpleasant things to me when I was unconscious. All of my stuff was thrown everywhere, including my satchel. My hands were bound and secured above my head to a headstone. My feet were likewise tied with the legs spread uncomfortably wide and attached to stakes driven into the ground. The other handicap was being on my stomach. I couldn't see a thing. Worse, I couldn't hear a thing but the occasional sound of the wind which carried the smell of the still-burning buildings a couple of miles away at the military base.

I lay still for what seemed like forever. I kept waiting for the degradation or death. When darkness fell, and still nothing, I figured he must have gone to the base to scavenge. Naturally, I began going to work on the bindings. I was sore, very thirsty, hungry, and scared. Combine that with the poor job of tying me up and eventually I got loose.

It was fully dark by now and I was crawling around trying to find my stuff when I found the body. I *probably* screamed. I definitely moved away and felt for anything that I could use as a weapon. Nothing happened. Even with the distant glow from the fires, I could not see. I didn't move for a while, waiting for an attack. I must have dozed off after the adrenaline backed down a notch. And here I am. I've dressed and grabbed what few things I still have.

My best guess is that I managed to stick the bastard just as—or just before—he punched me in the temple. The idiot was so obsessed with raping me that he bled out. Seriously, men can be such dumbasses.

There is too much activity to the west for me to risk the base. Besides, I already know that the best stuff is already gone. Seriously, I hope to God that I can find a water source by this evening. I won't move until it gets cooler. My body is already hot, but I am not sweating. If I am…it's evaporating before it can be noticed.

Thursday, August 26

I didn't realize how bad off I was. Apparently I passed out in the cemetery. I am inside what I am pretty sure was a bar.

Two ladies, a pretty teen girl, and an old man saved my butt. They brought me to this place—wherever the heck it is—and have been pumping me full of water, rabbit stew, and some mashed vegetables that I can't identify.

The thing is…they're all deaf and dumb. I don't speak sign language and only one of them knows how to read and write…the young girl. She's kinda skittish. I imagine that the still angry-looking scars that make up most of the left side of her face—including the dark hole where her eyeball used to be—is a big part of that reason.

I tried to helpful after I recovered. I even went out yesterday and set some snares for rabbits, just like Eric showed me. I brought five in and after the one I ate, I wrote a thank you note that I will leave where the girl is sure to find it. Best I can tell, all I have to do is to head south following the road out of town. I'm pretty sure that I will eventually find a sign that will tell me where I am and eventually, how far it is to Vegas.

Saturday, August 28

Not a lot to see out here. There are mountains to either side of me so I seem to be walking in a perpetual shadow except for midday. The going is slower than normal because of all the rock slides and such that make it so that I am always climbing over things.

I've not seen a drop of rain in I don't remember how long, however, I do hear thunder in the late afternoon and early evening. I've found one tiny creek since I left those people, and it didn't smell right. I'm rationing myself with much too infrequent sips from my canteen. I'm down to one full and one empty.

Tuesday, August 31

Followed a sign that led me off the main highway. My best guess is that this was some sort of tourist stop or something. I'm inside of a wasted building. It does not have any windows remaining intact. Everything has the words "Quartz Mountain" stamped on it. I found a few of those big plastic containers that you swap out of an office water cooler. The seals were still intact, so I've been quite the little water piggy.

Also, now that my biggest problem of finding water is solved, it rained today. An awesome thunderstorm rolled through. I sat in the middle of the room and managed to remain dry. I am willing to bet that this place was some science geek's dream vacation once upon a time.

Wednesday, September 1

Gabbs Airport. That's where I am now. I've met five people who are headed the same way. The thing is, I'm not sure if I want to travel with them or not. There are three guys and two girls. I haven't really tried to learn their names yet. They do have some interesting stories about Vegas. Since I haven't had a radio in quite a while, I can't confirm them.

According to these people, Vegas is online and accepting newcomers. Supposedly they broadcasted for two weeks straight after the "Battle for Vegas" was over. Now they start every hour with the message that peace has been restored to Vegas and every living soul willing to work. Anyone willing to put in for a full time job is welcome to apply for citizenship. Additionally, visitors are welcome. It seems that a day's work is the new currency. They have a variety of jobs that offer an exchange of credit for each day worked.

It's not quite the vacation Mecca that it use to be. Still, according to these people, pretty much everything under the sun is available there: food, weapons, vehicles, you name it. One of the men said that there are even organized caravans leaving for various destinations all over the states; from the central plains to Alaska. The East Coast is gaining a reputation as some sort of Chernobyl-type wasteland. If even half of what these people say is true, then I picked the right destination. From Vegas, I can choose a caravan to anyplace. I bet they hire on scouts for advance teams.

It's hard not to be giddy. I'm sitting here waiting for the night's broadcast like a kid waits for Christmas. This would at least confirm some of their story. They say that the broadcast starts shortly after dark.

I don't think I realized just how excited I could be to reach my destination. I tried to take each day as it came, putting one foot in front of the other and hoping for a little progress. Maybe, somewhere in the back of my head, I didn't really think I would make it. Then, there's the whole thing about how there is a real doubt when it comes to my sanity. Would a sane person do what

I have done? If I examine my actions too much, or really took a moment to think about what I am doing…

Thursday, September 2

WOW! Heard a lot of interesting things on the radio last night. Vegas sounds like it has a lot going on.

Right now, I have to get over what I saw in Gabbs. I guess it was some sort of mining town way back in the Old World. Now, it is the closest thing that I have seen to match up with how I always imagine the Old West to have been.

The town is actually two parts, connected by Brucite Road. They've done some serious fortifications to this place, and the two parts are individual entities with very different ideologies. They co-exist like siblings.

The northern part has a real cult feeling to it. They have giant crosses everywhere with zombies nailed and bound to them. The people all wear robes. The colors vary according to where the individual brother or sister is deemed to be in his or her "walk towards Godliness." That was according to Brother Frank. There was a *real* Genesis Brotherhood feel to these people, but there didn't seem to be any of that nasty subjugation of the women-folk.

When I asked about the crosses, I was told that they were once citizens, and now they are *beacons*. I was almost afraid to ask what that meant. Apparently, when Jesus makes his return, he will take up the dead first…or something like that. When the zombies stop squirming on the cross, I guess that will be the sign that Jesus has returned.

As for the southern part, it's like a John Wayne or Clint Eastwood movie come to life. There are saloons and brothels and people with bad teeth. There is even a sheriff with a badge.

The group I was with wanted to stay for a few days. As for me, hearing that broadcast got me fired up all over again. I know I still have a long way to go, but I wanted to keep moving. It's almost like I can see the finish line. I did accept an invitation to dinner from the mayor; I figured one day was okay.

Of course, I'd be lying if I didn't say that I keep expecting the family from *Texas Chainsaw Massacre* to pop out at any moment. I enjoyed my meal right up to the point when every-body was summoned to the fire house to "bear witness" to the hanging of a citizen accused of colony endangerment. It seems this guy led a small horde back to Gabbs when he was returning from a scavenger run. It seemed a bit harsh, but I'm just an out-sider.

In the morning, I will head south once more. The owner of the Gabbs Saloon was kind enough to give me a gas station roadmap. There is a lot of empty territory between here and Ve-gas. I didn't see much in the way of streams and such; that means another long, rough stretch.

I can't stop now. I've come so far that I have to see this through. And the possibility that there are caravans radiating out from Vegas is exactly what I want. Who knows? Maybe I'll make a name for myself as some sort of fearless caravan scout. I'll have a special suite or home in Vegas, and people will line up on waiting lists to ride out on a caravan being escorted by Meredith Gainey.

Friday, September 3

It's like being on the moon or something. I haven't seen a sign of anything—living, dead, or undead—all day. And the ter-rain is so alien to anything I have ever experienced. That is a testimony as to how little I've travelled.

I had no idea that mining was such a big deal in Nevada. I'm always passing signs or remnants of signs for some mine or another. Tonight, I'm making one my camp. It sits just off of the highway; and I've found a ratty little trailer to rest my head. I've really noticed the temperature drop overnight these last few days.

I looked around and didn't find anything useful at all. Sure, there are tools and such, but most of it is far too awkward to yield and too heavy to carry. I am running with the bare necessi-ties and have come to the realization that anytime I've tried to get fancy—bikes, carts, and such—I just end up losing it and then spend the next two or three days missing it.

A fairly ominous storm is rolling in. I'm glad I found this trailer. Anybody sleeping out in the elements tonight is in for a miserable one. Already, the thunder and lightning are here and some pea-sized hail fell just about an hour or so ago.

Sunday, September 5

It's strange how something so innocuous can completely change your luck and your day. According to the signs, I'm in Luning, Nevada. This place looks to have been empty since shortly after the onset of the zombie uprising. There are maybe a dozen bodies I have found so far going door-to-door.

My lucky day came in the form of a train at the south end of town. All of those pretty cars that never got to their destination are now just worthless lumps of dingy metal. It was in the caboose—I didn't even know that they still existed—that I discovered plenty of water. That's a good thing, because the town of Luning has been stripped of anything useful.

My guess is that the train arrived late in the collapse. The only challenge was the four zombies I had to deal with when I opened the door to the cab of the caboose. One particularly obese man was standing there with his face leaving greasy smears on the window to the left of the door. He might have been enough to scare most folks away. Also, the window appears to be bullet-proof. I guess that the folks who came through and stripped this town over the years decided that it wasn't worth the hassle when their bullets didn't damage the door. They probable figured that it wasn't worth the risk when the town itself was so empty and easy to pillage.

I'm not exaggerating when I say that this town is empty. It even looks like people have picked through the cars on the train. Not just the automobiles being hauled—which couldn't have yielded much of value I don't think—but every single cargo bay is open on every car on the train. In the main locomotive, there is a long-since-dead body shot in the face with obvious zombie markings.

Anyways, I have water and I don't care how heavy it is. I filled my canteens and found a suitcase with wheels that I rigged with a harness. I'll play sled dog if means that I've got water.

My map tells me that the town of Mina is about eight miles away. I may be able to ditch my harness as early as tomorrow but quite frankly, I am sick of being thirsty. I won't risk it.

Water is the new gold.

Monday, September 6

I'm in Mina, Nevada. There are some ruins and a cemetery before you enter town. The citizens obviously reacted in the same way as other communities when the dead started walking: they went crazy on their local cemetery. It is little more than a charred mess. They took it to an extreme. There are backhoes and all sorts of digging equipment around the fence. It looks like most of the graves were dug up and whatever was found was put to the torch.

I wonder how the zombie problem got all the way out here. I mean, did a trucker die while passing through? Or maybe a family on vacation? Or did they watch it on television until everybody stopped broadcasting, then just sat in scared uncertainty until a horde showed up weeks or months later? I'm curious as to whether some folks waited as long as they could, then broke under the strain and ran…only to fall into the hands of zombies miles away.

When I see some places as remote as this and the last town affected the way they are, I try to picture someplace that might have remained unaffected, and I can't. Over the past few years of the Old World we made everything so small. I remember all the flu bugs and viruses that would pop up. It seemed that if a duck sneezed in some remote village in China, folks in Mexico would start falling victim to a new illness ten days later.

Even in this nowhere town, the sign—what's left of it—for the RV park, boasts of wireless internet. Seriously? And that might be why we fell so fast. We had our noses buried so deep in all our devices that we left out collective asses up in the air for the zombies to take a big bite out of.

I remember a camping trip I went on with some friends the summer before all of this happened. We chose the sight because it promised a tower that meant our iPhones and Blackberries would all still work. How did folks camp before that?

Thursday, September 9

Still in Mina.

I've gone through every single shop, building and residence in town. I hauled everything of value to the elementary school. I had to take out a few creepers, and in some of the residences I had to deal with a few of the formal locals that had been left behind or refused to leave.

I wasn't going to stay, but then I saw the humongous herd of horses galloping across the grounds to the west of town. I've never seen so many horses in one place in my life. And all of that was interesting, but when I woke up after the first night and several deer were clomping down the main street, my mouth started to water. I'm not exactly proud, but I snuck around some buildings to put myself in position, and when the deer came past, I managed to nail a little one with my spear.

I roasted big chunks of the tender meat; enough to get me to the next town. According to my map, it is Tonopah. If those folks I left behind eventually come, they will have a sign telling them that there are supplies inside the school. Also, they will be able to avail themselves to my makeshift barbeque.

In the morning I will be on the move once more. Even with this brief stopover, my desire and excitement about reaching Las Vegas has not dimmed. I know I may be setting myself up for disappointment, but the possibility does exist that I will find what I have been looking for when I finally get there. I've likened this to joining the military...the chance to travel and see things coupled with a (relatively) safe and secure place to return to once your mission is complete.

Saturday, September 18

According to the map, this is Tonopah, Nevada. Too bad there isn't enough left to identify it as such. I have no idea what happened but it looks like the military bombed the crap out of this place. The worst aspect of that is my water situation. It hasn't rained in I can't remember how long and I haven't found anything drinkable since leaving Mina.

There was one cool thing. I found a mostly intact Stealth-Bomber. I'm fairly sure that's what it was. Bad news, the pilots were both zombies. I don't even want to know what has happened here. And as flattened as everything is…I have one worry that won't go away.

Did they nuke this place?

Seriously, I have never seen the kind of absolute obliteration that exists here. I bet that if I could get an overhead view, I would see a well-defined blast radius.

Also, other than the two pilots in the crash-landed bomber, there is nothing living here. I haven't seen the rustle of jackrabbits or even a fluttering bird in two days. To make matters worse, I've been walking through some undisturbed ash and debris.

Tonight, I'm camping in the payload area of the downed aircraft. I stuck a blade in the sides of the heads of the zombies in the cockpit. I know they seemed strapped in and all, but I just couldn't get comfortable knowing they were right there straining against their harnesses. Also, what good does it do to leave any of those things alive when you have the chance to put them down?

I sure hope that I find water soon.

Sunday, September 19

Holy crap! It is freezing cold. It feels like somebody threw a giant switch. Normally it gets cold at night, but today it never felt like it warmed up at all.

I've passed all these so-called National and State parks. Really? They just seem like dead volcanoes. Some of the distant hills and mountains look like they got dusted with powdered sugar overnight.

There are lots of trenches and gullies carved into the earth around these parts, but not a drop of water that I could see or hear. I am checking any and all abandoned vehicles that I passed, but so far…nothing.

I'm too far out in the middle of nowhere to turn around. All I can do is press on and pray that I find water soon. Being extra careful, I'll be down to my last canteen by the end of tomorrow.

Monday, September 20

Damn.

I'm trapped on the second floor of the Esmeralda County Courthouse in a town called Goldfield. Using the word 'town' might be stretching things just a bit.

This place doesn't even qualify as a pencil dot on a map. It seems more like it was left in tribute or something to miners of the old days. There couldn't have been as many people living here as there are zombies on the street. The biggest problem is that I didn't see where they came from. I ducked inside this big, brick building looking for water, next thing I know, the streets were crawling with the undead. There weren't even any inside when I arrived! That is what has me so confused.

I'd already checked out what passed as an airstrip at the north end of town and made my way through a few residences. I went in to check out the courthouse which has no windows left on the ground floor—but all of them still in place upstairs. That's when things went wrong.

I heard the crash of something heavy and metallic hitting the ground. Hurrying up the stairs, I looked out the window and was stunned. Hundreds of those things were on the street. They weren't focused on any one building—several were pouring inside mine and I quickly barred and braced the emergency exit—but the largest number converged on this four-story building up the road a ways.

The thing is, I keep hearing something. At first it took me a while to recognize what I am certain is conversation. There are others in this town. Living, breathing, talking people.

I'm left wondering if it is these people that brought the zombies. Perhaps they were on the run from a herd. The only problem with that possibility is that anybody that has survived for this long knows not to run someplace and trap yourself with those things on your tail. Zombies don't get bored and will stay outside, clawing at your doors and walls until something comes along to distract them and lead them away. Even then, if it is a big herd like this one, (I'm guessing it at well over a thousand) then you can't be sure that all of them will leave. The only way to survive a herd is to lead them on a wild goose chase and lose them as soon as possible.

Since the zombies seemed to be clustered to various degrees around every building in town, I'm not entirely certain what happened. All I know right now is that there are a frightening number clawing at the two doors that would allow access to this floor. If I get any sleep tonight it will be a miracle.

Tuesday, September 21

I don't know who they are, but I hate them. It's a large group; of that much I am certain. Most can't be out of their teens yet. It's a mix of boys and girls from what I can see, and there doesn't seem to be one main leader.

This bunch has a real *Lord of the Flies* nature about them. On multiple occasions I saw them fighting each other as viciously as they do the zombies. I don't have a clue as to how these idiots have survived this long. I even witnessed a pair of very pregnant girls—the older one was *maybe* fifteen—go at each other with knives.

Twice they tried to gain my building. Once they even made it to the second floor and tried to get in. I've become very proficient at setting a barricade these past couple of years. They gave up when traffic got too heavy.

I've heard a few of *those* screams. Once, I even saw a boy tossed out from a window into the waiting mob below.

The boys and the girls seem to be almost primal with their urges. I've looked out a few times to see a boy just run up behind a girl and yank her pants down while she looked out a window or over the edge of a roof. But nothing blew me away more than when I saw a girl tackle a boy, roll him onto his back, and straddle him at knifepoint. This group seems to have no filters whatsoever.

I hope they don't get any sort of clarity any time soon and mount an assault on my position. I have no doubts as to the chances of my survival. What I need is to get the hell out of here.

Friday, September 24

I'm where a lot of people always thought I would end up: a brothel. This is the first compound of survivors that I have found that isn't fenced and fortified. Stranger still, this place is a *functioning* brothel.

Let me correct myself. There is some fortification; all of the doors and windows are barred, and the gun turrets on the roof are iron-plated. But that's it. According to Jasmine, the house madam, that's all they need. There are concrete pill-boxes set up two miles out and spaced at five hundred yard intervals around this place. They rely on Morse code and flags to indicate when there are approaching parties, whether they are living or undead, and in what numbers. It's primitive, but it seems to work.

Besides the madam and her dozen working girls, there are three hundred soldiers here. They weren't from either faction that fought over Vegas, but they are aware of them. I doubt they'll have any problem though. This is the largest concentration of weapons I've see yet. They have the building that once functioned as the truck stop packed from floor-to-ceiling with ammo, RPGs and all sorts of stuff.

The head honcho of the soldiers, Eddie Scott, said that they've held meetings with some of the leaders from Las Vegas and there's no concern that an attack will be coming. When I asked about the apparent issue between the folks at Winnemucca and Las Vegas, Eddie said that their beef was an issue between the two unit commanders that spilled over to the men. His group came from Colorado, and has been here for just over a year.

I asked about civilian traffic and he said that I was the first they'd seen in two months. Then I mentioned that pack of feral children. He said that they lost a few men to them last winter. Supposedly, one of the young girls lured a patrol into a secured place. He was sketchy on the details, but I got the idea that it had been very ugly. With what I witnessed, I can only imagine; and even then, I'm probably coming up short.

He asked how I managed to escape a town full of them *and* zombies. It turned out to be no big feat. The kids apparently grew bored with whatever twisted games they were playing and went on a rampage. And even then, that was some sort of game. They were intentionally beheading the zombies so that they would remain animated. Then they strung the heads from poles, stuck them on fence posts, and all sorts of varieties on that theme.

It was during this event that I made my break for it. I had to take out a few zombies on the way, but I knew that I had to get out of town before they brought their attention back to my building, and more specifically, my locked door. I'm really glad that I didn't encounter any of those kids on my way out. I don't know if I would have just been able to kill yet another living being—much less a child—unless they did something first. And my guess is that by then it would have been too late.

This place runs like clockwork. The men and women come and go as they start their shifts. I guess the brothel only had eight girls to start, but a few of the soldiers opted out of the military unit and went to work for Jasmine. It all seems a bit surreal, but this is the world that we live in. Goods and luxuries are the currency of today. The soldiers bring in the goods, and the girls provide the luxuries.

I did the math in my head, and if my guess of two hundred and twenty-ish is close when it comes to how many men are in this group, I figure those twelve 'working girls' are getting ridden twice a day every day if each guy only gets one turn per week. And I'm thinking my guess may be conservative because the six bedrooms are in use around the clock.

Fun fact: each one of the girls is sterile. Three of them were before; I guess the others had a procedure done by the company's medic. Additionally, almost two dozen of the men were forbidden contact with all but one of the women—one of the female soldiers it turns out—because of STDs. The woman in question is infected with something, none of my business. She is also the only one that is required to use condoms with every customer.

Here's where it gets a little stranger. The men restricted to her have made runs as far away as Salt Lake City to bring back hundreds of thousands of condoms. I'm no expert, but I know those things have a shelf life. I wonder what happens when those things either go bad or they finally run out. The whole thing is a bit dark and creepy if you ask me, but it is a reminder of what we are as a species...pleasure seekers. When it comes down to it, we want to feel good.

I asked about the women in the company. It seems that they are all encouraged to "play the field." I don't see anything good coming from that. We are also a possessive species, one day, someone's going to snap.

There are seven children here between the ages of a couple of months to what I am guessing to be about a nine-month-old. They really take the 'it takes a village to raise a child' adage to heart in this place. There is an RV that is used as the nursery, and it appears that everybody rotates through just like a watch shift to care for the children. I've never lived in a commune, but I imagine that this is what it would look like.

These folks hunt, fish—although I have no idea where—and even grow stuff. They didn't tell me where the greenhouses were, only that they have some constructed in the hills. There are windmills set up all over the place, but none of it is used to power lights. When night falls, this whole facility goes into blackout mode. Nothing more than fire pits provide lights after sunset.

I'll stay here a couple of days. I offered to go out with the hunting group, and in exchange I am getting a water pack. It's like a backpack but it holds water. The drawback is that I will have to fill it with my canteens because it doesn't have any filtration device. Which reminds me, I'm down to my last two changeable filters for my canteens. I really need to reach a bigger town and hope they have some sort of sporting goods store and hope further still that they haven't been completely looted. The filling time on this pack if I use my canteens would be most of a day, and that would also mean that I would be lugging about sixty-four pounds on my back. The more likely scenario would be filling it a little over half way and keeping my canteens full. Honestly, I don't short change myself, but I can't see me toting almost seventy pounds on my back for any length of time.

Saturday, September 25

Left this morning to go up into the hills and hunt. I sure wish I could bring this rifle with me when I leave, but I've been told that there is absolutely no way that will happen.

I spent the early part of the afternoon on this rocky outcropping. I bagged a nice buck. Being the owner of the first kill was a little source of pride for me. I think a few of the guys—and even the one female soldier—were impressed.

Everywhere I look it is brown. The ground is brown, the plants are brown, and I think this place is starting to get to me. All I want to do is to get moving again. Once I reach Vegas, if I sign on to be a caravan escort, l like I am hoping to, I'd like to do some traveling that takes me into places with a little more color. However, I can't knock the sunsets out here. They're incredible.

Tuesday, September 28

Back to what I've titled Brothel Base.

I leave tomorrow. Oh yeah! And I'll have company. Her name is Justine Cash and she has family that is rumored to still be alive in Las Vegas.

I guess it will be nice to have somebody to talk to. She was one of the soldiers. Apparently, while I was on the hunting trip, a team returned from some sort of mission to Beatty, a town about thirty-five to forty-five miles south of here. They ran into a team from someplace called Pahrump. So, based on third or fourth hand information, Justine is heading for Vegas by way of Beatty. Since they knew I was headed that way already, Eddie, the commander or whatever he is—everyone just calls him Eddie, nobody uses rank or anything like that around here—asked Justine to wait. I guess the idea is safety in numbers or something like that.

Wednesday, September 29

On the road. Absolutely nothing to see.

It didn't take long for Justine and me to get chatty. She asked me why I was headed for Vegas. That kind of surprised me. I assumed that Eddie or somebody had filled her in.

I explained that I'd been in a few compounds and fortified towns, and it just wasn't for me. I told her how I'd never been anyplace *before* the zombie apocalypse and how I heard a radio broadcast one night. I decided on the spot that I wanted to go see for myself.

We probably walked in silence for almost twenty minutes. I actually started to feel a bit uncomfortable. Then…Justine let me have it. She told me how she's fought at least fifty intense battles—I guess that meant battles lasting longer than an hour—against living and undead. She's been close to starving at least a dozen times, nearly killed by dehydration three times and considers herself lucky. She thinks I'm an idiot.

"You survived the worst disaster in all of history and you run around seeing how close you can get to death. How can you value your life so little?" she asked.

I explained that I didn't think I valued my life so little. I feel that I am actually turning a terrible situation into an opportunity. She retorted that I was suicidal and that everything that *she'd* done to risk her life had been in the line of duty. She went on to say that this trip was the extent of her carelessness, and that if her brother wasn't actually in Las Vegas, she would either join their military security regiment or wait for the first chance to join a team that would take her back to her original unit. Going out on her own wasn't even a remote consideration.

The rest of the day, we just walked. We made good time, but the silence was a bit oppressive. If I'd known that I was gonna get preached to and told that I'd basically lived the last two-plus years wrong…I would have gone alone. Good thing I didn't tell her about my baby.

Thursday, September 30

Spending tonight in the trailer of a jackknifed semi. The sky is clear, which means that the night will be very cold. We did luck out; last night we had to sleep out in the brush in shifts. This trailer is hard to get into. That means that zombies won't be a problem even if they pass by. Not that I expect them to, we haven't seen a single thing since we hit the road.

Today was more of the same uncomfortable silence. I hope we reach Beatty tomorrow so I can ditch her and go back to being alone. I thought it would be nice to have somebody to travel with. I was wrong.

She did actually ask me what I was writing at some point last night after we made camp. I told her it was none of her damn business. If that was her attempt to bridge the gap or whatever…too bad. I mean really, who is she to judge me?

Friday, October 1

The sign says "Welcome to Beatty Nevada...the gateway to death!"

I'm in this domed building that obviously served as a library. I honestly have no idea where Justine is. A few miles outside of town, we stopped at these warm springs. They weren't any good for filling my water supply, but I took the most amazing bath.

Justine was kind enough to lend me some honest-to-goodness soap and—gasp!—a razor. That last part was more cruel than kind. Even with a shiny new blade, my legs and underarms now feel like giant strips of road rash. Still, I *think* she meant it as a nice gesture.

Next, we went to this other stream and replenished our water supply. I first knew that things would be different when we were filling up our canteens and water packs. I put down four zombies in about two hours. I was starting to wonder what the hell was going on...and that's when I looked around and realized that Justine was gone.

I searched the area where I'd last seen her. I even risked calling her name...twice. Finally I started south along the highway. It wasn't long before I saw the sign that 'welcomed' me to Beatty.

There was movement almost instantly. A glance around revealed that many of the buildings had black X's painted on them. I assumed that that meant they'd been searched. Twice I heard gunshots. Both times scared the crap out of me.

I found a few hotels and the requisite numbers of bars and long-since-looted grocery stores. I decided not to stick around. As I crept out of town, I'm certain that I saw movement that was much too fast to be a zombie. In fact, I was chasing after the third such sighting when I found the library. I ducked inside and was disappointed to discover that it was empty of books.

It's getting dark and the main entry of this place has a reinforced gate that bars on the inside. Somebody has used this location to hide out before. I won't feel guilty treating myself to some of the supplies that I found boxed up in a few of the closets.

Part of me wants to look for Justine, but I'm not convinced that she was grabbed as much as I think that she crept away. There are obviously people living here; or in the vicinity at any rate. I'm fairly certain that, if I've seen signs of *them*, then they know I'm here. However, nobody has made a move to reveal themselves to me.

Saturday, October 2

Tonight, I'll be sleeping in this church at the south end of town. I know I should have left, but something here doesn't sit right. The voice in my head is telling me to leave, but I can't.

Late last night I heard somebody crying. No it wasn't the baby cry, it was honest-to-God weeping. Only, in the darkness, and with the occasional moan and groan of the zombies roaming this place, I couldn't go out and look for the source.

Yes, I tried. I got about three blocks when five of those shambling bastards came out from what I am fairly sure was a playground or a park. They came right for me. And while I have no doubt that I could take them, it was the sound of crashing glass from somewhere else close by, that made me retreat. I have no idea how crowded this town might be.

I searched today and found a busted in door on a building that I am certain was an elementary school. There was blood everywhere. I don't know what it is, but something here is bothering me. I looked around all day, but didn't find a thing. At least not a living thing.

Monday, October 4

Today I tried something different.

After two days in town of finding nothing while I scurried about searching for whoever is running around here, I went up this naked, ugly hill on the north end of town. I found a telescope in the high school. And, while it's not the greatest, it works.

I went into this horseshoe-shaped hill and climbed up the back side. When I got to the top, I lay down and scanned the town. From up here, movement was obvious. Funny thing …there aren't nearly as many zombies wandering the streets as I had guessed. I would put their numbers at three hundred tops. And while I wouldn't want to deal with them as a group, they are spread out.

The movement of those that are obviously living is centered on the high school on the *south* end of town and a hotel to the north. It is obvious that these are two competing factions.

The school compound is bigger and has more people. This little microcosm is interesting to say the least. The folks at the hotel are obviously military and those at the school are civilians. If I had to guess, I'd be willing to bet that Justine went to the hotel. Did she know about the societal rift here? And did she see me as one of "them" along the lines of the divisions here? Is that why she was so snotty? My worst fears seem to be realized. We've stopped fighting the zombies. We are now more worried about each other.

Friday, October 8

I chased him for three days.

I never caught him, but today I caught up with him. He is hanging from a sign over the highway. I'm in the burned out ruins of another—I had no idea there were so many of the damn things—airport, and I pray to God that the band of men I managed to evade don't find my trail…or me.

I don't know if these guys are new arrivals or what. However, there are a large group of badasses running all over what the sign said is Indian Springs. Funny, I thought the folks at Winnemucca had people here. If they did, they ain't here now. This place was wrecked *before* that gang showed up. There are at least a dozen fires burning now. I think—although this may just be the paranoia talking—that they are trying to flush me out.

When I first arrived, after seeing the guy that I was chasing swinging from the sign, I thought that there were a bunch of zombies here. It turned out to be mannequins. *That* was creepy.

Now, about the guy I was chasing.

I was up in the hill looking around town when I saw this girl running down the street. Chasing her were two guys. I knew that, as far away as I was, there would be no way that I could get there in time to help. They were going to catch her. Still, I had to do something. I made my way down the hill and lost sight of them the moment before the screaming started.

I came up the steep bank of the trickle of water that passed itself off for as the Amargosa River just as one of the guys—a fat, greasy-haired, Hispanic-looking guy with tattoos all over his body, including his face—was standing up and buckling his pants. He ended up staring at the point of my spike-tipped walking stick that jutted from his chest. The other guy—a scrawny, acne-scarred white guy—took one look at his friend, then me as I was drawing my machete...and took off running.

I was between him and the girl sprawled in the dirt not moving. I didn't have to check. She was dead. I did not have time to really take a close look, but the dark splotches around her white, freckled throat told me all I needed to know.

For the next few days we played our deadly cat-and-mouse game. The first day, he sealed his fate. I'd lost him in these ratty looking houses on the southeast end of town. Then he came out on some type of motocross bike. I was certain that I'd lost him. I watched helpless as he pedaled away. I knew that, even if I could find another bicycle to give chase, I doubted I could ride worth a damn with my water pack sloshing around.

I returned to the scene of the brief skirmish and was given another setback. I'd taken off in such a hurry after the second guy that I'd left my walking stick-spear sticking out of the fat guy. It was snapped in half. I don't know if it happened when I stuck the guy, or if it happened when he fell to the ground or what...but it was unfixable. That's when I started crying.

Hell, I don't know why. Maybe it was because that weapon was the last thing I had left from the beginning. I'd been through hell with that thing. Every other weapon I have has been swapped out a dozen times or more. Half the time, I'd see a new knife or machete and simply toss the one I was currently carrying aside for the newest find. But the walking stick...my trusty spear...I've had that thing for what seems like forever. My hands had worn grooves into the wood that allowed it to fit perfectly in them when I walked.

I no longer cared about what was happening in Beatty. I resumed my journey. I would get to Vegas, find out who was in charge, and get a job with the caravans. I would have my cake and eat it, too. I'd have a permanent residence *and* I would get to travel; go and see all those places I longed to see. Maybe I'd even have a semi-regular sex life. The possibilities were endless.

By the first night that I made camp, I'd forgotten all about the guy who'd gotten away. It was midday the following afternoon when I came across the bicycle. The back tire was flat. That would mean that he was on foot. I highly doubted that he'd circled back.

Later in the day, I came across an abandoned old pick-up truck. A zombified corpse had been dragged out and its head bashed in. Judging by the scuffs in the sand, it hadn't been an easy kill. The big rock was still sorta lodged in the skull where the last blow had finally put the thing down for good. My guess was that there was something in the cab of that truck that the skinny guy has wanted really badly.

That night, I found a clump of scrub brush to nestle in and sleep. It was a rough night. The wind was constantly blowing which added to my cold misery. I expected that if I did ever find that guy, he'd be dead from exposure.

The next day, today, I found him hanging from that sign. The body was just swinging in the breeze. In an instant, I went from fox…to rabbit mode.

I considered the ruined residential area, but decided that the airport was a better choice. Also, more of the structures were intact; more places to hide. As an added bonus, there were a number of aircraft. I counted two dozen private luxury jets parked all over this facility. There was even a large, commercial passenger plane; but without any stairs or a ladder, there would be no way to get inside.

Right now I am in one of those luxury airplanes. It is parked underneath the partially collapsed roof of a hangar. I actually had to move a big panel of aluminum, and then it was still a tight squeeze to get inside. I'm hoping that I didn't disturb much when I got in. That way, if those crazy people running wild around here come past, hopefully they won't even notice that I am here. There is no doubt as to my fate if I am discovered. That is a rough looking bunch.

The last thing that I saw before I ducked into this plane was the lighting of what I am positive was a church on fire.

Saturday, October 9

Mystery solved. Heading south on Highway 95, I followed my gang of looting maniacs. Staying out of sight wasn't too hard for a number of reasons. First, they were loaded down with a strange assortment of things that they found in Indian Springs. (That included a number of mannequins, a screen door …like I said…strange.) Second, I don't think that these guys have faced any serious sort of resistance.

There is a pair of prison complexes just south of town. Great big sprawling monstrosities that seem to take up as much area as the entire burned out town of Indian Springs. It's like a giant human warehouse. However, even as far away as I stayed while passing, the noise—mostly screams and what sounded like a crowd roaring—was incredible.

There looked to be a fairly impressive number of zombies milling about. Not to mention the huge bonfire blazing in the open space between the two main complexes.

I cannot begin to imagine what sort of nightmare is taking place behind those razor wire-topped fences. I couldn't put enough distance between myself and that place fast enough. For the rest of the day I felt like I was being chased by a horrible monster. Even once I was out of range of the place—both audibly and visually—I still had the feeling that I was being watched. That feeling kept the hair up on the back of my neck.

I've come to realize that the vastly unpopulated state of Nevada is quite different from Oregon in a lot of ways; the sparse and spread out population didn't keep the zombie outbreak from reaching even the most remote corners. But the pockets of humanity that survived have a much different life where the environment actually is an ally. If I use that logic, then I would be willing to bet that population-heavy places like New York and California are a waste.

Of course using logic like that makes it hard to imagine how a city like Las Vegas managed to withstand the onslaught. That would make it a bit of a miracle. I hold this sliver of hope in my heart that I will find what I've been looking for once I get there.

Tonight I will be sleeping in a place that was probably once some geek's wet dream: a watch tower on the perimeter of Nellis Air Force Base. The sign on the highway told me that *this* is the infamous Area 51. Funny…it just looks like more of the same empty desert.

If an alien spaceship shows up…maybe I'll hitch a ride. Talk about getting the chance to travel! However, it is getting chilly and the sky is turning a bruised purple color. I'm going to settle in and get some shut-eye.

Sunday, October 10

Hmmm…no aliens came.

Well I guess that place turned out to be a bit of a disappointment. I have to admit, I did stay awake for a considerable time after dark…and not one single thing happened. No flashing lights in the sky, no strange whirring sounds.

So, if aliens got bitten by a zombie, what would happen? I bet all those crazies who were so into that crap before have had fist fights over the possible answers. I wonder if we would get Space Zombies? Wow…that sounds like the premise for a *really bad* SyFy Channel Original Movie. It also sounds like Meredith is getting a little bit bonkers spending all of this time alone.

Strange. None of the zombie stories that I *do* remember were so devoid of zombies. I haven't seen any for a while. Didn't they always have hordes of undead trapping a small band of survivors in an unlikely location? I mean, really…a mall? How would you secure a place like that? And while I have certainly seen my fair share, there are times like now where I am just totally alone. I've walked across Oregon and much of Nevada this year. Much of that time I have only been in danger of being bored to death.

Tonight I am in some park; Floyd Lamb State Park according to the faded wooden sign hanging above the door of this log cabin-style building that I'm calling home for the night. Tomorrow…I will be in Vegas. Perfect timing. I've been careful with my water and food, but am starting to run a bit low. I *think* I hear some moans and baby cries in the distance. Oh well, the doors are sturdy and all the windows have heavy shutters that are still rolled down and locked.

Tuesday, October 12

What is it that they say about the best laid plans of mice and men? Oh yeah…they're destined to be fucked.

I won't be going to Vegas it seems. All of my hopes and dreams are now just this sour taste of rot.

I woke yesterday filled with excitement. It really is my own fault. So much time out in the middle of nowhere took its toll. I was roused from my sleep by the sounds of pounding on the door. There were at least two dozen of those things out there. Worse still, I could see movement in the trees. More were coming.

I went upstairs to the windows that I could see out of and was upset to discover that I was surrounded by a couple dozen of them. They were at both doors clawing and scratching to be let in. I ditched the water pack and topped off one canteen. After checking my two knives strapped to my thighs, I drew my machete and went to the front door. I've never missed my spear as much as I did in that moment.

After making short work of the two right in the doorway, I launched myself into the pre-dawn, chilly morning air. The place was swarming with them. They were moths to my living flame. And hadn't I just bitched about not seeing that many zombies like in the movies? Be careful what you ask for…right?

At some point I got turned around. I knew that I should be arriving at the highway…yet I was still in the park. Actually, I was in these sparse woods. When I burst out into a clearing, the sun hit me right in the face as it crested the distant mountains, bathing the world in a glorious sunrise. Crap! That meant that I was facing east; the wrong way. I knew that the highway was *west* of where I'd spent the night.

I turned around and he was right there. Barely old enough to start growing whiskers, the boy had the look of the long dead.

His skin was split in places and his wounds were so dried out that not even maggots nested in them. Instead, I am pretty sure that I saw *growth*; it looked like mold or something with stuff sprouting from it. One eyeball remained; glossed over in putrid off-white and shot full of black tracers. The other socket had sealed shut like the skin had melted over the hole and fused together.

My coat saved me. Initially. Unfortunately, I'd been sans gloves for longer than I can remember. I brought my machete up and he clawed at my arm. That caused me to miss badly. The blade went into the shoulder, shattering the collarbone and wedging itself in rather firmly.

I went for a knife, but the zombie-boy lunged and we both went to the ground. I kicked and bucked, but we were such a tangled mess that it wasn't doing any good. By the time that I got my knife free of its sheath, I had my free hand around its throat, keeping the gnashing teeth just far enough away. The smell coming from its mouth was surprisingly bad for how dried out and long dead this thing was. It was making my guts do rolls, threatening to spew what little may have been in my stomach.

The clicking and grinding sound of those teeth caused me to wince every single time. Finally, I drove the blade into its temple. I shoved the body off and scrambled to my feet…and right into the arms of the pair of zombies that were so torn up, the only way that I knew one of them was female was the sagging breast that remained on one side. Once again I found myself sprawled on the ground in a life-or-death struggle.

I fought, kicked, bucked, and squirmed. Finally I got myself free and crawled away. I made it to my feet a second time and looked around frantically. No direction was clear, but I took off in the way that seemed most likely to give me a chance.

When I finally reached the road, I fell to my knees gasping for breath. I puked up a scalding mixture of bile and a tiny smidge of food to give it some texture. It was while I was on my hands and knees that I noticed the nasty bite on my left hand.

I hoped desperately that I was one of the lucky immune. Then a handful of those bastards came barging through the brush beside the road and I had to get to my feet and run. I don't think that I ever once considered running *towards* Vegas.

In all of the chaos, I'd lost my weapons and canteen. The only thing I still had was my satchel. It seems right that I am left with nothing but this journal. I'm in the old watchtower that I slept in a couple of nights back. Along the way, I saw my reflection in the side mirror of a car. The tracers are already visible in my eyes even in the filthy mirror that I looked in.

I know that I don't have much time left. Writing this is taking all of the energy that I have. There are moments when it is like I can feel the infection spreading throughout my body. Down below, about a hundred of those things have gathered around the base of the tower. Their growls and cries and mewling keep jarring me back to the task at hand which is to finish this last...this final entry.

To whoever finds this, if anybody does, please—if at all possible—get this to my daughter. I've included enough information so that she can be found. When I set this book down, my plan is to secure the strap of my satchel around my neck and the other end around the railing. I realize that I will come back as one of those things, but my hope is that somebody will come along and see me. If they come up to investigate, they will find the book.

I wish that I had something profound to say now, but honestly, this headache is beating every thought out of my skull before it has a chance to gel. So...I guess that all there is left is to say goodbye.

Epilogue

Tuesday, August 1, 2023

My name is Orlando Scott. Las Vegas, 1st Regiment-Expeditionary Unit. I found this book a few weeks ago while returning from Correctional City.

The originals of this document were returned to me after Command Control inspected and copied each of the three separate texts. A convoy bound for the Northwest and the Rainier settlement will be taking the originals. If the assumption is correct, Ms. Gainey referred to what is now know as Corridor 26, a series of trading posts just west of the ruins of Old Portland.

Saturday, June 8, 2024

My name is Snoe. My father's name was Samuel Todd. My mother's name was Meredith Gainey.

CONTINUE READING AND ENJOY
AN EXCERPT FROM TW BROWN'S
BOOK ...

DEAD: THE UGLY BEGINNING

1

The Ugly Beginnings

I ain't no hero. I never thought of being one. When I was young, I didn't dream about being a police or fireman. I never considered joining the military, even after 9-11 when so many others my age flocked to the recruiter's office.

Hell, I was the guy who picked a desk in the middle of the classroom on the first day of school when all the Brains rushed for front row seats and the Jocks and Stoners roamed to the back. I didn't play sports, at least not in any organized way. When sides were chosen (even if it was just a pick-up game with my buddies), I was pointed out someplace in the middle. Sometimes I would pull off a play in football, basketball, kickball...whatever, which was only amazing because it was me doing it.

I had my share of girlfriends. I lost my virginity my senior year. On prom night. To a girl who played flute in the high school marching band. Her name was Kerri or Kathy...or Kari or Cathy.

So you're starting to get the point. Right?

I worked in an office complex after I graduated college ...B minus GPA. Never married, but I was engaged a few times. My one bedroom apartment was small, but it suited me and my dog just fine. Well, that was until the horror movies jumped off the screen and landed right in the middle of an atypically un-believing real world.

Some of the stuff about zombies proved to be true.

Some not.

Most of how humanity was predicted to act was drastically underestimated. The best. The worst. Sometimes I wonder how in the hell we've survived as a species.

That will likely be answered definitively sooner than I would like.

It may seem corny, but no one I've met since it began can give me a solid answer as to how it all rolled into motion. Sure, there are theories: Government Bio-weapon gone awry; Super-virus; alien particles from space; demons from Hell; and global warming. Each gets equal billing when you hear the topic come up. Maybe it's a mix of all of the above. Or, maybe God got tired of us messing up his toy. And if you don't believe in God...well then you can refer back to the list and pick your favorite. Honestly, I don't give a damn. I'm too tired from running. How I ended up leading a band of survivors in this Romero-Hell is my new reality. The time for blame has long passed.

Since things began, I've seen...we've all seen...things best forgotten. Yet, I, as well as anybody still alive, know that forgetting is impossible. The best you can hope for now is sleep without the nightmares coming back to refresh those images you desperately try to shove into a hard to reach spot in your mind. There are some things that the movies missed, or could not accurately convey. The biggest would be the smell; that, and the psychological toll of hearing a person scream as they are ripped apart and fed upon.

***

"...seem to see no pattern in what is being called *The Blue Plague*, due to the discoloration common in the final stages where it is theorized that the body is starved for oxygen."

Click.

"Sars. West Nile. Crap. What's next?" I turned off the television and tossed the remote onto a stack of unread magazines scattered across my coffee table.

Pluck, my Basset Hound, twitched a big, floppy ear and closed his eyes in disinterest. I scratched him behind one of those ears, earning a contented doggie sound.

I got off the couch and made one of those habitual trips to the fridge. I popped it open knowing deep down that I didn't really want anything. A thud from the living room signaled that Pluck was on his way, just in case I might produce some tasty treat that would undoubtedly be shared. I'm pretty sure Pavlov's dogs are hidden somewhere in Pluck's family tree.

As is often the case when I'm about to make a major life choice, this one being leftover Chinese take-out, or last night's pizza, the phone rang. I passed Pluck just as his paws smacked the linoleum with a scrabble of clicking claws that were in dire need of trimming. His exasperated huff caused his thick jowls to flutter.

"Yeah?" No need for formality since I could see Bill Wright, a friend of mine's name, in the caller ID on my phone.

"Steve, are you watching this?" My friend Bill was naturally excitable, but something in his voice was off.

"Is this sports related?" I made no attempt to hide how totally *not* interested I was. "Unless it involves a female gymnast losing some or all of her outfit—"

"Turn to Channel Seven now!"

The near-hysterical timbre in his voice had me grabbing my remote before I realized it. I punched the buttons with my thumb. The green volume bar inched across the bottom of my screen as I tried to comprehend what I was seeing.

"...of the local police force along with a detachment from the National Guard have set up around the town's perimeter. No contact has been established with any of the residents up to this point. Reports from the air indicate that it is unlikely that any survivors exist."

The buzzing in my ear reminded me that I was still on the phone with Bill. Also, my arm remained extended towards the television. My hand was empty because, at some point, I had dropped the remote.

"Another 9-11?" I felt my chest tighten.

"I don't think so," Bill said. I could hear his keyboard rattling in the background. "This shit is all over the place. And not just in our country. It's global!"

"What the hell is going on?"

"Straight-up horror movie shit!"

"Uh-huh." My enthusiasm and interest began to recede quickly.

"Dude, I'm totally serious! Packs of crazed people are going on rampages and just tearing people apart. *YouTube* already has like a thousand postings under "Zombie Attack" that show some twisted stuff. At least it did until the site locked up and crashed."

"So you're telling me that zombies are out there going all *George Romero* on the unsuspecting citizens of the world?" I was still watching my now muted television while sitting on my coffee table rubbing Pluck's head as it rested on my knee. It wasn't showing me any zombies, just a talking head and a caption that read: *Possible Small Town Epidemic.*

"If you saw any of these clips, you'd be grabbin' a gun and headin' to the nearest shopping mall!"

No, I didn't believe Bill in the slightest. That was mostly due to the hours he, I, and others spent imagining just such a scenario; usually after viewing any of the *Dead* flicks. Take your pick…*Night, Dawn, Day, Land.* Original. Remake. We'd seen them all enough to recite lines like *Rocky Horror* fans. It always led to the "what if" conversation.

One of the oldest, most overused sayings is, "Be careful what you ask for…" You know the rest. So, I did what anybody else would do if their friend called to say that the zombies were coming. I hung up.

***

Sometimes you will see something in life that makes you say or think, "That's just like that movie…." Or, if you're the literary type, it could be in a book. I've read or seen lots of 'zombie-esque' stuff over the years. I always thought it would be so cool. Of course, I'd never go into that dark place *that so many fall prey to. Plus, those zombies move so slow…at least until the British influence brought on the sprinting zombie. Man, am I glad they got that wrong.*

***

I went to bed watching *Talk Show with Spike Ferensten.* Overall, a normal Saturday night for me. Ironically, it was the utter darkness that woke me.

My eyes opened to that total blackness that modern man had grown so unaccustomed to experiencing. The first moments were disorienting. Usually there is a blue glow that filters through my curtains from a car rental place that casts its light on my closet door. I live near the airport, so I can count on two fingers the number of times I've lost power. Both times were due to terrible ice storms.

It was late April.

In the distance I heard sirens. That is nothing unusual near the airport at any time of day or night. So, I closed my eyes with the intention of going back to sleep. An unfamiliar growl signaled the change in my world...I just didn't realize how drastic at that particular moment.

The growl changed register. Suddenly, my droopy-faced, foot-warmer of a dog began barking furiously. There was no mistaking the message.

Danger!

I climbed out of the covers and tried to creep to my bedroom doorway. If there was a creaky board in the floor that I missed, I'd be shocked. I peeked down the hallway. My front door was in a direct line of sight, and on the right was my living room window with the curtains closed. Through an arch on the left would be my kitchen and a much smaller window. My apartment was on the second floor and in the corner of the small thirty-unit complex. Usually, at night, the big lit sign from the luxury hotel across the street shone brightly in my living room; even through closed curtains.

Not tonight.

"Pluck!" I whispered.

I could see his dark shape, barely discernable against my front door in the blackness. The shape moved and was at my feet pushing against me with its bulky head. I reached down to scratch behind his ears and noticed that Pluck's hackles were standing straight on end.

"What the hell?"

That was all I managed before something outside brushed up against my front door. In a flash, my normally docile companion was lunging towards the door barking furiously. Not thinking, I ran after him yelling his name and that he quiet down.

A dull thud.

I moved my agitated dog aside with one leg and leaned over just enough to ease the curtains aside so that I could take a peek out my living room window. A man stood at my door. To be more precise, he was leaning against it with his back to me. That was the first time I got a hint of that smell.

I watched as one hand raised and brushed the doorknob. It fell listlessly back to his side. My first thought was that this guy had been hurt and was seeking help. He wore coveralls and a heavy utility jacket. I figured him to be from the power company.

There are moments in life that you never forget. Ones that never erase themselves from memory and end up in that permanent photo gallery your mind keeps. Some of those images blur over time. Others become glossier, as if they've received a bit of mental airbrushing. The first girl you kissed becomes a vision of pure beauty. That first car loses all the dents, dings, and rust spots.

Some memories do the opposite.

That body leaning against my door jerked like it was convulsing. The head snapped around so suddenly that I'm pretty sure I heard something pop…right before I screamed and fell backwards on my ass.

Something heavy struck my doorknob. That sound was like a slap on the face. I scrambled to my feet and did one of those stupid things I said I'd never do. You know what I am talking about. The person in the movie has to take that 'one last look.'
Of course that is usually when he or she gets their face eaten off. So, I pulled the curtain aside just enough to get that peek.

I know in my logical mind how dark it was that night. Over time, my brain has filled in the shadows. His name was Ed. I know that because it was embroidered on the left breast of his dark jacket with white thread. There was a milky film over his eyes that looked like a thin coat of Elmer's wood glue. Black blood filled the vessels in his eyes, which add a particularly nasty effect to that vacant, soulless look that lets you know you're dealing with a monster (oddly it is also a giveaway for somebody in the latter phases of infection). The dark smears around his mouth are the bright red of arterial blood in my nightmares. Ed's mouth is open and his face is pressed against my living room window.

The apartments I called home for over a decade were not the greatest: leaky faucets; poor insulation; and cheesy carpet from an era that was long out of style way before I moved in. But back to the windows…they are thin enough that you can feel a cold breeze through them on a blustery fall or winter day. I knew seconds before it happened that the glass was not going to hold.

Crash!

And just that quick, everything I knew, loved, did for fun…gone. My world had been shaken violently, and the pieces would never settle into anything resembling normal ever again.

Ed's stench hit me hard. The smell was so thick that I could taste it in the back of my throat. Two things happened almost instantaneously; Pluck lunged at the body that was halfway through my living room window, and I puked. To say "vomited" or "threw up" would diminish the true nature of that moment. It was as if my stomach heaved so violently that my intestines reversed flow and joined in the event. My mouth and nose burned from the bile-laced mixture that spewed from deep inside my guts. I staggered back, unable to see for a moment. Over the ringing in my ears I heard Pluck snarl and bark as he threw himself at the unnatural thing that threatened his master. I probably owe my life to that stupid dog.

His sudden yelp brought me back.

My eyes cleared, and I could see Ed holding something in his hands. It took another second to overcome the shock of what I was seeing. It held Pluck by a hind leg and his collar as it buried its face into that soft, warm, scratchable belly. When its head snapped up, long strands of skin and viscera pulled away. My best friend howled loud enough to drown out my own cry. But for a moment anyway, Ed was occupied.

God help me.

I ran.

I scrambled for the door, fumbling with the lock for seconds which seemed eternal before I could yank it open, and I ran away. I ran away from my apartment. I ran away from all my stuff. I ran away from that smell of death, and blood, and puke. I ran away from Ed.

I ran away from Pluck!

At the bottom of the stairs was a small, pink bicycle with training wheels. My mind held up a mental flash card of a tiny Mexican girl. She would ride that bike around the square inner-courtyard of the complex. She always rang the little bell on her handlebars if she came up on somebody from behind. She would laugh.

So I ran.

I reached the parking lot and realized that I had never bothered to grab my keys. The stupid ones in the movies always go back. My mind flashed on that image of the Ed-thing taking a bite out of the middle of my dog. Every hero in the movies knows how to hotwire a car. I had no clue. I still wasn't going back.

I stood there like an idiot for a moment, then heard a low steady sound. The backside of my apartment complex's parking lot is a steep, tree-covered embankment. There is a wall made of river rock that forms about a five foot base before the earthen slope begins and rises up to the street above. That street is like a border between my apartments and a quiet residential neighborhood. Parked on the edge of that street, just visible through the trees that overhung most of the parking lot, was a big power company truck.

It was running!

Hoisting myself, and scrambling up the embankment, I reached the road. Typical for this time of night (it was 3:42 a.m. according to my watch) it was quiet. I sorta turned a slow circle to make sure all was clear. Farther down the road from me something may have moved in the darkness. I wasn't about to wait and find out. Still, rushing to the truck without at least a little caution could be as fatal as a stroll down this road into the deep, black shadows.

I moved out into the middle of the street so as to allow myself the greatest amount of open space, then crept towards the idling vehicle. A large, dark smear marred the driver's side door. I wondered briefly if it belonged to Ed...or worse...his co-worker. Just as I neared close enough to peer in the open window, a scream unlike anything I'd ever heard—before that night anyway—shattered the relative quiet. That piercing sound seemed to reach inside me and clamp down hard on my bladder.

Yeah. I wet my pants.

Now I realize that something like that never happens to action heroes. Well, I guaran-damn-tee that he or she never heard a scream like that before. Not for real anyways.

It sounded like a woman or a child.

I yanked open the truck door deciding it was time to move a little quicker. Thankfully, no surprises leapt out at me, and I slid into the cab. I took quick visual inventory: keys, big flashlight, clipboard, brown paper sack. Great.

I popped the column shifter into drive and stomped on the gas pedal while twisting the steering wheel hard left. Making a big U-turn, I raced to the corner and did a bouncy power-slide. Turning sharp left again, I dropped into the entrance of my complex. I veered slightly left clipping a beat up Buick parked in the first tenant's parking spot. The truck fish-tailed the short length of the lot where an opening in the two-story building on my right indicated the entrance existed to one of two breezeways. Slamming on the brakes, the truck screeched to a halt and banked right just enough to have the nose pointing into the void. I found the knob and pulled, turning on my headlights.

The scene in that dark tunnel-like breezeway threatened to cause another upheaval from my stomach. Ed, along with two more of those things were clawing at this short, pudgy, Mexican woman. One of them was tearing out what looked to be a strand of intestine from a gaping hole in her abdomen. Another was jerking back with a chunk of left forearm between its teeth. Ed was on hands and knees chewing away at a thigh. Backing toward the steps was a little girl.

I struggled to remember the name I'd heard when her mom or dad had called for her. It was my little bicycle rider.

Thalia!

I leaned out the window and called her name. She spun, and I could see her clothing was splattered with blood.

Please don't be a zombie.

The three things feasting on what I was pretty sure had been her mom glanced up, then went back to what they'd been doing. Thalia, on the other hand, ran towards me.

Zombies don't run. Right?

"*Ayuda me, por favor! Ayuda mi mamá, señor!*"

"English, sweetie." I reached down and grabbed the tiny girl, yanking her rather unceremoniously through the window.

"Please to help my mamá, Mister Steve!"

Her accent was kinda thick. "Mister" sounded like 'meester', but her family was the sort that worked hard at their English. Good thing, because my Spanish was limited to a poor Speedy Gonzalez impersonation.

She looked at me with large, pleading eyes. I didn't have time to explain. Besides, I felt that any help on behalf of her *mamá* at this point would be useless. *Mamá* was done. I shifted into reverse and backed out as quick, and still cautious, as I could. It would be really stupid to wreck now.

As the headlights drifted across that horrific scene, I took one more look. My mind was screaming that this could not possibly be happening the way I was seeing it. I slammed on the brakes causing Thalia to fly forward and hit her head on the dashboard. She started crying, but I didn't hear it. Creeping into the breezeway was a short, squat shadowy figure.

Pluck.

I watched in painful fascination as my constant companion for so many years nosed into the body sprawled on the concrete. His head pulled back, and a flap of torn flesh hung from his mouth.

Slowly, I regained awareness of my surroundings. Tiny fists were pounding on my right shoulder. I glanced at Thalia in confusion as the sounds of her sobs poured into my consciousness. The blurred vision and burning sensation in my eyes made me realize that I was crying, but that wasn't why the little girl was pummeling me.

A bloodless face stared at me through the closed window of the passenger side door. The mouth opened and pressed against the glass. My mind focused on the weirdest thing.

No fog.

The window didn't fog up! This thing's mouth was all over the glass, and it wasn't fogging up even a teensy bit. Crazy.

An equally pale hand with a chunk missing, and what looked like just a stub for a thumb, smacked against the increasingly slime-smeared window. I heard a rattle of the door handle. This thing was trying to open the door, albeit clumsily. Time to go!

I made sure I was still in reverse and goosed the accelerator. Our friend came with us as he still had a grip on the door handle. I swung around and brought that side of the truck almost flush with the rock wall. A gout of blackish fluid made a macabre Rorschach pattern on the glass. Thalia screamed again and was practically in my lap. Her arms clutched about my neck so that I had to crane around her to see. My head turned just enough to allow me to see a shape rising in the shadows of the breezeway.

I eased the little girl down next to me and wrapped one arm protectively around her. She buried her face in my side and for that I am grateful. She didn't need to see what was staggering our way. The thing outside the passenger's side was not letting up in its effort to try and get at us, so I gave another tap on the gas. Gripping Thalia, I hit the brakes and shifted back in to drive.

Directly in front of me was Pluck. Without any further thought, I floored it. The time was long past to be outta here. The big truck lurched just a bit as our tag-along fell free and ended up under the rear wheels. Then the front sorta bounced like we'd hit a speed bump.

That "speed bump" was the end of my boon companion. My best friend. My foot warmer. I looked in the rearview mirror long enough to know I'd crushed his head like a jack-o-lantern in November. My dog, good old Pluck, lay still in the middle of the *Villa la Puerta* apartment complex parking lot. I think, in a lot of ways, I was relieved.

***

One sentiment that popped up in most of the zombie books and movies was the desire to ensure friends and companions didn't "come back." I get it now. Not just the fact that I didn't want him wandering around as one of them, *it was much more. Honestly, that thing wasn't Pluck. It is just so vile to see somebody you knew and loved become a part of the cause. To think that his body would still be moving after his... essence?...soul?...whatever the hell you want to call it, is long gone? It just ain't natural.*

***

I pulled out onto the street just as I saw Thalia's mom appear in my rearview mirror. I'm really glad that sweet little girl never saw what I did at that moment. What she had seen moments before, as well as what she would see in the next hours...days...weeks...would provide enough nightmare fodder.

I turned right. Away from the airport and towards the freeway seemed the best choice. A few blocks ahead, I could see that the power was on! That held some definite plusses and minuses.

Plus—I could see. I did a quick look-over of Thalia. Not that I'm heartless, but I had to make sure. Thankfully, there were no bites or scratches. I was really hoping there weren't any that I couldn't see. Her face was nestled right in my side. If she turned...

Minus—I could see. Here and there, singles, doubles, and mini-herds of those things were on the move. Or worse, feeding. Again, really glad Thalia couldn't see this. A couple of times, I had to swerve to avoid one of those things as they wandered out into the street after the few passing cars. I saw no reason to play Death Race with...

Zombies. That's it. That's what they are, and I can't avoid it. After Pluck and Thalia's mom, I have no doubts that the dead are, in fact, returning. For whatever reason...instinct, anger, hunger...they are attacking and feeding off the living.

As I hit the I-5 South on-ramp, it dawned on me to switch on the radio. A monotone, obviously recorded message, was repeating on every station I scanned to:

"The Emergency Broadcasting System has been activated. Please stay tuned to this local station for information..."

The message was on a loop. I tried the two-way radio. It came alive with all sorts of frantic chatter.

"...advised, we have lost contact with units seven, nine, twelve, and seventeen."

"...came out of no place and just grabbed Duran..."

"...where the hell is anybody!"

"...damn lady just bit me! I mean took a chunk out of my arm!"

As I drove down the interstate listening to the insanity unfold, I passed a couple of cars that were pulled only partially off the road. In the opposite lane, a few cars whisked past heading north. There was no way I would even consider heading into downtown Seattle. Within hours, if not already, that place would be a chaotic death trap. I was considering my options when a snippet of conversation caught my attention.

"...of people grabbed Ed. I heard him scream as they dragged him into the bushes. I stayed up on the pole. God forgive me, but I was scared to death."

"Then what?" a female voice demanded. "You said you lost the truck. So what the heck happened?"

"A few minutes later...five, maybe ten...one of them came out of the bushes and took off with the vehicle."

I turned off the two-way. There was nothing I could say or do now that wouldn't take forever to explain or clear things up in any manner. There was little doubt that it was my 'Ed' they were discussing. The problem being, I was pretty sure my explanation would not be very welcome. Not yet. If things held true to form, nobody would acknowledge or believe what this was until too late.

I reached over and opened the glove box. Thalia didn't make any attempt to move away, not that I blamed her. I wasn't sure what I was looking for. I rummaged, keeping one eye on the road as I felt around. Two wallets! That was the same moment I realized that I left mine. For somebody determined not to make stupid mistakes, I wasn't doing so well.

I spotted an off-ramp that advertised FOOD-GAS-LODGING. Veering right, I decided it was time to get just a little proactive. I made up my mind that I *knew* what was going on, and it was my responsibility to this child beside me to start taking steps to prepare for the worst eventuality.

A fully lit service station was perched at the top of the off-ramp. You know the kind; the mini-mart disguised as a gas station with a garage added as an afterthought that was good for nothing beyond a tire change. A small car was parked in a dark corner across the expansive asphalt lot from where the entrance was—probably the on-duty cashier's.

I pulled up to the pump station closest to the doors. No surprise, I saw no sign of an attendant...or cashier...whatever. My head was on a swivel, searching for any movement. Inside or out. I pried Thalia loose and took her tear-streaked face in my hands.

"I'm gonna take care of you, but I have to get out of the truck for a minute. I will lock the door. Don't open it until I say. Can you do that?"

She nodded.

"I will leave the engine running. So don't touch anything. Okay?"

More nodding.

I looked around again. This was a bad time for any surprises. At the moment, the coast was clear. I climbed out, locking the door, closing it carefully, and checking it to be certain. So far, so good. I fast-walked to the glass door and tugged.

Damn. Locked. Naturally.

Trying to watch everywhere at once, I scooted to another set of doors around the corner. Nothing was moving inside or out of the store. Yet. I could hear the occasional vehicle speed by on the nearby freeway. I think I heard gunshots from somewhere distant. I briefly wondered what I would do if another vehicle arrived with people having the same idea as me.

Also locked!

Damn! Damn! Damn!

Just a tiny bit desperate and a whole lot scared now. I looked everywhere for an idea. Turning my attention fully inside, I knocked on the glass. I don't know if I wanted somebody to be there or not, but old habits die hard.

No answer.

I knocked again. Louder. Still no response from within, or thankfully, out. That left me with what I saw as my final option: the metal ashcan sitting next to the door. I picked it up, dumped the contents on the ground, backed up a few steps and hurled it as hard as I could at the glass door.

CRASH.

I had half-expected the thing to come bouncing back at me. Lucky me. The entire door exploded inwards. Fine cubes of glass glittered like fake diamonds under the white glare of the fluorescent lighting.

Now it was time to be quick. I glanced back at the truck. Thalia was staring wide-eyed but calmly back at me through the windshield. I noted that pump nine was closest. Peering over the counter to be assured of no nasty surprises, I quickly climbed over and found the panel allowing me to turn on my pump. In no time, I had the nozzle in place and put the lock on so that I could tend to other issues while the tank filled.

Back in the store, I stopped at a rack of those burlap carry bags imprinted with pictures of Mount Rainier, the Space Needle, and other local touristy things. Grabbing a few, I literally ran up and down the aisles scooping stuff from the shelves. The medicine aisle was almost empty by the time I finished. Mostly basic things, like allergy pills and aspirin mixed in with the first aid stuff, filled six of those bags. I grabbed food second, which made me sorta proud that I was thinking clearly. Food would be easier to grab than medicine or hygiene as this dragged on. At least that was my logic.

I decided that milk would likely become a luxury. It would do good to get some while I could. I paused at the wall of the glass-doored refrigerators when I came to the milk section. My hand grasped the handle and I totally froze, my heart pounding in my throat. I had found the clerk. Plus one.

Inside the refrigerated stock area, behind the tilted display shelves, stood two zombies. They were staring at me from the shadows, behind the orderly rows of beer, orange juice, and various name-brand sports drinks. A quick look behind them at the main door to the chill box helped ease my heart rate back under triple digits. The big, metal door looked shut.

I backed down the aisle a few steps away from the milk towards the soda. Sure enough, my 'friends' followed. I tapped the glass like you would an aquarium. They both lunged forward, tangling themselves in the shelving and each other. I bolted, popped the door where the milk was, grabbed a couple of cartons, and headed to the exit.

I ducked out into the open lot to hear Thalia pounding on the glass of the driver's side window. A quick glance confirmed that a small pack of zombies were crossing the asphalt towards us. They still had some ground to cover, and I transferred our haul to the truck pronto. That finished, I pulled out the nozzle and hung it up as I replaced the gas cap. I dashed around the front of the truck and Thalia opened my door.

"Please let us go now!"

"I totally agree, sweetie!"

Climbing into the cab, I gave the approaching zombies another look. It was like the introduction to a dirty joke. An Asian, a naked lady, and two policemen walk into a gas station parking lot...

Hmmm.

I revved the engine.

"Put on your seatbelt, *señorita*."

Without a word, Thalia did exactly what she was told. I heard the 'click' and fastened my own. I pulled away from the pumps and made a wide U-turn. A glance in the rearview...then side-view mirrors...now for a slight turn of the steering wheel to get things right. I shifted into reverse and stomped the gas.

Zombie Bowling.

I felt the impact and the ensuing bounces as I rolled over the bodies. Three of the four lay twitching on the ground. The fourth, Naked Lady, still stood. She turned towards me, arms outstretched, mouth open. Back into drive, and again I put the pedal to the floor. I swerved just enough to catch her with the driver's side corner of the bumper. A satisfying thud and crunch rewarded the effort, coupled with the body flying several feet. Down, but not...dead? I briefly pondered the idea.

Twice-dead?

Fitting.

Thalia exclaimed her surprise when I slammed on the brakes and flung open the door. All of the zombies were in varied stages of struggling to their feet. On their backs they are a lot like turtles.

I approached the first downed policeman and was very disappointed. No gun. The second was my payoff, though. His wide, black leather belt held several toys for me to examine later once I had more time. I grabbed a window squeegee as I closed in on my target. With one swing I brought it down as hard as I could. My blow found an eye socket which exploded with thick jelly-like fluid. This thing began thrashing, arms flailing, hands grasping. A second swing…another…and another as the face shattered and the eye socket hole expanded. Finally the brass and hard plastic squeegee broke through to something softer. The thing at my feet quit struggling. Instantly. It's like hitting an *off* switch.

I worked the belt off the *twice-dead* while watching the others. The other policeman and the Asian were back on their feet, headed my way. Naked Lady was bent almost entirely backwards. She was trying to pull her unnaturally vee-shaped self along the asphalt. Yuck. Prize in hand, I made it back to the truck with relative ease.

Dropping the gun belt on the seat, I closed the door and headed for the exit. A car zoomed past, heading for the interstate presumably. A screech of tires sounded as it slammed on the brakes, then sped back to us in reverse.

The car, a sporty foreign model by the looks…what can I say, I'm not much into cars…halted directly in front of us. I considered our chances of ramming the little car without taking too much damage ourselves, but decided to wait a second and see what this person wanted. He or she could be just like Thalia and me. Still, no sense in being stupid. I pulled the gun from the holster and glanced to see if it was loaded. Check. Safety off. Check. I'm savvy enough to know it is a nine millimeter. I glanced in the rearview. The zombies were still a fair distance away. Problem was that now there were seven. I had enough time to at least give this person in the car a moment. I wouldn't waste time, but I also was not about to let my guard slip.

"Get down, Thalia."

She obeyed without protest. Unbuckling her seatbelt, she slid to the floor on the passenger's side, pulled her knees in tight, and wrapped her arms around them. Sort of like a tiny ball.

The door to the sports car opened. A tall, very attractive in an out-of-my-league sort of way, brunette emerged. My mind sped through several scenarios. All of which ended up with me as the hero and her falling into my arms. She proceeds to show her gratitude and admiration for my heroism...

"Thank God!" she screamed, and ran to my truck.

I rolled down the window, seeing no reason to open the door. I mean seriously, there are a bunch of walking dead shambling this way. Sure they're still a ways off and moving slow, but my mind is still trying to process what's happening.

"Ummm...you probably shouldn't be out of your car."

I am so smooth.

"Please help me! What the hell is going on?"

"You *really* shouldn't be out of your car." I glanced again at the group of undead closing the distance slowly and steadily. One of them was outdistancing the others and had his arms outstretched.

"My neighbor did this!" the pretty brunette said, holding up her left arm. Blood dripped from a shallow but jagged rip below the elbow.

My look must've given something away, because she hastily covered up. Her expression was a crazy mix of fear, embarrassment, and confusion. Without warning, she lunged at my door, pulling wildly on the handle. I went for the lock, but a shade too late as the door opened and I tumbled gracelessly to the ground.

Thalia screamed.

Scrambling up as quickly as I could with the wind only partially knocked out of me, I had no idea what to do. Was this lady one of *them*? Maybe the newly turned are different. Perhaps the brain died slowly, and they kept certain functions for a while. I really had no clue where the movie stuff was right or wrong. Hell, maybe it was *all* wrong. All of that jumbled around in my mind like rocks in a dryer as I came to my feet.

She was apologizing over and over. Maybe she was sorry she had to eat me now. All I truly knew at that exact moment was that she was beside me with a vise-like grip on my arm. There were several of those things about twenty feet or so away, and I was not ready to die.

I shoved her as hard as I could, sending my closest threat stumbling back towards the street. I snatched the gun from the cab where it had fallen to the floorboard in all this insanity. My finger curled around the trigger as I spun and fired.

She was in the process of climbing back to her feet. With an expression of astonishment, she looked down as a bloom of red spread across her blouse. Her eyes returned to mine in shock.

"Why?" She staggered sideways a step and fell…hard.

I still heard screaming. While I was shaking my head rapidly to clear it, something grabbed my shoulder. I whirled around face-to-face with the speed-walker of the bunch. It was a woman. Or had been. Her dark hair clung to her face, glued in place by dried blood. Most of the left cheek had been ripped away. Greyish gums and blood-smeared teeth greeted me in what looked like an exaggeratedly evil grin. I raised the pistol and fired. The bullet tore through its throat, jolting the upper body backwards. I felt the grip upon my shoulder tighten, and the head snapped back toward me with mouth open wide.

It's strange, the little things that capture our attention in a crisis. I noticed that the flat, lifeless, black-blood veined eyes never changed expression. No anger, hunger, victory, desire, pain…just empty. Truly empty.

I jammed the barrel of the gun into the now gaping maw and fired. The creature simply dropped. Again, it was as if the plug were suddenly pulled, like on a radio.

Without waiting for more bad things to happen, I jumped into the truck, slamming the door, locking it, and rolling up the window seemingly all at once. I shifted into drive and launched the big truck into the street, clipping the sports car enough to turn it a little sideways. My hard right turn aimed us back towards the interstate.

***

I've risked my life a whole bunch of times since that night. But at no time was I as stupid or out-of-control as I was in the way I left that gas station parking lot. Six more inches to the left, and I catch enough of that sports car to probably end our ride.

***

Looking in my rearview mirror, I got a sick feeling in the pit of my stomach. The zombies had fallen on the brunette. That could only mean one thing. Since they ignored, and even stepped over the zombie that I had just blown the back of its skull off, the brunette was not, at the time just before I shot her at least, dead.

Adding one plus one, I had just killed someone. My mind began to argue vigorously the varying points.

She was bitten.

It was only a matter of time.

You saved her much misery.

All the way to the interstate, and for the next several miles, my mind continued. It tried to offer me the solace that no other living, breathing human being would if they'd seen what I'd done.

Eventually, Thalia fell into a fitful sleep. If things were as I suspected, and if they had just started…this was only the ugly beginning.

It would get worse.

DEAD- the 12 book series

The unthinkable has happened.
The dead are walking!
Humanity's fragile thread may
be reaching its bitter end.
Individuals and groups struggle
to survive…some at any cost.
Will there be anybody left?
Or, is this just…
The Ugly Beginning?

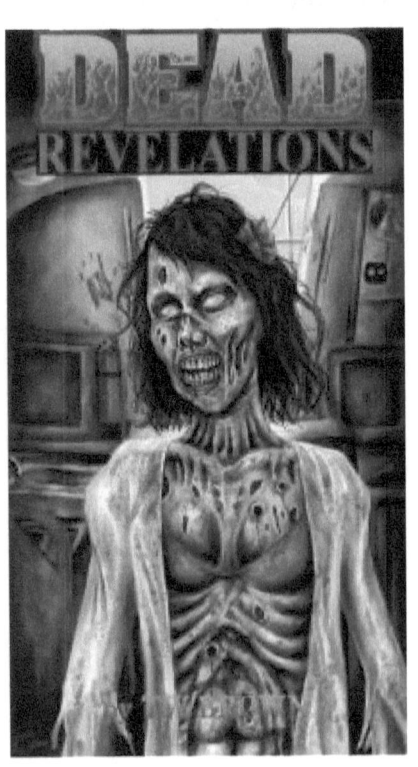

The Dead Walk:

Samuel Todd is a regular guy:
...Failed husband...
...Loving father...
...Dutiful worker...
...Aspiring rock star.
He had no idea if anyone
would care, or take the time,
to read his daily blog entries
about his late night observa-
tions. But what started as an
open monologue of his day-to-
day life became a running
journal of the first-hand ac-
count detailing the rising of
the dead and the downfall and
degradation of mankind...

Catch all 3 books in the Zomblog Trilogy

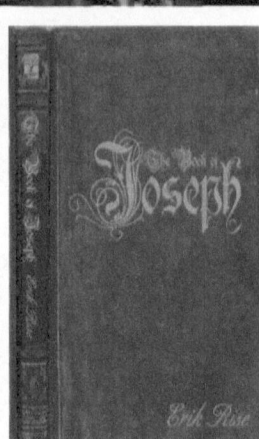

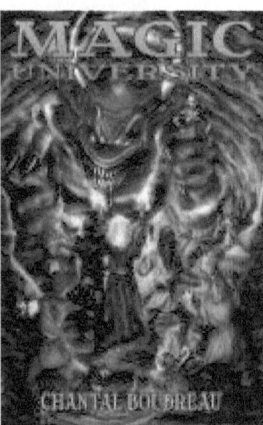

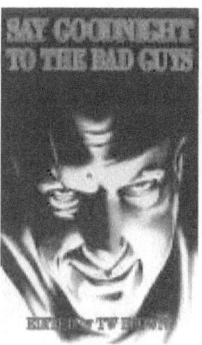

C. W. LASART

AD NAUSEUM

13 Tales of Extreme Horror

Exotic, Erotic, Gruesome and Gory! What if your Muse really was a twisted bitch, and she lived in your spare bedroom? And how far would you go to improve your station in life? In this premiere collection by C.W. LaSart, you will find 13 gruesome tales of the macabre, from a simpleton who forms an unnatural obsession with his own backyard to a lonely woman whose suitor is not heaven-sent. These stories, ranging from the supernatural to the darkness that lives within the human heart, are sure to send a chill down your spine and a flush to your face. Certain to disturb and delight, Ad Nauseam is a walk through the twisted imagination of one of horror's rising stars.

GOT HORROR?
ATOMIC
DEAD GUY
THE ART OF SHAWN CONN
ATOMICDEADGUY-COM

LOOK CLOSELY
THESE ARE DRAWINGS, NOT PICTURES

To have your pet art done, Contact Denise @
dlbrown@maydecemberpublications.com

MAY DECEMBER
Publications

**The growing voice in horror
and speculative fiction.**

Find us at www.maydecemberpublications.com
Or
Email us at contact@maydecemberpublications.com

TW Brown is the author of the **Zomblog** series and the **Dead** series. He is deeply immersed in pursuing his dream of being a "full-time" writer while trying to balance the duties of husband, father, friend, and Border Collie owner. He keeps busy reading and editing the numerous submissions for a variety of upcoming anthologies and full-length titles for May December Publications. He has had short stories published by Pill Hill Press, Living Dead Press, and others. You can contact him at: twbrown@maydecemberpublications.com or visit his website at www.maydecemberpublications.com. You can follow him on twitter @maydecpub and on Facebook under Todd Brown, Author TW Brown, and also under May December Publications.

www.ingramcontent.com/pod-product-compliance
Lightning Source LLC
Chambersburg PA
CBHW020244150626
46552CB00020B/165